M000080505

FAULTS

Orion Gregory

Copyright © 2021 by Orion Gregory

All rights reserved. No part of this publication may be reproduced, distributed or transmitted in any form or by any means, including photocopying, recording or other electronic or mechanical methods, without the prior written permission of the author, except in the case of brief quotations embodied in reviews and certain other non-commercial uses permitted by copyright law.

This is a work of fiction. Any characters, businesses, places, events, and incidents are either the products of the author's imagination or used in a fictitious manner. Any resemblance to actual persons, living or dead, or actual events is purely coincidental.

Printed in the United States of America
ISBN 978-1-736683-90-3 (paperback)
ISBN 978-1-736683-91-0 (ebook)

Canoe Tree
Press

4697 Main Street
Manchester Center, VT 05255

Canoe Tree Press is a division of DartFrog Books.

To Fran, Carli, Jill, and Neptune,
whose optimism and humor breathes life into my characters.

And to my friends, the greatest people in the world.
You know who you are.

And to Joann & Jerry,
for being the best fans ever.

"I play each point like my life depends on it."
--Rafael Nadal

CHAPTER 1

Milena Lombardi had no idea what her suicide would trigger.

She assumed she was killing only herself but couldn't have been more wrong. Her death would eventually cause a ripple effect, leading to despair, heartbreak, and even murder.

If she knew the ramifications of her actions, she would've reconsidered. Suicidal people often don't understand how much they mean to others.

The truth is, depression lies. It deceives. It filters out the good and brings the bad to the forefront.

No one cares. Things will improve after I'm gone. In time, everyone will forget me.

Lies. Untruths. Falsehoods.

Milena would end her life today. It would be the one task she'd accomplish this month. She meticulously planned the event, accepting all of the consequences that came with the decision. In a few minutes, she'd never experience hopelessness or despair again.

She would reminisce about the past today while reflecting on her life and its purpose.

But in the end, it wouldn't matter. They would discover her body on the balcony of her seventh-floor studio apartment in Milan, Italy.

If only she could turn back time.

Why didn't she complete her education at Savannah State University instead of turning pro two years early? A career in professional tennis would have still been waiting for her. Now there was no money to return to school.

Why did she decide to experiment with an illegal drug, hoping to enhance her tennis career?

Why did she waste so much time with Peter O'Malley, a fickle lover and a self-centered human being?

Why did she allow Sydney Livingstone to depart from her life? She was the best friend she ever had. Their relationship was beyond special. Milena and Sydney knew what each other was thinking. They often finished sentences for each other. Milena appreciated Syd's quick wit and dry sense of humor. To Syd, Milena was the sister she never had. When they were together, they giggled like school children. On the tennis court, they knew exactly where to go and how to proceed. It was like they were reading the other's mind without using words. They were on the precipice of achieving greatness as a doubles team.

The reason for the breakup was Milena's petty and immature jealousy. Once the damage was done, there was no turning back. They were also doubles partners in college, earning All-America status. They combined forces on the pro tour and ranked among the top sixty doubles teams in the world. But the relationship was permanently damaged. No going back.

Milena noticed a 2011 runner-up trophy gathering dust on the shelf. She'd earned the award at the Australian Junior Open. She nearly won the title that day, leading 3-1 in the third set, before defaulting because of a torn calf muscle.

Milena remembered her father and tennis coach, Paulo, attempting to comfort her. She wanted to continue but couldn't apply weight to her right leg. The loss was distressing, but it was also the highlight of her junior career. The Italian newspapers hailed Milena as a "Tennis Menace" and Italy's best hope for the future. And she was only seventeen.

Milena spotted a picture of her parents hanging on her austere gray wall. It was taken several years before she was born. Her father, Paulo, was a handsome, powerful man. His 250-pound frame belied his proficiency as a tennis player. Daria Lombardi, Milena's mother, was a striking beauty with shoulder-length black hair and dark brown eyes. Her head rested on Paulo's right shoulder, and her arms surrounded his waist. Hills and a small line of trees filled in the background.

Milena's parents couldn't afford the stifling cost of high-end tennis lessons. Paulo knew that Milena, at a young age, had the talent to become a special player. As a youngster, Paulo was a ferocious competitor but lacked the early training to contend on a national level. He passed his knowledge onto Milena, who achieved her first national ranking at age ten.

There was a drawer in Milena's home that she hadn't

opened for 316 days. But that streak would end today during the final hours of her life.

Inside the drawer was a letter from the International Tennis Federation (ITF). She remembered how devastated she was when she read it for the first time. Human Growth Hormone (HGH) was detected in her urine, prompting the ITF to suspend Milena from competition for three years.

The scenario surrounding her suspension had been strange. A few weeks before her suspension, she passed a drug test with flying colors. Feeling confident, she experimented with HGH shortly afterward. Her rationale for taking HGH was to heal injuries and to restore her fading confidence.

Out of the blue, the ITF insisted Milena take another drug test. Did someone turn her in? She'd never live to find out.

Milena finished reading her letter of suspension from the ITF. In a perverse way, she hoped to find something she had previously missed. Perhaps parentheses or an asterisk would change the suspension to a warning. No such luck.

Then, in early 2017, the unthinkable happened. Milena's mother passed away. No one saw it coming. Doctors said her death was caused by an aneurysm in her stomach. Even if Daria had been in the hospital during the attack, doctors would've been unable to save her. The event happened on a Saturday morning as Daria and Paulo vacationed in Rome. An inconsolable Paulo phoned Milena to break the news.

And then there was Milena's lover, Peter O'Malley. He was six feet, eight inches tall, and a brown-haired Irishman who made his living on the professional tour with a powerful serve and a dominant net game.

Their relationship was tenuous because of Peter's wandering eye and Milena's overprotective family. Milena loved Peter until he dropped a bombshell six months into their relationship. Peter admitted that he was in love with her friend, Sydney Livingstone.

Milena and Sydney were opposites in most ways. Milena sported medium-length brown hair and a strong, compact build. Sydney was five feet, nine inches tall, sleek, and well-toned. Her personality was bouncy and upbeat. She attracted men like a magnet.

Deep down, Milena knew it wasn't fair to blame Sydney because of the way Peter felt. But she was overwhelmed by jealousy and resentment, prompting her to make the biggest mistake of her life. She confronted Sydney and accused her of destroying the relationship between her and Peter. In no time, their relationship was over.

Shortly afterward, the ITF announced Milena's suspension from tennis. Milena and Sydney would never speak again.

Now, in 2017, Milena knew her chances of reviving a struggling career were minuscule. She stopped training and practicing and added thirteen pounds to her small five-foot-five-inch frame. Her superior muscle tone deteriorated due to muscle atrophy. Milena felt like she had nowhere to turn and few chances to earn a livable wage.

A special delivery she'd been awaiting arrived today. Inside the box was a large white envelope that contained a letter and a small pouch of seeds.

The return address listed Bhubaneswar, India, as its origin. The note inside seemed like it was produced on a

typewriter in the 1970s. Some letters were bold; others extremely light. Some appeared higher than others, as if the
device may have skipped during the typing. The letter read:

Horizon Resource Company
Bhubaneswar, India
Thank you for [sic] order.
En closed [sic] are samples from odollam tree. Seed
[sic] are for research only. Do not ingest or take
internally. Toxic and poisonous.
Use at [sic] own risk.

There's no risk, Milena thought. *They'll do exactly as*
intended.

The odollom, known as the "suicide tree" in India,
produces seeds containing the deadly toxin cerberin.
After several days of research, Milena found a source for
the seeds.

Earlier in the day, Milena had accomplished something she'd delayed for months. An envelope, with a
handwritten farewell and apology, was en route to Sydney's home in Savannah. Also enclosed was a locket with
a picture of them accepting their first-place doubles trophy at the 2015 Bucharest Open. It would be an olive
branch from the grave. And it made her feel better.

Milena placed four empty glasses on a table. At the
bottom of each glass, she placed two seeds. She filled
each glass halfway with Peter's favorite bourbon, Crystal
10. The bourbon was a gift from Peter two years earlier

after they reached a mixed-doubles semifinal in Tokyo. The note attached to the bottle stated, "Cheers to my partner and my love!"

Milena watched seeds plunge to the bottom of each glass, reminding her of a defeated warship. The two shots she'd previously consumed relaxed her, at least as much as anyone can relax before taking her own life. Milena had heard that the seeds were extremely bitter. Her plan was to hold her nose while chugging the bourbon.

Her thoughts shifted to her father. Should she call him to say goodbye? Daria's death nearly killed him, and her suicide would probably finish the job. She was relieved when her father's cell forwarded the call to voicemail. He would find out soon enough.

Perhaps she'd be with her mother shortly, in a place where there was no mental illness, physical pain, or three-year suspensions. She took a deep breath and wrapped her right hand around the first glass. In three gulps, the glass was empty and the bourbon's strength overcame a sickening, strange taste. She grabbed the second glass and swallowed the bourbon, along with its seeds, in the same way.

A stabbing pain in her chest made her forget about the remaining two glasses. Milena placed her right hand over her heart and her left hand on her throat. She fell from her sitting position and ended up horizontally on the loveseat, staring at the swirling plaster design in the ceiling. Just when the pain in her chest couldn't get any worse, she was overcome by a feeling of peace. An ever-so-slight smile appeared on her face. She took a final breath and closed her eyes.

CHAPTER 2

FOUR YEARS LATER

The site of a three-star hotel emerging from the left side of her red and black Corvette rental car wasn't something that would normally excite Sydney Livingstone. Today was different. Syd completed a ten-hour-plus drive from Savannah, Georgia, that had begun at four in the morning. She had nearly fallen asleep at the wheel about an hour earlier while driving north on I-77 near Athens, Ohio. A coffee, supercharged with a shot of espresso, provided the energy to finish her trip. By the time she reached her destination in Silverhill, Ohio, the Hampton Inn had resembled an oasis in the desert.

Syd's digital clock displayed 2:37 p.m. as she pulled into the parking lot. She figured she'd have enough time to check-in, jump into the shower, unpack, and take a ninety-minute snooze. A serial coffee consumer, Syd didn't worry about the lingering effects of caffeine on her sleep. When truly fatigued, no stimulant in the world could keep her awake. Upon waking, she'd grab a light meal, peruse a bookstore, and relax before heading for practice at the Wukeson Family Tennis Center, home of the annual Mainspring Mutual Open (MMO) tournament.

Silverhill, an affluent town of 37,000, is located fifteen miles northwest of downtown Columbus. Wealthy suburbs nearby include Westerville, Upper Arlington, Dublin, and Bexley. Silverhill is also the home of the Early Television Museum, dedicated to the preservation of technology from the early days of television.

As Sydney rode the elevator to her hotel room on the third floor, her thoughts reverted to the clerk behind the desk who checked her in a few minutes earlier. She had barely gotten her name out when the clerk jumped to attention and said, "Yes, Sydney, I've been expecting you. Here's the card to your room. Please let me know if you need anything else."

Syd smiled and thanked the man for his hospitality. It seemed like he'd been expecting her, or as if her name was fresh in his mind. *I'm a decent tennis player*, she thought, *but far from a household name*. Perhaps the clerk was really a rabid fan, although he never mentioned the tournament or anything about tennis. The more Syd thought about it, the less sense the encounter made.

I'm being paranoid, she thought as the elevator's ding reminded her she'd reached the third floor. Paranoia, anxiety, and "what-if" thinking were not foreign to Syd. Her doctor prescribed a medication called venlafaxine a year earlier. Weeks after starting the drug, Sydney's anxiety plummeted from severe to manageable.

The venlafaxine allowed her to tolerate claustrophobic situations like riding in airplanes or squeezing into tight elevators. Looking at her five-foot-nine, 130-pound mus-cular frame, you'd never know that the drug's weight-gain inducing side effects were a major concern. In order to keep her weight within the range to compete at the world level, she had to increase her weekly running workload by nine miles per week. The extra miles caused an increased strain on her body, but it also provided a calming effect that made her anti-anxiety drug work more effectively.

A few days earlier, she discussed her fears with an on-line counselor. Although she had received threats in the last year, she accepted that menacing was commonplace among female players. There's always a love-struck per-vert lurking somewhere, monitoring the women's tour from a computer in his grandma's basement. For a deter-mined tormentor, it's relatively easy to invade Twitter or Instagram accounts and issue a veiled threat—one that's too nebulous for police to investigate.

Syd followed the hotel's display arrows until she locat-ed room 317 and slid her card into the door's slot. The light blinked twice, and she pushed the door open with her left hand. She placed her left foot slightly inside the door to prevent it from closing, grabbed the handle of the suitcase with her right hand, and wheeled it into her room.

She released the handle of her suitcase and allowed the door to close behind her. After a few steps, she spotted the king-sized bed on the right. The site of the mattress, bed coverings, and fluffy pillows made her realize just how tired she was. Syd loosened her hair from its ponytail, peeled off her gray shorts, removed her shoes and socks, and collapsed on the bed wearing nothing except under-wear and a blue halter. But there was one more task she needed to accomplish before she slipped away. The cof-fee and espresso had worked their way into Syd's bladder, providing enough discomfort to prevent her from falling asleep. A quick bathroom visit would be a precursor to a serious power nap.

While emptying her bladder, she turned to her left to face the shower, which was obstructed by an ugly green curtain. Perhaps a good body-cleansing experience could wait until after her nap. The shower would invigorate her for the practice session. She was so tired; she wondered if she could make it through the shower without falling asleep and taking a header into the tub.

Syd stood up and headed toward the bed, oblivious to the fact that she wasn't alone. Someone on the bath-tub-side of the curtain—a strong and sleek clothesless Af-rican-American male—lay cramped and motionless across the bottom of the tub. He clutched a knife firmly in his left hand as blood seemed to flow out of his left eye socket, all the way down to the base of his neck. Once he heard Syd-ney flop onto the bed, he slowly pulled the curtain open and rose out of the tub. A sudden knock at the door caused him to slip back to his previous position, drawing the cur-tain to a close again.

Who could be knocking? thought Sydney. Her boyfriend, Enzo Martin, an English player ranked eighty-ninth in the world, shouldn't arrive until at least six tonight. Clean-ing staff? No, the room was fine. Room service? Nope.

Maintenance? Not unless something had gone wrong that she didn't know about.

The feeling that something wasn't right returned with a vengeance. As Syd slipped her shorts on, she remembered she had packed a self-defense mechanism called Tiger Claw. She'd purchased it on the internet shortly after receiving those online threats. Syd pulled down the zipper of her suitcase and reached into a mesh pocket. She removed the Tiger Claw and pressed a release button on the device, exposing four sharp metal claws designed to tear human flesh.

Syd approached the door and peered out of the view hole. A young woman appearing to be in her late twenties stood behind the door, holding a package wrapped in off-white paper and a clipboard. *She looks innocuous enough*, thought Syd. Definitely no need for the Tiger Claw. She pressed a button to retract its claws, placed the device into her pocket, and swung the door open.

CHAPTER 3

"Are you Sydney Livingstone?" said a small-statured, plain-looking young woman with shoulder-length brown hair. She wore a white "Summertime in Columbus" T-shirt and white Old Navy ankle jeans. Her left foot—covered by a red deck shoe—tapped the floor nervously.

"Yes, I am," said Syd. "Do you work for the hotel?"

"No, I'm here to deliver a package," she said, handing Syd a sealed envelope and a bottle covered by wrapping paper.

"Thanks," said Syd. "Do I need to sign anywhere?"

"That's not required," the woman responded.

"Do you know who it's from?"

"There's a card that comes with the package. That's really all I know."

The woman nodded quickly as if to signal the end of their interaction. She scurried down the hall, past the elevators, and disappeared through an entrance labeled "Stairway."

Syd took the package and its envelope to her bed, tossing the disabled Tiger Claw into her open suitcase among unpacked clothing.

The white envelope seemed somewhat crinkled like several people had handled it.

She opened the envelope and removed a piece of paper with the following letterhead: *Ominous Delivery Service.*

Strange name for a company, she thought, *as she read the handwritten words below:*

> *This bottle of Crystal 10*
> *I must send*
> *Hope you enjoy it*
> *More than your friend.*

Inside the package was a 750 ml bottle of Crystal 10 bourbon. Syd remembered that brand of bourbon. It was the type Milena had consumed while committing suicide. Milena's father discovered her body four days later. Syd heard the bourbon was a gift from Peter O'Malley, the Irish tennis player who caused a rift in the relationship between her and Milena.

Syd cried for weeks after Milena's death. At times, she broke down while competing, practicing, driving, and lovemaking. For a brief period, she considered taking her own life.

She remembered one of her own journal entries, written shortly after Milena's death.

> *When you needed me most, I wasn't there. How was I to know we'd never speak again? Now it's too late to tell you what you needed to hear:*

I love you unconditionally.
I need you in my life.
Our friendship will last forever.

Who sent this package? And why? Was the delivery from someone in her own inner circle, or was it sent by a deranged fan who gets his rocks off terrifying a twenty-four-year-old female player? But how would a fan know where she was staying in Silverhill? Few people had that information. A chill shot up her spine, and suddenly Syd's urge for a nice siesta had vanished.

Endless thoughts and scenarios ran through Syd's mind. *Who was that woman at the door? Why didn't I ask for her name or take a picture of her? Does the hotel have cameras? Why isn't Enzo answering his phone? Was he going through airport security, or had he already adjusted his phone to airplane mode?*

Mom flew into town last night to watch me play. Should I alarm her with a silly call about a bourbon delivery? Should I call my doubles partner—Anja Radanovic—to inform her I won't be practicing with her tonight, given the circumstances? She's staying at a nearby hotel. Should I tell her to come to my room until I sort this out?

Syd turned on her back and buried her face into one of the five pillows on her bed. She couldn't let some weirdo take up residence in her head and affect her performance on the court. If she won both pre-tourney matches on Sunday, she would qualify for the main draw of the MMO. A first-round loss in the main draw would provide a decent payday, while subsequent victories would double and possibly triple those earnings. With much-needed prize money and ranking points on the line, she couldn't afford to be distracted.

Syd rolled over onto her right side and attempted to take control of her stress through rhythmic breathing. Inhale to a count of four, hold for four, and then exhale for seven. She repeated the process several times before she suddenly stopped breathing. What did she see sticking out from under the bed? She reached her left hand underneath the frame and grabbed what felt like fabric. She pulled the item—a pair of men's underwear—up and onto the bed. Then she leaned over the bed, her head nearly touching the floor. But there was nothing but more clothes—a tan short-sleeved shirt and jeans, all unfolded. Had someone thrown them hurriedly under the bed? What the hell? Who would toss clothes beneath a hotel bed? A past visitor? That thought made little sense. Or worse, what if it were someone still in the r—

Syd leaped out of bed, grabbed the Tiger Claw from her suitcase, and extended the device's razor-sharp nails. She'd search the kitchenette area first because she couldn't see behind the counter. Upon closer inspection, the kitchenette was vacant. She turned her attention to the closet, just to the left of the room entry door.

Closets terrified her as a child, even more so than monsters living under her bed. As a child, she had seen a haunting movie where a closet creature grabbed kids who opened the door and yanked them into the netherworld. Syd considered bypassing the closet, bolting out of the room, and screaming for help. Then she pictured the interrogation:

"Let me get this straight, ma'am. You created a chaotic scene—running and screaming through our hotel—just because you found a discarded pair of tightie-whities? Do I understand correctly?"

No, she thought, *I won't be the laughingstock of the third floor.* She'd check out the closet herself. Syd turned the knob slowly to the right and flung the closet door open violently, expecting a creature to reach out and grab her elbow. But unless the creature disguised itself as an ironing board, the closet was free of danger. A small iron hung on a wall hook, and a translucent plastic bag encompassed a sheet, an extra blanket, and a pillow—apparently for someone willing to sleep on the room's fold-out couch.

But then Syd remembered the bathroom curtain. If someone had removed their clothes in her room today, could they be hiding in the bathtub?

Syd walked hesitantly past her bed and turned toward the bathroom. She couldn't take her eyes off the drawn shower curtain. She strained to listen for the sound of breathing. With the air-conditioning unit blowing noisily, she couldn't be sure. She moved the Tiger Claw to her right hand and tip-toed across the burnt red quarry tile leading to the shower. She grabbed the curtain and swung it open.

A man lay on his left side, eyes closed, his head resting at the end of the tub opposite the faucets. Brown dreadlocks partially covered his face, and fresh blood flowed from his left eye socket, down the side of his face, and onto his neck. At six-foot-three, his body barely fit in the tub. He opened his eyes, grabbed a knife in his right hand, and rolled on his back to meet Syd's horrified gaze.

"Enzo, are you crazy?" Sydney screamed. "You scared the life out of me!"

Enzo rolled over on his back and laughed so loudly that it would have disturbed adjacent sleeping guests if it were nighttime. He sat up, pawing at laughter-generated tears which now streamed from his eyes, mixing with the pseudo-blood on his face.

"I owed you one!" he said, tossing the rubber knife out of the tub and onto the tile. "Remember last month when I walked in your front door? You were lying on the floor with your head surrounded by fake blood and that goofy-looking wound stuck to the side of your head?"

Sydney was still partially in shock but knew she couldn't be angry with Enzo. She enjoyed this bogus death game as much as he did.

"I really scared you that time," said Syd, trying to regulate her breathing. "But this scene today was a monumental effort on your part. How long were you waiting in the bathroom?"

"At least forty-five minutes," he said. "You wouldn't believe how slowly time passes when you're buck-ass naked lying in a cold bathtub."

"Well, I guess we're even now," said Sydney. "But no more death scenes until this tournament is over."

"I promise," said Enzo, still shivering. "Do you think I'm in the mood to pull another stunt like this any time soon?"

"Hopefully not. But I can see you're freezing to death. And coincidentally, I have adrenaline pumping through me like an active fire hydrant. How about joining me under the covers so we can address both dilemmas?"

Enzo emerged from the tub and carried Syd to the bed. He put her down gently, lay down next to her, and pulled the covers over the both of them. Syd placed her tongue on Enzo's chest, crept it slowly up his neck, and finally into the wetness of his mouth. She wrapped both arms around him, rolled over on her back, and pulled him on top of her. Maybe she could enjoy a little stress relief and still leave some time for a nap.

Upon waking at 4:45 p.m., Syd and Enzo showered, dressed, and headed downstairs to the hotel restaurant for dinner. A light meal would serve her well before their Saturday night practice session. A cheerful, tall server with flowing dark hair escorted them to a table in the dining room, which was at one-quarter capacity.

"I take it you caught an early flight?" Syd asked as the two shared a small pre-dinner loaf of bread and butter.

"Yeah, and that's when I got the idea to sneak into your room. I told the guy at the desk to let me in so I could surprise you," he said. "Remember, I was the one who booked it."

"I knew there was something funny about the way he was acting," Syd laughed. "It seemed like he was expecting me.

"And that delivery of the Crystal 10 bourbon, that was a little overboard, wasn't it? I like a joke as much as anybody, but didn't you go a little too far by referencing Milena? I'm still struggling with that."

"Wait a minute!" said Enzo. "That's what the knock on the door was about? A delivery of bourbon? Crystal 10?"

"Well, you would know. And where did you find that nervous delivery girl? Certainly not at an acting school."

"Syd," Enzo replied, sitting straight up in his chair, "I know I shocked you today with my unconventional arrival, but you have to believe me. I had absolutely nothing to do with that bourbon delivery. It wasn't me!"

CHAPTER 4

At the MMO, Saturday is a practice day for all players. For players who had not yet qualified, Sunday was their opportunity. They would have to prevail in two matches to enter the main draw.

The forecast for the next few days was for partly cloudy conditions with a 20 to 30 percent chance of showers. Temperatures were expected to be in the upper eighties.

Hundreds of spectators passed through the turnstiles of the Wukeson Family Tennis Center, which houses sixteen courts and accommodates eleven thousand fans. Most fans enjoyed opening day. The relaxed atmosphere provided a wonderful opportunity for players and fans to interact. It was certainly the best time for autographs.

The previous year's MMO tourney moved to New York City because of COVID-19 restrictions, one week before the US Open. With the worst of COVID-19 over, Silverhill (Columbus) again hosted the MMO.

Syd pulled her rental corvette into the players' entrance of the Wukeson Tennis Center, which was located just to the west of the facility. They designated her practice time for seven under the lights on Court 15. She had parted ways with Enzo after dinner, but she planned to see him later that night after practice.

Enzo was scheduled to practice with his best friend, Rumanian Victor Dan, a fast-rising twenty-year-old whose claim to fame was a quarterfinal showing at the Australian Open. Syd met Dan twice—at the 2019 French Open and a pre-tournament dinner in Bucharest.

Syd beamed when she noticed her mother waiting inside the facility. Chelsea Livingstone-Crumhour waved excitedly with arms and hands crisscrossing over her head. Syd hadn't seen her mom in six months. They embraced eagerly.

"No more COVID elbow bumps!" said Syd, enjoying a long-overdue hug with the woman who gave her life in 1997.

The pandemic hadn't allowed for many personal visits between Syd and Chelsea during the last year. Her mother, a practicing Boston tax attorney, lived an on-the-go life for the past seven years. After turning fifty-five, Chelsea vowed to slow down to spend more time with her remaining child.

Syd's younger brother Anton died at nine, the victim of a car-bike accident. The event occurred in 2008 on a moderately traveled street in front of their historic Savannah home. No one claimed responsibility for the accident. Leads generated by Savannah police never led to an arrest. Around town, rumors persisted that a local nineteen-year-old named Harold Swift was a passenger in the car that killed Anton. Swift, diagnosed with a learning disability, denied being present when the accident occurred. He took a lie-detector test, but they deemed the results "inconclusive."

After Anton's death, Syd noticed a change in her mother. The once-carefree woman became withdrawn, rarely leaving her residence unless working. Chelsea enlisted the help of psychics, a profession that's plentiful in a ghost-obsessed city like Savannah. During one session, Chelsea heard Anton's voice whisper a message from beyond the grave. She carried a gold locket around her neck with Anton's words inscribed: "Love You Mom."

Anton's death put a major strain on the marriage of Michael and Chelsea Livingstone. Blame, guilt, and anger—and Chelsea's perpetual quest to reconnect with her son—divided a once-solid relationship. Michael, paralyzed by the heartbreak of losing both his wife and son, ended up moving away to a small town in Michigan.

Michael served as Syd's tennis coach when she was young. His intense and degrading style of coaching caused almost irreparable flaws in their relationship. Syd's most painful memory was of her father smashing her fourth-place trophy during a national fourteen-and-under tournament in Los Angeles.

"Almost ain't good enough!" he screamed while crashing her trophy into the concrete. Syd watched helplessly as hundreds of broken pieces of glass, metal, and plastic scattered across the ground like a fallen chandelier.

After the divorce and throughout her professional career, Sydney and her father seldom spoke. She'd heard her father dated a few women in the Michigan area, but nothing had materialized from those relationships. He'd ended up single and living alone.

"I'm so excited that I could fly in to watch you!" said Chelsea, now holding both of Sydney's cheeks in the palms of her hands. "I'll just hang around for an hour to watch practice, but I'll be here tomorrow for both of your matches.

"Remember, there's no pressure to win. I'm thrilled to spend time with you this weekend!"

"Yeah, Mom," Sydney laughed. "No pressure at all, except to pay the bills."

"Look, Syd, I know this tennis thing isn't all roses and rainbows," said Chelsea. "But I'm available if you ever need anything, including money. I know I was distracted by Anton's death and the divorce, but please know I'm here in your corner."

"Listen to me!" Syd replied, grabbing her mother's shoulders and straightening her. "You were a wonderful mother then, and you still are now. We went through a lot, but you know what? We're survivors. And we still have each other."

Chelsea stepped back for a moment and wrapped her arms around Syd, squeezing tightly. For a second, Syd thought her ribs might break.

"Let's plan on dinner tomorrow night," said Syd. "I want you to meet Enzo."

After saying goodbye to Chelsea, Syd removed her ID lanyard from her bag, displayed it to the guard at the gate, and headed inside the facility toward the players' lounge. Two excited teenage girls stopped her along the way. With a Head tennis bag draped over her shoulder and four rackets sticking out, most fans could tell she was a tournament player.

"Excuse me," said the taller girl, carrying a giant yellow faux tennis ball larger than her head. "May we get your autograph, please?"

"No problem," said Syd, scribbling her signature on the large ball.

One girl squinted to read the name, but she couldn't discern it.

"Pardon me, what's your name?" she asked.

"Sydney Livingstone."

The girls looked at each other quizzically.

"Sydney who?" asked the shorter one.

"Livingstone. Kinda like a stone that's come to life."

The girls shrugged and ran toward several other players who entered the gate.

I guess I'm not exactly a household name, thought Syd. *I wonder if that'll ever change?* But Syd knew her time was running out. She recalled an appointment with her orthopedic doctor in Atlanta. The doctor's words resonated in her mind: *Degenerative hip disease.* They could treat her pain along the way, but there was no cure.

"You can play for two or three years at the most," said the doctor. "Define your legacy now."

Syd's first qualifying match was slated for 9:00 a.m. Sunday. She'd face Canada's Monica Rivet, a thirty-six-year-old trying to squeeze the most out of her remaining time left on the tour. If Syd prevailed, her final qualifying match would take place later in the day at five.

Tournament director Al "Fitz" Fitzgerald manned the registration desk inside the players' lounge. Fitz was a fireplug, five-foot-eight and 210 pounds, with a thriving mane of wavy black hair. Syd never cared for Fitz. She felt he suffered from "little man syndrome." He was a know-it-all with a boisterous, uncompromising personality. Most players on the tour disliked Fitz, partly because of his incompetence but more for his authoritarian style of officiating. Perched high in his chair, Fitz talked down to the players, both literally and figuratively.

Fitz resented Syd deeply. Two years earlier, she reported him to the WTA board for dining at a restaurant with Sweden's Alexandra Carnack, a top-ten player. The violation occurred during a tournament in Stockholm. Players and officials are prohibited from spending time together off the court.

Several players corroborated the story, but Fitz found that Syd was the one who had reported him. He received a six-month suspension from the WTA. The media ran with the story, and Fitz's reputation took a major hit.

Syd smiled when her eyes met Fitz's. He looked back with an emotionless, stoic stare. If looks could kill . . .

"What can I do for you, Ms. Livingstone?" said Fitz. "I hope my dining habits won't annoy you this week."

With important matches in her immediate future and a potential stalker to worry about, Syd decided this wouldn't be the time for a confrontation.

"I'm here for my seven o'clock practice court."

"Yes," said Fitz. "I've been expecting you. I have redirected you to Court 12. You'll be practicing with your doubles partner Anja, along with Peter O'Malley and Cassandra Flores."

Syd's blood pressure rose—and for more than one reason.

"Wait, just a second," she said. "I'm supposed to practice on a court with Anja only. I have qualifying matches tomorrow. Singles players should be on a court with only one player. And besides, didn't Flores already have a practice time today?"

"Ms. Flores requested additional time," said Fitz. "I complied with her request. And Mr. O'Malley said he'd be willing to join the three of you to make it a foursome."

"What's the big deal?" asked Fitz. "It's only a practice session."

CHAPTER 5

Court 12 was about a three-minute walk from MMO's massive Center Court, the marquee tennis stadium at the Wukeson Family Tennis Center. Syd walked behind a brick, brown-painted wall that ran along the south end of courts 11 through 14, sequestered from the rest of the courts. The interaction with Fitz annoyed her, but she knew that she must stay in the right frame of mind in today's practice and tomorrow's qualifying rounds. Winning two qualifying matches wouldn't be easy.

The seven o'clock practice continued until nine, although Syd hoped most of her heavy-hitting would conclude by 8:30. With her first qualifying match scheduled for 9:00 a.m., she wanted to conserve her energy. Four players on one court cramped her style, but she needed to get the most out of the session.

Syd emerged from behind the wall and onto Court 12, where Anja sat on a courtside chair next to her coach, Paul Russo. Anja and Syd played doubles together in a tournament in Indianapolis where they won several matches before falling to the number-four seeds in round sixteen.

The strong showing put several thousands of dollars into their pockets and buoyed their dreams of becoming a credible doubles team.

Syd and Anja did not enter the doubles tournament at the MMO because Anja preferred to concentrate on singles. A lingering calf injury also factored into her decision. They still planned to play in several tournaments before the end of the year.

Syd was halfway onto the court when Anja intercepted her. Anja wrapped her arms around Syd's waist, lifted her off her feet, and twirled her. Anja was three inches shorter than Syd, but her powerful thighs and calf muscles provided almost superhuman strength. When Anja wasn't playing tennis, she was working out or enjoying an adult beverage. The muscles in her arms popped when she struck a ball, making her one of *Tennis* magazine's most photographed players. She dated several male players on the tour, but her current partner was a Russian female player, Marisha Belov.

"You're gonna kill it tomorrow!" said Anja, lowering Syd after several vertigo-inducing spins. "You're going to win both matches and join me in the main draw. But let me warn you, if we end up playing against each other, I'll definitely kick your ass!"

Syd loved Anja's positivity and enthusiasm. When Syd suffered a heartbreaking loss in April, Anja stayed by her side for an hour, attempting to console her.

"You're going to be among the elite players very soon, girl," she said. "You have to go through some shit. I believe in you!"

Russo became Anja's coach six months earlier after she ended her relationship with her former coach. She seemed content with Russo, whose knowledge of court strategy and high-percentage play made up for his shortcomings as a stroke technician. Russo instilled a renewed sense of confidence in Anja. Her ranking improved, and her tennis intelligence soared. Syd couldn't afford a full-time coach, but Anja suggested Russo.

Russo handed Syd a piece of paper with scrawled handwriting on it.

"Here's my take on your first opponent," he said with a slightly detectable European accent. "I've listed her strengths, weaknesses, and her tendencies," he said. "This will help you."

"If—or I should say, when—you beat her tomorrow, we can discuss your second opponent."

Syd had only met Russo twice. She'd heard that he maintained a file with an analytical profile on nearly every player. Anja said that she knew exactly what to expect when she faced a particular opponent, thanks to Russo. He did not come cheap, but a good showing in the main draw would help Syd pay for Russo's services.

Russo seemed to be just shy of six feet, but his arms were thin and his body frail. Syd guessed Russo to be in his mid-fifties. He almost appeared to be malnourished and, when combined with his analytical personality, he reminded her of a disheveled, bearded mad scientist. Because of sunlight-induced migraines, Russo's sunglasses rarely left his face.

"I have one question to ask you, Coach Russo," said Syd. "Do you have a file on me, and when can I see it?"

"Some things are not shareable," he replied, smiling wryly. "Unless you become one of my students."

Sydney stuffed the report into a pocket of her warmup jacket. She saw Peter O'Malley approaching with Cassandra Flores. Clad in a white Lacoste performance dress with black trim and loud yellow bursts, Flores was one of the most recognizable players at the tournament. Spectators applauded at the sight of Flores. She waved politely at the crowd but turned down autograph seekers.

"Maybe I'll sign after practice," she said. "I need 100 percent concentration."

O'Malley smiled at Syd and greeted her in his thick Irish accent.

"You look quite good today, Sydney," he said. "I'm so happy you're trying to qualify for this tournament. You're only two wins away!"

Syd looked into Peter's eyes, trying to detect any hint of sorrow over the way he treated Milena. She detected nothing.

"Glad you could join us, Peter," she said. "It's so nice of you to volunteer to hit with three female players."

"I didn't volunteer," replied Peter. "Cassie needs some extra time to prepare for her first-round match on Tuesday, and she asked me to tag along."

The foursome proceeded through the entire gamut of practice drills for the first ninety minutes—backhand and forehand crosscourt shots, down-the-line groundstrokes, serves, service returns, overheads, and volleys.

"I always wanted to take on three ladies at once," said O'Malley, dancing wildly in the center of the court.

His tone was so childlike; it didn't come off as offensive.

"I don't know about you, Peter," said Flores, "but I'm here to make money. Please stop distracting me with your juvenile sense of humor."

Flores continued to crush baseline strokes toward her opponents. Syd nodded at Flores to show her appreciation for the effort, knowing it would prepare her for what lay ahead tomorrow.

Syd heard that Flores' recent lover was Belgium's Jules Willems, the world's top-ranked male player. In the eyes of fans, Willems possessed an ego larger than his ranking. But Syd knew him more intimately. During a three-month cooling-off period with Enzo, she hooked up with Willems at a tournament in Monte Carlo. She'd found him charming, polite, and even somewhat shy. It was a non-committal two-night affair with no expectations.

Enzo heard about the brief affair and never claimed to be okay with it. The cooling-off period was his idea, and he hooked up with several women during that time.

The lights illuminated the courts as darkness set in. At nine, Flores called it a day and rushed past the remaining spectators, waiting patiently for her to fulfill her promise of an autograph.

Anja and Syd walked to their courtside chairs next to the bleachers where Belov awaited.

"Syd, we're going to a restaurant. Would you like to join us?" asked Anja. "We'll eat quickly since you play in the morning."

Syd glanced toward Belov, whose expression had not

changed. She didn't appear angry over the invitation but didn't seem pleased, either. Syd politely passed on the offer, blaming the late hour.

Anja and Belov left the court and soon disappeared into the night. O'Malley had been fumbling at courtside with his tennis bag, but it was obvious to Syd that he was waiting for her.

"I see something that needs improvement on your forehand volley," said O'Malley. "Can you stay on the court with me for a few minutes? I can show you something that will help."

Syd scanned the facility. Several nearby courts were dark, and most players were gone or in the process of leaving. Peter could tell by her facial expression that she wasn't buying his offer.

"Look, I know it's late, and you have to play early tomorrow, but I think I can really help you. I need fifteen minutes and not a second more."

Syd remembered the delivery of Crystal 10—the same bourbon Milena consumed during her suicide. Peter purchased the bottle for Milena as a gift.

Was he the one who sent the bourbon to her room? And was the delivery meant to intimidate, or was Crystal 10 simply his beverage of choice? Her head was spinning.

Syd's thoughts pivoted from bourbon to her forehand volley. If Peter was fibbing about a weakness in the stroke, he had gotten lucky. The forehand volley frequently broke down, especially during crucial points. The stroke deficiency caused her to lose several matches, costing her thousands in prize money. Would it hurt for Peter to offer advice? No, it wouldn't.

Peter's suggestions helped. He said the follow-through on her forehand volley had become too exaggerated. The stroke had become more about the timing and less about control. By the end of the fifteen-minute session, Syd's forehand volley was accurate and powerful. Now she could apply the technique in future matches.

She thanked Peter for his advice as they were packing to leave. On her cell was a text from Enzo:

Playing w/ O'Malley? Surprising, but X-tra practice is good. Riding w/Victor back to hotel. See U when you get back!

"It emptied out fast here," said O'Malley. "I parked on the north side next to Fitz's car. May I give you a ride to your car?"

"I'll be okay," she said. "It's a short walk. And besides, I've got to get to the hotel quickly so I can rest for tomorrow's match. The fun begins at nine."

"Okay, be safe," said Peter. "It's been nice spending time with you. And say hi to your father for me."

Syd stopped in her tracks.

"What do you mean 'say hi to my father'? I haven't spoken to him in two years. My mother issued a restraining order against him. He shouldn't be here."

"Oh, um—" Peter stammered. "I thought for sure I saw him standing behind our court tonight. You didn't know he was there?"

"No, he's not here, or at least he shouldn't be," she said. "He lives in Michigan. We don't talk anymore. Are you absolutely sure it was him?"

"Well, *absolutely* sure? I guess not. It could have been someone else. I waved, but he didn't acknowledge me. I haven't seen him since we were junior players, so he probably looks nothing like the way I remember him. Come to think about it, it was probably my eyes playing tricks on me. Are you sure you don't need a ride to your car?"

"No, I'm really okay. And thanks for your help. Maybe someday you should be a coach."

"Now, that would be an interesting career choice," he said. "Teaching beautiful women to play tennis. Maybe I'd work for free."

Unsure where the conversation might lead, Syd smiled, hoisted her tennis bag on her back, and nodded goodbye to Peter. As she headed toward the exit, she noticed Fitz across the complex, trash bag in hand, searching for cups and cans left behind by spectators.

A few stragglers remained, hoping to snag an autograph or picture with one of the remaining players. A small group of teens surrounded Syd at the exit, each with their own cell phone camera, ready to snap a quick photo.

"How about we take one giant picture?" said Syd, motioning to the tallest boy in the group. "Then you can text it to your friends after I'm gone."

The group bunched together with Syd in the middle, and the camera flashed brightly.

"I need to go," said Syd, glancing at her cell, which now read 9:39. "Big day for me tomorrow."

Syd walked through the dimly lit parking lot on the west side of the facility. She didn't want to focus on Peter's sighting. Tomorrow's match was hours away, and he was probably mistaken anyway. A loss on Sunday would mean an early departure from the tournament. She would stay in Silverhill to watch Enzo compete, but a defeat would be another step toward the end of her career. If she was ever going to achieve success, it needed to happen soon.

A white van, lights on and engine running, obstructed the view of her car. As she moved closer, she could see a driver and passenger, both men, waiting inside.

When she was nearly at the van, both men sat up quickly in their seats, motivated by her arrival. Nearby, a tall parking lot light flickered, creating a strobe-like effect. Why hadn't she accepted Peter's offer of a ride?

Her fingers groped for the Tiger Claw. Damn! She forgot to bring it. Maybe she'd run back toward the tournament site.

As she moved, the men emerged from the van, approaching from opposite directions. One was burly with tattoos running down his arm, and the other was tall and rangy. Neither looked familiar.

"Please stay away!" said Syd, backpedaling slowly. "I don't have money, and I want to get back to my hotel."

The men looked at each other, surprised by Syd's statement.

"Ma'am, please," said the burly guy. "We're just maintenance workers here. Is this your Corvette?"

"Yes, it's mine, but it's not for sale or anything," she said. "It's just a rental."

"We don't think you should drive this car home," said the taller guy. "Someone has done something bad to your car."

"Bad?" she asked. "What do you mean, 'bad'?"

Syd walked past the men and toward the back of her car. The passenger side looked untouched, and the trunk closed. As she walked to the driver's side, one man shouted, "Wait a second! I don't know if you should—"

Syd suddenly stopped, her brain attempting to make sense of what she was seeing. She felt a pounding in her chest, and her breathing turned shallow. An electrical-like charge shot up her spine. Painted on the driver's side door in thick black letters was a foreboding message:

Die Bitch!

CHAPTER 6

A chubby Caucasian man approached three attractive but unsuspecting women on a beach. Covering his face was a full beard, and his shoulder-length black hair flipped up at the end. He was barefoot, dressed in khakis and a blue muscle shirt.

The women were on their backs wearing bikinis. Two listened to music, and one read a novel. In the man's ear, apart from anyone's view, was a listening device designed to relay instructions from three men nearby. The man's mission was to obey the instructions provided to him. One woman sat up as she saw the man approach.

"Make these women feel your chest hair," said a voice through the device. "But you can't ask them to do it. It needs to be their idea." The other men giggled hysterically, like young adolescent school children who placed a fake spider on their teacher's desk.

Enzo's eyes surrendered the fight to stay open, but the sound of "Impractical Jokers" still resonated across the room. He'd hoped the comedy show would keep him awake until Syd returned. But a four-mile run in the heat, combined with a two-hour evening practice, turned his need for sleep into a bigger priority than lovemaking. The sound of the door swinging open interrupted Enzo's slumber.

"I'm packing up and leaving!" said Syd, tossing her empty suitcase on the side of the bed reserved for her. "I need to leave before anything else happens."

"Whoa, Syd, what are you doing?" asked Enzo. "Leaving? You're playing tomorrow!"

"Nope," said Syd, hurriedly throwing clothes in the suitcase without folding them. "Not going to happen. I'm leaving, and *this* is why."

Syd shoved her phone into Enzo's face. He lay horizontally, and his eyes hadn't quite cleared yet. Enzo searched blindly for the remote, which was inches from his left hand. He pressed the power button, ending the view of the bearded man getting a chest massage from one of the women.

"Wait," he said, still attempting to wake up. "What is that?"

Displayed on Syd's cell was a picture of the driver's side door of the Corvette with the inscription "Die Bitch" plainly in view.

"I'm definitely leaving," she said. "First, bourbon arrives via special delivery, and now my life's being threatened by a psycho with a can of spray paint."

She forced her bulging suitcase shut, failing to include some additional clothes she had placed on a table across the room.

"Hold on," said Enzo. "Someone wrote this on your car tonight? Where did that happen?"

"Outside the tennis center," said Syd. "It appeared two guys were going to attack me, but they were maintenance workers bracing me for what I was about to see."

"Syd," Enzo interrupted, "you're giving up a chance to qualify for this tournament because some jerk-off painted two words on your car?"

Syd looked into Enzo's bloodshot eyes as he sat up in the bed.

"Two words?" she said. "Really? If the words were 'live well' or 'be happy,' I'd be annoyed about my rental being defaced. But the words were 'Die Bitch,' which makes me not give a damn about the car or tournament."

"Did you call the police?"

"You know, I really thought about doing that," she said. "But I didn't feel like sitting in a police station until two in the morning, especially when I have to play at nine.

"But as I'm driving back to the hotel, I noticed people staring, trying to catch a glimpse of the 'Die Bitch' lady. So I decided to shitcan this tournament. It's not worth my life.

"Oh, and did I mention that my estranged father may have made an impromptu appearance at my practice session tonight? Unless O'Malley sees ghosts, and he's the one who sent the bourbon."

"Syd!" he shouted. "You can't let whoever is doing this to you win. You've worked too hard, and you're so close to breaking through. Why don't I pour you a drink? We'll continue to talk it out. If you want to leave after one hour, then you can go. Fair enough?"

"Okay," said Syd. "An hour it is. But there's one question you're not allowed to ask me."

"What's that?"

"Did I opt for the rental car insurance?"

Consuming two glasses of chardonnay hours before a match is not standard protocol, but the wine relaxed Syd. A few minutes later, she was lying next to Enzo, snoring away.

The sound of Enzo's cell phone alarm awakened Syd with a jolt. She sprung to her feet and located the glowing, pulsating phone on a table across the room. *What time is it? Did I oversleep my match? Were last night's events a dream?*

"Hey, relax, girl!" said Enzo, emerging from his sopor. "I set my alarm for you, just in case. You're going to play, right?"

She grabbed Enzo's phone, which displayed 6:45. Syd was just late enough to be stressed, considering she hadn't showered or consumed a bite of breakfast. And what about her car? The media would love to know the story behind a player driving with the words 'Die Bitch' displayed on her car.

"I'm showering and going downstairs to eat a light breakfast. I guess I'm going to play. Are you with me?"

"Yeah, sure," he said. "But we may have to shower together because we don't have much time."

"That's fine," said Syd, "but keep your hands to yourself. I'm not in the mood, and I have to conserve my energy."

At 7:15, Syd and Enzo sat downstairs in the small breakfast area of the hotel. A few players scheduled to play in tomorrow's main draw were either eating breakfast or passing through the lobby. Brianna Garvey, an American player ranked eighth in the world, sat a few tables away. She dined with a man, presumably her husband.

The server, matronly and probably in her mid-fifties, strolled leisurely to their table, order pad in hand.

"I'm ready to take your order," she smiled.

Syd told the server they were under a time constraint. She ordered a scrambled egg, a slice of wheat toast, and a small bowl of assorted fruit. Enzo, with no match scheduled until tomorrow, ordered the big farm breakfast complete with eggs, pancakes, hash browns, and sausage links.

"I assume you're going to eat quickly," said Syd.

"I promise," he laughed. "I'll finish with my breakfast before you."

"Hey, isn't that Kei Nishikori?" asked Enzo, pointing to a fit Asian man lugging a suitcase out the hotel door.

"Yep," she said. "He was number four in the world. At least he's got a few good years left."

"Unlike you," said Enzo. "That's what you're saying, isn't it?"

"I know," said Syd, straightening up in her seat. "Today brings enough challenges. And don't I know it."

As promised, Enzo's breakfast was gone before Syd's. He sometimes reminded her of a Shop-Vac, voraciously sucking solids and liquids into his holding tank, completely bypassing his tastebuds. Usually, she had to turn her head away when Enzo was in what she called "attack mode," but today was different. They needed to finish breakfast so she could begin the digestion process and arrive at the MMO in time for at least a fifteen-minute warm-up session with Enzo.

"One more thing before we leave," said Syd. "I need to call hotel maintenance to ask them if they have an extra can of spray paint."

"Why would you need spray paint at 7:45 a.m.?"

"I want to paint the letter T on my car right after the E. At least 'Diet Bitch' would make me look like a weight-loss nut instead of someone destined for doom."

Enzo thought about Syd's words and started to laugh. Every time he composed himself, his eyes met Syd's, and the process started over again.

"That's what I love about you," he said, wiping tears from his eyes with the restaurant's cloth napkin. "You find something funny in every situation. But in case you're wondering, I'll drive today."

As Enzo regained his composure, Syd's phone buzzed.

"Do you recognize the number?" asked Enzo.

"No."

"Then don't answer it. It's probably one of those robocalls."

"It shows a 614 area code. That's Columbus. Maybe I'd better take it."

"It's Al Fitzgerald," said the voice. "You know, Fitz?"

"Yes, I know you well, Fitz," said Syd. "What can I do for you?"

"There are a couple of things," he said. "The maintenance people told me about the car incident last night. Are you sure that occurred at our facility?"

"Yes," replied Syd. "When someone scrawls 'Die Bitch' in large black letters on my driver's side door, I usually notice it before I drive away."

"Do you know who painted that on your car?"

"Not really. I don't want to accuse anyone unless I'm sure."

"I'm sorry about what happened," he said. "I've hired extra security to monitor the players' parking area. It's probably some bored neighborhood kid who couldn't resist the urge to defile a nice car."

"Yeah, I'm sure that's it," she said. "Is there anything else, Fitz?"

"Yes, one more important thing," he said. "It looks like you've won your morning match by default. Your opponent, Monica Rivet, didn't return to her hotel last night, according to her significant other. They found her rental car abandoned this morning in a Columbus suburb called Powell. The police are trying to figure out what happened to her.

"But the good news is that you're one victory away from qualifying. We'll see you on the courts today at five."

CHAPTER 7

Sixteen-year-old Jessica Lovejoy was the talk of Columbus. Nobody expected her to defeat Canadian veteran Camille Watson, ranked eighty-third in the world. But Lovejoy rolled to a somewhat easy 6-2, 6-4 victory. Lovejoy, a high school junior, turned professional six weeks earlier, forsaking the opportunity to play college tennis amid a multitude of Division One offers.

Because of her ability to generate local interest, the MMO tournament committee allowed Lovejoy to participate in the tournament as a wildcard entry. No one expected her to survive her first-round encounter against Watson. A contingent of about a thousand fans arrived to support Lovejoy, a Columbus native. Her father and coach, Brooks Lovejoy, is the head pro and owner of Maplewood Tennis Club, located in a suburb called Dublin.

Nearly all of Lovejoy's powerful groundstrokes reached their intended targets during the first set, transforming an apprehensive crowd into a raucous, mob-like bunch. Whenever Lovejoy came up with a winning shot, the noise at Court 8 was deafening. Watson seemed distracted by the chaos early in the match but eventually rallied in the second set. The crowd refused to let up, and their energy and enthusiasm propelled the youngster to victory. Lovejoy ended the match with a down-the-line backhand that Watson could only watch helplessly.

Russo phoned Syd at noon, warning her of what she'd soon be up against.

"I just finished watching the Watson match," he said. "She lost to that sixteen-year-old. The crowd was crazy, and they've got the kid believing in herself. Be prepared to play hard and deal with the crowd."

"Let me talk to her!" Anja said to her coach, grabbing the phone out of his hand.

"Congrats on your victory this morning," she laughed. "I hear you didn't miss a single shot in the entire match."

"I was perfect today," said Syd. "I didn't know I could win and eat breakfast at the same time."

Anja was a courtside spectator at Lovejoy's match and was eager to share a scouting report.

"She's so young; she doesn't understand her limitations yet," said Anja. "And that makes her dangerous, especially with the crowd behind her. Hopefully, this girl will realize she's too young to win matches like this. I'll be cheering you on the entire time. After you win and qualify for the main draw, we can share a drink."

Syd thanked Anja, and they agreed to hit the practice court together for a pre-match warmup. Enzo scheduled an early practice session with Victor Dan, so Syd arranged a ride with best friend Nicole Hase, who'd made the ten-hour trip from Savannah.

Nicole and Syd were close friends since the first grade. Mrs. Murray, their elderly teacher, loved to share her modest spider collection with the class. While Syd bristled at the sight of arachnids, the young Nicole became fascinated with the species. Her interest continued to grow year after year. As of 2019, Nicole's collection was the fourth-largest in the world, according to the-scientist.com.

Nicole's white 2020 Buick Enclave zoomed into the hotel's lot and parked at the circle in front of the main entrance. Despite living in the same town, busy schedules hadn't allowed Syd and Nicole to see each other for eight months.

"This is quite a car," said Syd, placing her tennis bag in the rear cargo area and slipping into the seat next to Nicole. "I didn't know the spider industry paid so well."

"Well, since you mentioned that, I'm publishing my first book," said Nicole. "It'll be available in hardcover and online. It's titled *Arachnids and Us*, and Insect Planet may sign on for a five-episode trial series. Syd, I might become a celebrity like you!"

"If things work out, you'll be the genuine celebrity," said Syd. "I'm a twenty-four-year-old trying to squeeze the last bit of life out of my damaged body."

"Stop being modest," said Nicole. "The world will know exactly who you are after this tournament."

They arrived at the Wukeson Family Tennis Center and pulled into the same parking lot where Syd's car was defaced. This time, two guards patrolled the area, with one asking Syd for her ID before allowing Nicole to park.

Nicole turned off her motor and then looked to Syd.

"This is exciting!" she said. "I have a friend who's dying to meet you."

Nicole reached into the back seat and opened up a large blue cooler. She pulled out a fiberglass box equipped with a capful of water and several live grasshoppers. Taking up the biggest part of the enclosure was a large, brown-ish-black, hairy spider with robust legs and pads under each of its feet. Set in its forward-protruding jaws were two intimidating large black fangs running parallel to each other. Syd counted eight eyes and let out a gasp as Nicole reached inside and picked up the creature.

"Syd, I'd like you to meet Scarlet."

"Please!" said Syd, her heart pounding. "I'm scared of tarantulas. Please put him back into the cage!"

"Well, actually," said Nicole, "it's a she, not a he. And she's not a tarantula. She's what's known as a Theraphosidae, a member of the baboon spider family from South Africa."

"So I can assume by the way you're handling him—I mean her—that she's not poisonous?"

"To humans, she's not poisonous, although you might go into shock if her fangs puncture your skin. The intense pain usually goes away within eighteen hours after treatment."

"Well, that makes me feel a lot better," said Syd. "Do you think she'd like to sleep between Enzo and me tonight?"

"Oh, gosh no," said Nicole, gently placing Scarlet back into the enclosure. "She's my baby. And not only that, but she's also worth ten grand, so I can't have you squishing her."

"Okay then, have it your way," said Syd. "Scarlet stays with you."

"Remember when one of my spiders bit you after I told you to pet it?" asked Nicole. "I think that was in sixth grade."

"I still have the mark," said Syd, opening her left hand and displaying a pair of red dots on the skin between her forefinger and thumb. "I felt dizzy after it bit me, but the feeling faded the next day. My mother asked me to stop playing with you after that."

"That was probably excellent advice," laughed Nicole. "Do you remember what that spider's name was? I called it Siggy, but its full name was Sigourney Weaver."

"And didn't you have a black widow?" asked Syd. "And you named it—"

"Venom Miss America!" interrupted Nicole.

"You know we can't go eight months anymore without seeing each other," said Syd. "Our conversations are too stimulating."

While in the parking lot, Nicole introduced Syd to Matilda, a smaller Brazilian Wandering Spider she kept in a separate container. "I don't dare take Matilda out in mixed company. Her venom is toxic to the nervous system. Believe it or not, a bite from a spider like Matilda sometimes causes prolonged erections in men," said Nicole. "If you ever have a need, she's available for rent. Or perhaps you'd like me to slip her into your opponent's tennis bag. We can work out some kind of financial arrangement." Nicole's expression was stoic. Then she broke into a smile.

"I'm just trying to be funny," she said. "You know, to relax you before the match."

"Won't your friends be in danger in this hot car?" asked Syd. "It's in the mid-eighties here."

"The cooling container is battery-powered and completely climate-controlled," said Nicole. "It keeps insects safe in all kinds of weather. Anyway, it's time to worry about you, Syd, and how you're going to win today!"

After Nicole and Syd parted, Anja met her for a warm-up session at Court 11, an hour before Syd's five o'clock match. Anja took pride in her fitness, but she appeared even more muscled and well-toned for this tournament. She already qualified for the main draw and earned the fifteenth seed among the contingent of 64 players. To complement her strict physical training regimen, Anja enrolled in a sports nutrition program in her home country of Bulgaria. Her diet included seven servings of fruits and vegetables, whole-grain carbohydrates, and healthy protein sources such as chicken, fish, turkey, nuts, and legumes.

"I'm prepared to die to win this tournament," said Anja. "Let's hope we don't face each other along the way."

At the end of their hitting session, a horde of noisy pro-Lovejoy fans paraded toward Center Court Stadium, carrying signs and banners.

"Do you see them?" said Anja. "They are all hoping their hometown child beats you. But they are underestimating the power of us old girls," she said, flexing the bulging bicep of her right arm. "And you have the power to win this match."

"Thanks, Anja," said Syd, a shot of adrenaline moving through her system like a Ferrari. "I can accomplish anything with you in my corner."

Syd noticed that Anja's forearm was bandaged.

"Did you get into a fight with an alley cat?"

"No, it was the weirdest thing," said Anja. "Paul restrung my racquet this morning, and a section of sharp string was sticking out where he cut the tying knot. My arm brushed across it during practice. He should have been more careful. I told Paul I was going to sue him for 'malpractice.' Do you get it?"

"Unfortunately, I do," said Syd. She placed her left arm around Anja's shoulders and squeezed tightly.

"Thanks for being here for me."

Syd turned and headed toward Center Court, feeling like a gladiator walking into the coliseum. *But this was different*, she thought. *No one would get killed or anything.*

CHAPTER 8

Part of me wants Sydney to win this match, while the other part wants her to lose disgracefully. This sixteen-year-old child wouldn't be here, except that she was born in this town. Local favorite, my ass!

And why in hell would part of me want Sydney to win this match? Because I need her to remain in this city long enough to kill her. An embarrassing loss today may motivate her to leave town quickly, her shapely butt hauling down I-75 toward Savannah in that Corvette I meticulously defaced.

Getting out of town early wouldn't save her life; it would just buy her more time. But my time is important, too. I need to proceed with life. The sooner she's rotting in the ground, the better.

Planning to kill someone is easy. The hard part is implementing the act without getting caught. What good is revenge if I spend my remaining days confined in a claustrophobic cell, dreaming about nothing but a parole hearing every five years? That's not revenge; that's stupidity.

I need her to die, and I must get away scot-free. I've suffered enough, but I don't think I'll resent Sydney anymore after she's dead. No, death will be the great equalizer. In fact, maybe our relationship will improve in the next world.

Perhaps the best-case scenario is that someone else gets arrested, prosecuted, convicted, and sentenced for her murder. Then, I wouldn't spend my remaining days worrying that a cold-case detective will get a hair up his ass and hire a forensics team to uncover the DNA I left behind. They almost never reopen solved crimes. I need peace of mind.

In a perverted way, I feel sorry for Sydney. She's warming up with Southwest Ohio's newest goody-two-shoes. To the Columbus fans, Sydney's the Big Bad Wolf, trying to destroy the innocent dreams of their little Goldilocks.

Sure, I'll play the political game and pretend to like this young girl, but I'll bet she's one entitled brat. A Miss Priss who's been told by everyone how wonderful she is. I'll bet she's never had a good ass-whoopin' in her entire life. Come to think of it—I hope Sydney wins. She deserves a little fun before I snuff out her life.

Before I kill Sydney, I need to talk with her. First, she owes me a big thank-you for removing Monica Rivet from the equation. She would have probably beaten Sydney. But Monica's disappearance casts suspicion on Sydney or anyone else close to her. Who benefits when a player defaults? That's easy: Syd or anyone who's a friend to her. While removing Monica from the equation wasn't easy, it guaranteed Sydney would spend more time in town—and we know why that's important.

Wow! The crowd's loud, and I can't believe Lovejoy's leading 2-0 in the first set. She's shaking her fist in defiance and screaming every time she wins a point. But Sydney doesn't look rattled yet. My guess is she'll adjust and get back into the match. That's something I've always admired about Sydney. She's a cerebral competitor who uses analytical skills to figure out her opponent's game plan.

Back to Monica. She was so naïve. She knew who I was, and she thought she could trust me. Knowing who someone is and knowing their motivations are two entirely different things. How does a well-traveled, thirty-six-year-old not understand something so basic?

I approached Monica and told her I knew the president of Atlas Sportswear, a premier tennis clothing manufacturer. I'd even looked up the guy's name—Stephen Covington—on the internet, in case she decided to fact-check me.

Covington wanted to deviate from the norm—I told her—and find a veteran player to represent his company's apparel line. He was in town for the tournament and mentioned Monica's name to me. All she had to do was agree to wear his company's apparel during tournaments. It would guarantee her a two-year contract with a six-figure income. I know, that was quite a fish story.

Rivet made a decent living in seventeen years on the tour, especially in her late twenties. At thirty-six, she wasn't qualifying for most main-draws anymore, and her earnings had slipped significantly. The allure of signing a lucrative contract near the end of her career was too enticing to dismiss.

The success of the meeting with Covington, I said, hinged on their interaction. Covington was a particular man. She would have to tolerate his eccentric ways to please him. I informed her that Covington abhorred interruptions and preferred no cell phones at meetings.

"If he hears your cell ring or even a buzzing sound, the whole deal could go up in smoke," I'd said. "Give him what he wants, and you'll get what you need."

Man, I've become a good liar. I believed for a moment that I understood Covington's idiosyncrasies. I've heard if you lie enough, you'll eventually believe those lies. Maybe I'm at that point now.

Speaking of lies, there was one more thing I told Monica. Whatever you do, don't refer to Covington as "Steve." He prefers "Stephen." If she wants to be 100 percent safe, refer to him as "Mr. Covington."

Wow! Lovejoy's game is breaking down. Sydney's leading 4-2 in the first set, and the crowd's much less vocal. Instead of matching the younger girl's power, Sydney's using a variety of shots—slices, looping top spins, and drop shots—to break her rhythm. Lovejoy likes to hit with a lot of pace, but Sydney's not cooperating. I'm not surprised by Sydney's tactics, but I am impressed. It's now 5-2, and Sydney's serving to win the first set. I hope she keeps it up because my plan needs a few days to play out.

I'm laughing out loud now because Lovejoy looked over at her father and screamed, "She's supposed to be a pro, but she won't hit hard. I'm playing in the twelve-and-unders again!"

Pampered little imbecile! Although I hate to admit it, she's going to be a helluva player someday. At sixteen, she's hitting as hard as 95 percent of the women on the tour. Once she grows into her body, she'll become a household name. And if she gets her shit together in this match, she has enough talent to beat Sydney.

By the way, I harbored no ill will against Monica. She seemed like a decent person who struggled during the twilight of her career. Her ultimate downfall was bad luck, having to face Sydney in the draw.

The plan was for Monica to meet Covington and me at a small Vietnamese restaurant called Saigon Adventure. I dined there for lunch earlier in the day. I overheard the owner mention that she stored the key underneath the mat at closing time.

The hours listed showed the restaurant would close at eight on Saturday night. Knowing the restaurant would be vacant, I informed Monica that Covington would meet us at the restaurant at nine. I asked her to drive. Monica didn't know I'd already stolen the key at 8:15 and left the restaurant unlocked with the lights on.

We arrived at Saigon Adventure a few minutes before nine. I informed Monica that Covington had reserved the restaurant exclusively for us. Fortunately, she bought my story. Hopefully, police wouldn't notice the lights and come inside to inquire.

We entered the restaurant together and, of course, there was no staff available to show us to our table. Monica looked at me quizzically. Thinking on the fly, I told her Mr. Covington had arranged for staff, but they wouldn't arrive until 9:15.

"What about Mr. Covington?" she asked. "Isn't he supposed to meet us here?"

I said I received a text and that he would arrive shortly. I asked her to remain at the table and peruse the menu. I mentioned the bahn xeo was to die for, a poor choice of words given the circumstances. On my way to the restroom, I chastised myself.

The cleaver knife I'd removed from their kitchen earlier in the day was exactly where I left it—inside the restroom, underneath the circular brown metal trash can. I stashed it under my shirt and walked back to the table.

As I sat down and attempted to make small talk, I could feel Monica's eyes burning a hole through me. She stopped listening to anything I was saying. She began putting things together. We were all alone—no servers, no cell phones, no staff, and no Covington. I tried to distract her, but she would have none of it.

"Tell me what's going on. Because if it's sex, I go a different direction than you, if you know what I mean. And besides, I'm at this tournament with Jamie, whom I dearly love."

Monica rose to her feet. "I'm leaving," she said, fumbling inside her pocket for car keys. "I think it's best that you call a taxi."

I apologized to Monica. She was correct, I said. She was beautiful, and I longed to know her better. I'd been harboring a crush for a long time. I had gone about it all wrong, but I desired her more than she could imagine.

Monica's anger dissipated. Or at least I thought so. She seemed irritated but a little flattered.

"I have to play in the morning," she said. "But I will give you a ride to your hotel. Please sit in the back. We don't have to tell anyone about this."

We left the restaurant and returned to her car. I slipped into the back seat behind Monica. She grabbed a plastic container of gum labeled "fresh mint with green tea extract" from the console. "Take two and pass them back to me," she said. "Let's pretend nothing happened tonight."

I pulled out the knife as she placed her keys into the ignition. "Yes, nothing happened at all."

But then I mumbled imperceptibly, "At least not yet."

As the engine fired, I reached from the back seat, grabbed Monica's hair with my left hand, and yanked her head backward toward me. I placed the clever against her throat.

Monica finally understood the situation now, as the blade cut into her vocal cords. No time for small talk, reasoning, or bargaining. In an act of desperation, she grabbed my cleaver-wielding arm with both hands and dug her nails deep into my skin. My adrenaline was pumping too hard to feel pain, but I knew in an instant my DNA would be at the scene. Even though my DNA wasn't on any database, it could come back to haunt me. I hardly remember the next part, except that Monica was lying motionless in the front seat and bleeding out.

Wait, why is the crowd roaring? In my reverie, I'd stopped focusing on the match. Holy shit! The young girl won the second set, 6-4. The crowd is going ape-shit! Now they're going into the third and final set. I'd better stop daydreaming. Pay fucking attention!

CHAPTER 9

Going into her final qualifying match, Sydney didn't know what to expect. Her young opponent had little experience as a pro but believed in herself enough to pose a significant threat. Fresh off a win over a seasoned veteran, Jessica Lovejoy entered the match sassy and confident.

Sydney noticed that Cassandra Flores was seated in Lovejoy's players' box. Why would the world's second-best player give a damn about a local sixteen-year-old? Was Flores angry about Syd's brief affair with Willems, the world's number-one player? Certainly, Willems hooked up with hundreds of women, so why would that matter?

Syd knew a loss today would send her home nearly bankrupt and pondering the end of her career. One match away from qualifying, she couldn't allow the crowd to distract her. She had twenty-four thousand reasons to win today because that would be the amount of her prize money. Anything beyond qualifying would be a bonus.

When she was young, Syd's father trained her to block out courtside distractions. As unsettled as her dad was in life, he had mastered the techniques of focus, relaxation, and concentration. When Syd wasn't playing a point, she used the RE-LAX method. Every time she breathed in, she would say "RE" to herself. And each time she exhaled, she would say "LAX." The RE-LAX technique allowed Syd to put aside all negative thoughts and focus on the only task she could control—hitting the next ball.

Her father developed another method of focusing. Each time the ball bounced, Syd said the word "bounce" to herself. Each time the ball struck a racquet—from either player—she mouthed the word "hit." Syd's thoughts consisted exclusively of "RE" and "LAX," and "bounce" and "hit." She felt like she was in a mini-trance during matches, blocking out negative thoughts and impulses.

Syd felt disrespected by Lovejoy during pre-match instructions. When Syd asked which player would call the coin flip, Lovejoy rolled her eyes.

"If she wants to call it, let her," Lovejoy said to the referee. "I don't really care."

Lovejoy's ability impressed Syd during the warmup. The amount of topspin generated by her backhand amazed her. But Lovejoy's forehand was her best shot. Its velocity matched many of the world's top players. Every time she'd hit a forehand past Syd, she'd thrust her fist in the air—a normal gesture during a match, but an absurd one in a warmup.

Syd's players' box consisted of Chelsea, Anja, Russo, Nicole, and Enzo. She was happy to have the "Fab Five" in her corner; they'd probably be the only ones cheering for her.

The warmup seemed short and fragmented. She couldn't dial in on the ball speed generated by Lovejoy. Lovejoy jumped out to a 2-0 lead in the first set.

But then the unthinkable happened. Her young opponent, hitting the ball as skillfully as any player in the world, abruptly cooled off. Instead of looking like a top-ten competitor, she resembled a confused, fumbling sixteen-year-old who couldn't figure out the combination to her high school locker. Syd won the next six games, winning the first set, 6-2.

Usually, when an inexperienced player falls behind an experienced pro, her tennis game circles a drain. Syd expected Lovejoy to throw in the towel, but it didn't happen. Lovejoy found a second gear, broke Syd's serve early, and rode her own big serve to a 6-4 victory in the second set.

During the break before the third and final set, Syd sat courtside with a towel draped over her head. She was angry about letting the second set slip away and for allowing Lovejoy to believe in herself again. She applied her father's breathing techniques in her courtside chair, and soon, her body and mind relaxed. Once her negativity subsided, she could think clearly. And as her mind cleared, a new strategy popped into her head.

Lovejoy won many points because of powerful serving, which Syd had no control over. But Lovejoy's overwhelming baseline shots were even more damaging. In her comfort zone, Lovejoy was on the verge of taking control of the match. Syd knew she needed to disrupt Lovejoy's rhythm before it was too late.

She mixed in a variety of shots in each rally, including low slices, high topspin lobs, and powerful flat strokes.

She provided Lovejoy with a new adventure on every shot. Lovejoy's shots started missing their destinations, most flying wide, but others landing in the net or beyond the baseline. Syd built a 5-2 lead in the third set, and she was just one game away from qualifying for the main draw. Lovejoy, meanwhile, was going ballistic on the court change, smashing several racquets to pieces.

As Syd prepared to serve what she hoped would be the last game, she felt weak. Something wasn't right. She tried to take a deep breath, but little oxygen flowed into her lungs. Nausea and dizziness overwhelmed her.

As she headed toward the back of the court to serve, a tingling sensation flowed through her body. Two double faults and a couple of Lovejoy winners later, the score was 5-3. The teenager easily held serve on four straight points, and suddenly Lovejoy had reduced Syd's lead to 5-4.

At the break, Syd slumped over her chair, looking at her undersized retinue in the stands. They were staring at her quizzically. Enzo spread his arms at his sides with palms up, asking for an explanation. Syd looked up at the tournament chair, who also seemed concerned.

"I need a medical timeout," she said, struggling to breathe. "Will you please send a trainer out?"

Victor Dan watched the match from above, sitting high in the stadium seats, far away from most spectators. In his presence was a young girl he met after a practice session. The woman surprised him, approaching while he was perspiring heavily. Before Victor knew it, he was showering in his room while she watched television in bed. And now, she draped over him like a blanket. Maybe this was his chance to escape.

"I need to head to the players' box to talk to Enzo," he said. "I want to make sure his girlfriend is okay. Maybe I'll catch you later."

The woman, in her late teens or early twenties, wore a halter top, which bulged in the chest area, and a pair of tight-fitting jeans. Her black hair ran to her waist. "Would you like me to go with you?" she asked.

"Why don't you stay up here instead?" said Victor. "The players' box is reserved for family and friends."

The woman released her grip on Victor's arm, sensing this might be her last encounter with the Romanian player. Victor dashed from the top of the stadium, several bleachers at a time, and circled around to join Syd's friends.

"Enzo, what the hell's going on with Syd?" asked Victor, grabbing Enzo's arm.

"Easy on the arm, pal!" he said. "You've got a grip like a vise."

"Sorry, man," said Victor. "I didn't think I squeezed you that hard, but maybe the weightlifting is paying off. I'm really concerned about Syd. Is she going to retire?"

"I don't know," said Enzo. "Here comes the trainer."

Syd lay courtside. Her breathing was labored.

The trainer arrived at courtside, knelt next to Syd, and examined her. The head linesperson, Larry Epps, climbed down from his chair and spoke to her.

"Ms. Livingstone, we allow three minutes from the time the trainer arrives. At that point, you must play or receive a code violation."

Three minutes seemed like hours away. She was more concerned with getting air into her lungs and stopping her head from spinning.

"Has this happened to you before?" asked Bob Hunsaker, one of several trainers working the tournament.

"No," said Syd. "I'm having trouble breathing."

Hunsaker placed a stethoscope to her heart and asked her to sit up. Her heart rate was slightly elevated but nothing abnormal, considering she was in a three-hour battle.

"Have you eaten something you're allergic to?" asked Hunsaker. "Or have you come into contact with some type of poisonous plant?"

"Not that I'm aware," said Syd. "Can you treat me?"

"I can give you a shot of an antihistamine," he said. "But the side effect is extreme fatigue. Since you're experiencing breathing problems, I'm going to recommend that you retire from the match."

"One minute and thirty seconds remaining in the injury timeout," interrupted the head linesperson.

"Look, I know you want what's best for me," said Syd. "And I appreciate it. But I need to finish. Please give me the shot."

Hunsaker objected, but Syd cut him off. "Please do it. It's my life."

The doctor administered the shot as the countdown reached fifteen seconds. Syd looked over to Enzo, who was making a throat-slashing gesture to convince Syd to abort the match.

"I'm going to finish," she said, rising to her feet and grabbing her racket.

Hunsaker appeared stunned by Syd's statement, and he walked to the chair for a private conversation. Epps turned his microphone off, and the two conversed for another minute.

"Ms. Livingstone," said Epps, raising his voice because his microphone was still off. "The trainer recommends that you retire. I have to say I agree. Why don't you live to play another day?"

Fitz, the director of the tournament, walked onto the court to speak with Epps.

"She's having trouble breathing, and she's dizzy," said Epps. "The trainer advises against continuing. She insists on playing. Am I allowed to end this match?"

Fitz perused Syd, who was standing on her side of the court, preparing to serve. Her complexion was white, and her breathing shallow.

"Ms. Livingstone," said Fitz. "Do you wish to continue on against the trainer's orders?"

"Absolutely," she said, trying to ignore the antihistamine's fatigue. "I want to finish this."

Fitz shrugged his shoulders, looked up at Epps, and said, "Let's resume play."

Fitz's announcement brought Lovejoy to her feet. She stormed the head linesman's chair next to where Fitz was standing.

"This is pure shit!" said Lovejoy, a vein bulging from her forehead. "You heard her; she says she can't fucking breathe. The trainer tells her to stop playing, and now you're allowing her to continue? You need to stop this match now!"

Fitz's eyes met Lovejoy's wild stare. "You have no say in the matter, Ms. Lovejoy," he said. "If Ms. Livingstone chooses to play, then that's what we'll do."

Apparently still in shock, Lovejoy picked up a ball and launched it into the upper deck of the stadium. She grabbed one of four remaining rackets and smashed it into the ground, crumpling it into a worthless pile of fiberglass.

"Bullshit!" she screamed at the top of her lungs. "I don't have to take this."

Then she looked at her players' box and located her father. "They're unfair, Daddy!"

Epps, back in his chair, returned his microphone to the "on" position.

"I have already warned you about your behavior," he said to Lovejoy. "Now I'm taking a point away. If you show another example of unsportsmanlike conduct, I will penalize you a game and then the match."

Lovejoy may have been a spoiled brat, but she was no fool. If she continued to harass Epps, he would take away a full game, giving her opponent a 6-4 win in the final set.

The crowd screamed loudly for Lovejoy, apparently unphased by her conduct. "C'mon, Jessica!" screamed a guy from somewhere on the east side of the stadium. "We love you!"

The Lovejoy faithful rose to their feet, cheering and applauding wildly, causing Syd to wait for the noise to die down before serving. Ahead 15-love, she was only three points from victory. But fatigue and inability to breathe properly made three points seem light-years away.

Syd's first serve floated feebly and bounced high into Lovejoy's forehand strike zone. Normally, her opponent would have ripped a winner down the line or smacked the ball at an extreme angle cross-court. But a still-seething Lovejoy ripped the ball a foot beyond the baseline. Syd was two points from victory.

Syd struck her next serve with more force, but the pace was nothing to brag about. Lovejoy returned a rocket back at Syd, who could barely get her racket frame on the ball. 30-15.

Her breathing failing and fatigue increasing, Syd double-faulted on the next point, making it 30-all. *The body's shutting down*, thought Syd. *I might collapse.*

On the next point, the ball rocketed back and forth for over twenty hits. Syd hit a weak return on the run, and Lovejoy ran forward, ready to crush a winner. As she prepared to strike the ball, the same voice from the stands yelled, "Kill it, Jessie!" The shout stunned Lovejoy, causing her to look up a second early. Her ball crashed into the top of the net.

"Can we play that point over?" begged Lovejoy. "That was a definite hindrance!"

"Unfortunately, the shout came from the crowd," said Epps. "That's not considered a hindrance. I'll caution the crowd to remain silent during the points. 40-30."

Lovejoy looked to her parents in the box but remained quiet. Syd was one point away.

As Syd bounced the ball before serving, her stomach cramped. She felt a rush coming from deep inside. She ran to a trash can stationed at courtside and vomited violently. She paused before vomiting again.

"Stop the match!" yelled Lovejoy from her side of the court. "She's going to make the rest of us sick!"

Epps stared straight ahead, trying to decide how to proceed. Syd knew they could default her, especially since she had introduced bodily fluids into the equation.

Syd glanced at the courtside clock, which showed ten seconds left to serve. She wiped her mouth with her towel and sprinted to the baseline. She tossed the ball and hit a slice into Lovejoy's body. Shocked that Syd had recovered so quickly, Lovejoy returned the ball with a slice of her own.

A low slice was not ideal for attacking, but these were desperate times. Syd ran around her backhand and attempted an inside-out crosscourt forehand. She didn't like the feel of the ball as it careened off her racquet. It seemed like she didn't get enough height on the shot. Her guess was that the ball was going to strike the net. And it did.

The ball hit the white stripe on top of the net. But instead of landing harmlessly on her own side, the ball crept over the stripe and onto her opponent's court. Lovejoy expected the ball to land short and charged forward. The net tape, however, diffused the speed of the ball, and it landed very close to the net. Lovejoy could not get her racket on it.

The match was over—a 6-2, 4-6, 6-4 victory for Sydney Livingstone. And at the very least, a $24,000 payday would be in her immediate future.

Syd had no strength to meet Lovejoy at the net to shake hands. She wobbled slightly and landed on her back, not in a celebratory way but a semiconscious one.

Enzo leaped over the box railings and sprinted to Syd's side. Several trainers and a doctor also rushed the court, along with photographers from news outlets from across the country. This match would surely be internet news in the morning.

Syd went in and out of consciousness before they placed her onto a stretcher. As she opened her eyes while being removed from the court, her eyes focused on a figure high in one corner of the stadium. Memories of her childhood flashed back into her mind. Perhaps she was dying.

Or then again, perhaps she had just laid eyes on her father.

Chapter 10

The transport to the hospital, via ambulance, was a blur to Syd. She vaguely remembered being loaded onto the stretcher and taken from the stadium. She had no memory of receiving treatment in the emergency room.

The next thing she remembered, she was in a private room with an IV stuck in her left arm and oxygen tubes in her nostrils.

"So happy you're back with us!" said a smiling Enzo, cradling her left hand. "The doctors said there was a five-minute period when it appeared we might lose you."

Standing behind Enzo was Syd's mother, Chelsea Livingstone-Crumhour, an attractive brunette in her fifties who passed her good looks onto her daughter.

"I love you, Syd!" said Chelsea. "I'm so glad you're going to be all right. You gave us—and the entire city of Columbus—a real scare!"

"Is Nicole here?" asked Syd.

"No," said Chelsea. "Evidently, one of her spiders exhibited strange behavior. She found an emergency vet who specializes in exotic animals. She freaked out about the cost. I offered to pay, but she declined. She sends her love and promises to call tomorrow."

Chelsea straightened out Syd's bed linens and moved the covers up to her chin.

"With Nicole and her spider collection, there's never a dull moment," said Chelsea. "But I adore that girl. Enzo, did you know Nicole was a great high school tennis player? She played on the same team with Syd. They go way back."

"Syd mentioned that," said Enzo. "She felt like Nicole lived in her shadow in high school, but she always handled it with class and dignity."

Syd moved her fingers up to her nose, where she could feel the oxygen tubes. "I guess I won't have to make any formal introductions?" she said, smiling weakly.

"We took care of that in the ER," said Enzo. "Your mother's very charming. Now I know where you get your looks—and your sense of humor."

Syd reached for a plastic cup of ice water on the extendable wooden table above her bed. She sucked on the straw until the water disappeared. "My mouth's really dry. I think I'm still dehydrated."

"The doctor says your IV will keep you hydrated until you're discharged tomorrow," said Enzo.

As if on cue, a man in his mid-to-late forties, salt and pepper hair, and dressed in a white lab coat entered the room.

"Ms. Livingstone, I presume," he said, trying to mask a wry smile. "I'm Dr. Greg Fair. I was your physician in the ER here at Countywide Hospital. How are you feeling?"

"I'd say pretty fair," said Syd, as laughter echoed from around the room. "I won my match, didn't I? If I'm mistaken, then I won't be able to pay my hospital bill."

"Oh, we checked on that before I administered treatment. I'll receive compensation for my work today."

"Today's still Sunday, isn't it?" asked Syd.

"It is," said Enzo. "For another two hours and ten minutes."

"Ms. Livingstone," said the doctor. "Although you put us through quite a scare, you're stable and out of danger. I'd recommend staying here overnight to build up your strength."

"Tomorrow's a day off," said Chelsea. "Her next match is at three o'clock on Tuesday."

"It depends on how you feel on Tuesday," said Dr. Fair. "I don't think your problem is fatigue or dehydration. Something else caused it. Did you have any exposure to an allergen or toxic plant? Or did a snake or insect bite you?"

"I don't think so," said Syd. "I make a habit of monitoring what goes into my body." She looked at Enzo and winked. Enzo hoped Chelsea hadn't seen that. She had.

"Get some rest, and we'll discharge you in the morning," said Fair. "And congratulations on your win. A Columbus television station was referring to you as 'Unstoppable Syd.' They're right about that, you know."

After Dr. Fair exited the room, Syd looked at her mother.

"Did you see Dad at the match tonight? I think I saw him in the corner of the stadium."

"Your father?" asked Chelsea. "No, I didn't see him. Have you two been communicating?"

"It's been a long time," said Syd. "Peter O'Malley—the tennis player—spotted him yesterday, although he said he wasn't completely sure. Maybe Peter put the idea in my brain. I may have been delirious, but I think that was him."

"Maybe it was the power of suggestion," said Enzo. "But if you say you saw your dad tonight, I believe you."

Chelsea said she filed a restraining order on Syd's father, Michael Livingstone, in 2020. Several of her colleagues testified that Michael had followed her throughout the Boston area. Brian Crumhour, Chelsea's current husband, claimed that Michael had tailed his car for several hours while he made business calls. The judge granted the order and forbade Michael to come within one hundred yards of Chelsea or Brian. The order would remain in force until the end of the year.

"I don't know if he's dangerous," said Chelsea, "but they diagnosed him with severe anxiety and depression. If someone is crazy enough to follow you, who knows what else they're capable of?"

"Why didn't you tell me, Mom? That's pretty important stuff."

"He's your father, Syd. I know that at one time, you were very close to him, despite his abusive nature. I'd like to see you salvage some kind of relationship. He has mental issues, but he's always loved you."

Syd looked at Enzo, who had moved to the corner of the room.

"I can't fathom this," she said. "I'm being stalked at this tournament, and now there's a legitimate chance that my dad is making an impromptu appearance."

"It's possible the stalker and your father are the same person," said a man in a dark blue suit, his polished shoes tapping on the tile as he entered the room.

Enzo and Chelsea jumped to attention, startled by the mysterious man who walked toward Syd. The man extended his hand.

"Gil Trent, Franklin County homicide division. I talked with Dr. Fair. He said I could ask you a few questions, as long as it doesn't stress you out."

"It's too late for that," said Syd, straightening into a sitting position. "Did you say 'homicide'? I'm not sure why you're talking to me."

"You're not in any trouble," said Gil, who reminded Syd of a cop you'd see on TV. "But I need to ask you a few questions."

Trent looked at Chelsea and Enzo.

"May I ask you both to leave the room for a few minutes? I'll let you know when I'm finished."

"Excuse me," said Enzo. "Is it Mr. Trent?"

"Lieutenant," said Trent, apparently not taking offense.

"Okay, Lieutenant Trent," continued Enzo. "Do you mind if I see your ID before we leave you alone with Syd?"

"That's understandable," said Trent, reaching into his pocket and flashing his badge for all to see. "It'll just be a moment."

* * * * *

Enzo and Chelsea left the room and returned to the waiting area. A rerun of *Sex and the City* blasted from above a
half-filled room of visitors. Anja and Russo emerged from
the elevator and spotted Enzo and Chelsea.

"Is Syd well enough to see visitors?" asked Anja.

"Probably, but I wouldn't go in there," said Chelsea.
"She's talking to a detective. Hang out with Enzo and me
for a few minutes."

The foursome huddled together, separating themselves from everyone else in the room. They shared
funny stories about Syd and her relentless determination
to win, despite all odds. It was a welcome distraction for
Chelsea.

"I'm mentally exhausted, and I'm starving," said Anja.
"There's a vending machine down the hall. Would anyone
like something?"

"I'll join you," said Russo. "I need to see what kind of
stuff they have."

Anja and Russo headed down the hall toward the machine, leaving Enzo and Chelsea alone.

"Enzo, explain to me what's been going on with Syd.
Someone was stalking her?"

Enzo discussed internet predators, dismissing them
as perverts who had nothing better to do. He also mentioned the "Die Bitch" message on Syd's car.

"That concerns me a little more," said Enzo, "although
the tournament director thinks it's a bunch of area kids

screwing around with spray paint. But why only on Syd's car? I can't figure that out."

He brought up the bourbon delivery but left out the part where he posed naked in the tub.

"I'm worried about Syd," said Chelsea. "I hope the police officer is taking it easy on her. She's in no condition to be interrogated."

Enzo scanned the room, leaned over to Chelsea, and spoke softly so no one would hear.

"Miss Crumhour," he said. "I love your daughter. And I hope you're okay with that because we're, um, you know, different."

"I've noticed the differences," said Chelsea, appearing concerned. "You hit serves with more spin. And Syd is way more aggressive from the baseline."

Enzo smiled as Chelsea put her arms around him and squeezed tightly.

* * * * *

Syd needed sleep. A combination of factors was kicking her ass: her energy loss, her body's allergic reaction to god-knows-what, and the side-effects of the antihistamine. She was in no mood to play the question-and-answer game, but she persevered.

"Lieutenant, you said you're from homicide. I won a grueling match today and almost died in the process. Why am I speaking with homicide if no one's been murdered?"

Trent reached into his suit pocket and pulled out a picture. Syd recognized her as Monica Rivet. "Do you know this woman?" he asked.

"Yes, of course, I know her," she said. "I was scheduled to play her this morning.

"Wait a minute, I know they found her car, but are you saying something bad happened to her?"

"Bad is an understatement, Ms. Livingstone. We found her car abandoned in a nearby suburb called Bexley. We found blood in the car, although most of it had been cleaned up. As you know, she's never returned to the tournament or her hotel. Her companion, Jamie Pendleton, reported her missing early Sunday morning. We questioned Pendleton, but there's no evidence to make an arrest."

"I'm horrified to hear that, detective," said Syd. "but why are you here asking me questions about her disappearance, considering my health right now?"

"I spoke with the tournament's director, Al Fitzgerald. Do you know him?"

"Everybody knows Fitz," said Syd.

"Well, he informed me of a threat painted on your car on Saturday. Do you have any clue who may have done that?"

Syd shook her head.

"Fitz, as you call him, suggested that you would be a good starting point, but we're unsure if there is a connection between the car threat and Ms. Rivet's disappearance. So, I'll just come right out and ask you. Do you know of anyone who would want either you or Ms. Rivet dead?"

"Some people may not like me, I guess, but want me dead? No. And I don't know Monica well enough to hazard a guess."

"You benefited from Ms. Rivet's absence. Is that correct?"

"Well, I guess," said Syd, not knowing where this line of questioning was going. "Her default moved me one step closer to qualifying. But I had nothing—"

"I'm not saying you caused her disappearance," Trent interrupted. "But who wants you to win so badly that they might hurt Ms. Rivet?"

"Nobody I know would do that," said Syd, feeling dizzy and a little nauseated.

"I need to get some rest. May we continue this discussion another time?"

"Absolutely," said Trent. "I'm just about to leave. There's one more question I have to ask. What was your relationship with Milena Lombardi?"

"Milena was my college teammate, my doubles partner, and my dearest friend," said Syd. "We had a falling out at the end, but I loved her. Why are you asking me about Milena?"

"Because we found something at the scene. Do you recognize this?"

Trent reached into the pocket of his trousers. He pulled out an item enclosed in a clear plastic bag. Inside was a locket on a gold chain. The clasp was open, displaying a picture of Syd and Milena, each smiling and holding a large trophy.

"Have you ever seen this before?" asked Trent.

"Yes. Where did you find that? Milena had the only other one. Mine's inside my tennis bag, sitting on that table over there. I always take it with me wherever I go."

Trent walked across the room, picked up the bag, and handed it to Syd. "Would you show me, please?"

"I always keep it in this pocket," said Syd, unzipping one of the bag's compartments.

Her hand moved back and forth but emerged with nothing. "Let me check the rest of my bag. It's got to be in here."

Several uncomfortable minutes passed. "It's missing," said Syd.

"Have you seen this pendant?" asked Trent, displaying it in front of Syd.

"That looks exactly like mine. I can tell by the chain. Someone must have taken it from my bag. Where did you find it?"

"On the floorboard of Ms. Rivet's abandoned car. Can you explain how it got there?"

"I have no explanation," said Syd. "None at all."

CHAPTER 11

Sleep always came easily to Syd. On an average day, her vigorous workout and tennis regimen left her fatigued by ten in the evening. But this was no ordinary night. She'd tried to close her eyes at around eleven after her discussion with Trent, but wild thoughts and what-if scenarios kept her awake most of the night. She'd considered asking for a sedative but decided her body had been through enough. At five in the morning, she was nervous, like a field mouse with an owl nearby.

Fortunately, Enzo had brought her laptop to the room, and she spent the morning hours returning Emails and surfing the net. ESPN caught wind of the Rivet missing-person case, much to the chagrin of the Franklin County prosecutor, who wanted the details to remain private for as long as possible. ESPN posted a story with the following headline at 4:44 a.m.: "Female Tennis Player Still Missing After Discovery of Bloody Vehicle."

The network quoted Trent in the article: "We are investigating the circumstances behind Ms. Rivet's disappearance. We have impounded the car, and we are conducting a ground search. That's all we're releasing right now. If anyone witnessed anything pertaining to the case, please contact our office."

Syd was relieved that Trent didn't mention the pendant, but she knew police were curious about why the item was in the victim's car.

Someone removed the pendant from her bag. Many people had access to it.

On Saturday night, Syd's tennis bag was courtside with her. On two occasions, she'd taken restroom breaks, leaving the bag exposed. She'd also left the court to speak with other players, with the bag unsupervised. A determined thief would've had access to the bag. If someone spotted the stealthy thief in the act, they hadn't come forward.

She opened the "Notes" app on her phone and began making a list of suspects:

> **Anja:** *Opportunity—yes. She was always near me. Difficulty—low; gut feeling—no way.*
> **Russo:** *Opportunity—yes. Obsessed with counting steps on Fit Bit. Always walking around. Was there with Anja; difficulty—low; gut feeling—probably not.*
> **O'Malley:** *Opportunity—yes. Watched me play and practiced with me; difficulty—low; gut feeling—unsure. Ask him about the bourbon.*
> **Mom:** *Opportunity—maybe (although someone probably would've seen her); difficulty—medium; gut feeling—never.*
> **Nicole:** *Opportunity—maybe (same as Mom); difficulty—medium, although showed spiders to a few*

players (a diversion, perhaps?); gut feeling—no way.
Fitz: *Opportunity—yes (he was everywhere); difficulty—low/medium; gut feeling—possibly.*
Jules: *Opportunity—yes (he was practicing); difficulty—medium (everybody knows him; he would stand out); gut feeling—probably not.*
Dad: *Opportunity—yes. Someone would have noticed; difficulty—high; gut feeling—can't imagine.*
Enzo: *Opportunity—yes; difficulty—low; gut feeling—no way!*
Belov: *Opportunity—yes; difficulty—low (she was there watching Anja); gut feeling—doubt it.*
Flores: *Opportunity—yes; difficulty—low (she was with us); gut feeling—hard to know.*
Monica: *Opportunity—maybe; difficulty—medium; gut feeling—possibly. (Maybe she stole it, then someone attacked her. But why?)*
Lovejoy: *Opportunity—slight; difficulty—high; gut feeling—doubt it because she gets everything she wants.*
The Field *(other players, officials, trainers, fans): Opportunity—yes; difficulty—medium; gut feeling—doubtful (but maybe).*

She planned to save these notes to go over them with Trent. Everyone on her list had the opportunity to steal the pendant. Some would've needed to work harder than others. Trent would probably disregard her "gut feelings" since cops care more about facts than hunches. One fact

95

was indisputable. She owned the pendant found in the bloody car of a missing woman. And that's not good.

Syd's phone read 5:45. Returning to sleep was a pipe dream. She smelled coffee brewing from down the hallway, possibly at the nurses' station. Several sleep-deprived people in the waiting area had already helped themselves to the coffee and were back in their seats, watching a morning news show. Syd grabbed one of the two remaining foam cups on the table. She emptied two packets of Stevia into the liquid but couldn't locate the cream. Enzo always teased Syd about her coffee preferences, which always included three creamer singles in every cup.

"Would you like a little coffee with your cream?" he'd say. The server usually laughed, but Syd heard the phrase so many times, she'd become immune.

She searched for a nurse to locate creamer, or the coffee experience would be ruined. She located a thin, tired-looking man, about five-foot-nine and in his early twenties, with a three-day beard shadow.

"Excuse me, sir," she said. "Do you have cream for this coffee? There's none on the table."

"I think so," he said. "There are probably creamers in the break area. Want to walk back there with me?"

The nurse handed Syd four cups of the cream, which he found lying around the kitchen. "Please leave the extra ones on the table," he said, not realizing there'd be only one remaining when Syd was through.

Syd's mind went back to the pendant as she proceeded down the hall toward her room, gently sipping at her steaming beverage. She was within a few yards of her room when an adjacent door swung open suddenly. A burly brown-haired man in a suit, at least six-foot-three and over 250 pounds, moved into the hallway, blocking Syd's path to her room.

"Where have you been?" said the man. "I've been looking for you."

Syd studied the man for a second before a feeling of terror overcame her. He was the size of a cape buffalo, with thick bushy eyebrows and a stare that penetrated her soul. She dropped the cup from her hands, sending steaming coffee onto the freshly waxed tile floor and onto her hospital-issued slippers.

"Come here!" the man said, attempting to grab her shoulders.

Syd took two steps backward before pivoting in the opposite direction and sprinting down the deserted hallway.

The man stepped toward Syd but slipped on the coffee, landing hard on his back.

"Sonofabitch!" he snarled, jumping back to his feet. He looked for Syd, but she had disappeared around one end of the oval hallway.

Turning the corner, Syd could no longer see the man. She knew he'd emerge soon, and he wouldn't be in a good mood.

Dialing 9-1-1 was not an option since her cell phone was back in the room. The visiting area was now vacant, with the sound of canned audience laughter resonating throughout the second floor. Syd considered dashing to the elevators but decided she didn't have time to wait for one. Instead, she noticed that the door of Room 276 was slightly ajar. Displayed above the door's threshold was the name "Emile Guttenberg." She pushed the door open, slinked inside, and closed it quickly behind her.

A frail, gray-haired man emerged from the restroom, wearing a hospital gown tied in the back. He noticed Syd's presence and shuffled to his bed quickly.

"I'm sorry I went to the bathroom by myself, but I needed to go when I woke up. Please don't tell Nurse Cavanaugh. She's been so angry with me."

"Don't worry, I won't tell," said Syd, opening the door just a crack to determine if anyone was coming down the hall. "It'll just be our little secret."

"Wait a minute," the man said. "You're not a nurse, are you? You slipped into my room uninvited, didn't you?"

"Um, kind of," said Syd, not knowing how he would react. "It's a long story, but I need to hide if that's all right."

"You can stay as long as you please," he said, relieved that he wasn't in trouble. "Pull your chair up to the bed. I have a chess set. We can play a nice game until everything blows over."

"Maybe I'll take a raincheck on the chess game," said Syd. "I just need to use your room phone for a minute."

"Okay," the man said, "but I'm having surgery tomorrow. I won't be able to play for a few days, but I'll be here at least until next Sunday. Maybe we can squeeze in a game on Thursday or Friday."

"It's a date," said Syd, picking up the receiver and dialing 9-1-1.

"I'm just getting a fast busy signal," she said. "Why doesn't this phone call out?"

"Dial 9 first," said Emile. "Or maybe it's 9 and then another 9. I haven't really called anyone. Usually, my daughter calls me. Let me push the nurse alert button right now. She usually arrives within five minutes, unless she's busy with another patient."

Emile looked more closely at Syd, who was doing her best not to hyperventilate.

"Who are you hiding from?" he asked. "And why?"

Syd was getting nowhere with the nines and double-nines as the sound of a fast busy signal filled the room. The old man tried to interrupt.

"Ma'am, excuse me," he said. "There's something you should know."

"Not now, sir," said Syd, speaking quickly with her back to the door. "I'm trying to get this phone to dial out."

"But ma'am, I really think you should—"

A huge hand grabbed Syd's forearm. The grip was tight and powerful.

"Put down the receiver," said the man. "And put it down right now!"

Syd swung around, facing the same man she'd encountered in the hallway. She closed her left fist and threw a roundhouse punch at his head. The man ducked, and the blow sailed over his head harmlessly. The man grabbed Syd's wrists with his hands, and she could no longer move her arms. She considered using her knees or biting, but the man's powerful grip sent shooting pains up her arms and into her shoulders.

"Stop fighting!" said the man. "You're going to hurt yourself, and you won't be able to play on Tuesday."

"Wait," said Syd. "Did you just say 'play on Tuesday'? Who are you?"

"My name is Christopher Samuels," he said. "Lieutenant Trent hired me to guard your room until morning. I needed to use the pisser, and the next thing I knew, your room was vacant. I was trying to find you."

Unknown to Samuels, Emile had grabbed his cane and moved around behind him.

"Leave this pretty woman alone," he yelled, crashing his cane into the back of Samuels' head.

"If you're going to hurt her, you'll have to go through me!"

"Please stop hitting him!" yelled Syd. "He's only here to help."

Emile took a step back and dropped the cane to the floor.

"It's okay," said Samuels, rubbing the back of his head and checking for blood. "My wife does worse to me every day."

Several nurses and doctors rushed into Room 276, trying to determine the source of the commotion.

"I didn't go to the bathroom by myself!" shouted Emile to a large nurse wearing a "Cavanaugh" name tag. "I'm just entertaining some visitors."

"It's all under control," said Syd. "Lieutenant Trent hired a bodyguard but didn't bother to tell me. Did the nursing staff know about him?"

"Yes," said Samuels, feeling a bump forming on the back of his head. "They knew about it too. We didn't tell you because you could have inadvertently tipped off the suspect. We were hoping to catch him in the act."

"What makes you think the suspect's a 'he'?" asked Syd.

"Poor word choice," said Samuels. "I was speaking generically. Why don't I get you another coffee so you can spend the rest of the morning in your room uneventfully, without disrupting the entire second floor?"

Good idea, thought Syd. She and Samuels started to leave the room.

"Hey!" said Emile. "I'll keep the chessboard ready, right beside my bed. But I get the first move."

CHAPTER 12

She's going to lose this match! I can't believe I'm seeing this. Can somebody explain what's happening? This match should've been over. She was leading 5-1 in the third set, and it's suddenly 5-4. And if that's not bad enough, Syd's lying in a supine position at courtside with a trainer attending to her.

I knew something was wrong by the way she's playing. She's stumbling across the court, her complexion is ghostly white, and she appears to be on drugs or something.

Maybe I should've taken care of that entitled teenage punk as I did her last opponent. My chances of getting her alone were virtually nil, though. She's always surrounded by an entourage of adoring adults, telling her what a wonderful person she is and how she's going to be a future star. And now she's going to ruin my entire plan by winning this match with an incredible comeback. My plan is going to be spoiled by a spoiled brat. How ironic!

Nobody's found the body yet, at least as far as I know. It was a pretty gross experience. Watching her bleed out and pass away wasn't such a big deal. The gross part came when I slid that bloody mess of a cadaver into the passenger seat and then placed my ass on the driver's side. Sitting in a puddle of warm blood is not for the squeamish. That red, flowing mess penetrated my shorts and soaked through to my underwear. I felt like I was driving while having a period. But I prepared for such a scenario. I had packed a tennis bag, and when Monica picked me up at the hotel, I tossed it in the back seat. Monica didn't say a word about the bag. Tennis people go everywhere with their bags, and carrying one on the road is commonplace.

I'd planned to get rid of the body in a dumpster. I didn't have enough time to bury her, and I wasn't going to throw a shovel and body bag in her backseat when she picked me up at the hotel. She would have noticed.

I located a dumpster in an isolated, dark place in the back of a large department store. As I was driving by, I noticed a sign that said, *"Dumping trash is a felony."* Now the word "felony" didn't strike fear in me, especially with a body resting next to me in the passenger seat. A good lawyer might save me from a dumping charge, but not a premeditated, cold-blooded murder. I didn't want to dispose of Monica in that dumpster because I noticed a camera stationed high above, pointing down at the receptacle from the store's rooftop. If the camera was real and not a rubber decoy, they would bust me. Case closed; game, set, and match.

I drove for hours, uneasy about finding another dumpster. Around midnight, a cop began tailing me. If he pulled me over, the gig would be up. I pictured the scenario in my mind; the officer shining the light into my car.

"May I see your ID, please?"

"Sure, officer. Please ignore this murdered bloody passenger while I reach into my pocket to remove it."

Yes, I still had the knife in my possession, but my chances of plunging it into the cop before he opened fire with his 9mm would be infinitesimal. The key to my survival was to avoid being pulled over. I obeyed the speed limit, activated my signal long before every turn, and tried my best to remain in the center of my lane. Eventually, he lost interest and turned off at an exit. Crisis averted.

Finally, I came to a bridge that crossed over a body of water called Alum Creek. The road was barely big enough for two lanes, with one undersized street light failing to provide adequate illumination. I parked the car in the right lane and turned on the hazard lights to warn approaching vehicles. Given the late hour and isolated location, I doubted that I'd see other cars on the bridge.

Moving quickly, I opened the passenger side, and Monica's head and upper body, slumped against the door, nearly fell completely out of the car. It took me about five minutes, but I finally removed her body from the car, with her back to me and my arms around her waist. I am in shape, which helped, but lifting 125 pounds of dead weight from the inside of a vehicle isn't easy for anyone.

I dragged her to the side of the bridge, where I encountered a two-foot-high concrete barrier wall positioned in front of a three-foot fence. I let out a groan as I placed my left foot on top of the wall, followed by my right while maintaining a firm grip on the body. Then came the toughest part. I turned Monica around to face me. I dropped my right shoulder below her midsection and lifted her up, using the strength of my legs. A lifetime of tennis and working out prepared me to do strenuous tasks, but I wasn't sure I could accomplish this one.

I looked over the fence. I could see the river below with its current flowing slowly and evenly. If I lost my grip on her now, she'd probably fall onto the barrier wall, and I'd never be able to budge her again. If I failed to hoist her over that fence and into the river, I'd be forced to leave her right where she was. The next driver passing through during the daylight hours would easily find her.

The next thing I remember, I was tossing her body over the fence and watching it fall in a somersault-like motion. It struck the water with a violent splash. At first, her body disappeared below the surface, but then it reappeared, floating away in the current. In a few seconds, she was out of sight, vanishing into the watery darkness.

I took the car to the back of a convenience store and parked it. I took off my bloody clothes, removed the clean ones from the gym bag, and then put them on. The soiled clothes went back inside of the bag. I walked about a mile to a nearby bar where I used my phone to call a car courier service for a ride back to a hotel near mine.

When the car arrived, the driver asked for ID. I pretended to be drunk and told him I'd lost my wallet inside the bar. All I had was a $100 bill, entirely his for a ride. Bingo! Mission accomplished.

Speaking of accomplishing missions, what the hell is happening down on the court? Is that a needle they're putting in Sydney's arm? What's that about? Is she having an allergic reaction? Did someone poison her? Does somebody else want her dead more than I do?

I don't want anyone else to kill Sydney. If someone else beats me to the punch, then I wouldn't truly be getting revenge. It's kind of like tennis. When someone defeats me in tennis, I want to beat them the next time. If another player beats them, I get no pleasure from that. I want to be the one who defeats them!

She's ahead 5-4 in the third set, but she can hardly walk out. She is definitely going to lose this match unless that sixteen-year-old goes into the tank.

I can't believe what I see now. Syd's one point away from winning. Sweet mother of ass! She just vomited in the trash can. You can't make this shit up. Last point . . . net cord . . . son of a bitch! She won! And now she's collapsed.

Watching in this stadium, I can hardly believe what I've witnessed. I must act concerned. I have to show empathy. Act the way people would expect. I can't stand out. That would appear suspicious. I'll remain calm because things have worked out well tonight. Tomorrow's a day off, and tennis resumes on Tuesday. Syd's staying in town for now, right where I'll be able to find her.

Shit! She's been down a while. I hear sirens. Who wins a match but can't shake hands? I've never seen that before. This situation is serious.

The paramedics are here. They're checking her vitals. C'mon, Syd. Pull through! I need to watch you die, not some volunteer first responder. It looks like they're going to load you in that ambulance and whisk you off to the hospital. Now, what does that mean for me? Should I go to the hospital? I think people would expect me to go, wouldn't they? I don't want to go. The more I talk, there's a greater chance of slipping up and saying something inconsistent or incriminating.

Maybe I can make up an excuse. Perhaps some kind of emergency came up and I couldn't make it. I don't know. Would that cast suspicion on me? Maybe I'm paranoid. I've got to decide.

Should I visit Syd in the hospital or not?

CHAPTER 13

At 9:00 a.m., Syd and Enzo walked through their hotel lobby and took an elevator to their room on the third floor. The inviting aroma of a hot breakfast from the first-floor dining room was enticing, but Syd had already consumed some toxic hospital food: a lukewarm poached egg, soggy wheat toast, and a bowl of instant oatmeal. Lunch would be an upgrade, with several inviting cafes within walking distance.

"Thanks for picking me up this morning," said Syd. "After having the wits scared out of me last night, I'm looking forward to a nice long nap. Hopefully, I won't get arrested before tomorrow's match."

"Nobody's going to charge you with anything," said Enzo. "Someone is setting you up. Who in their right mind leaves a pendant at a crime scene?"

"I don't know—maybe a stupid criminal or one who had it ripped off her neck? Like it or not, Enzo, I'm a person of interest."

"You're a person of interest to me," said Enzo, putting his arms around Syd's waist and allowing her to crash to the bed on top of him.

"I'm not exactly in a feisty mood," said Syd. "Why don't we take a quick nap and then practice for an hour after lunch?"

"That works too," said Enzo. "You checked out your position in the main draw, right?"

"Believe it or not, I haven't seen it. I've been a little preoccupied."

Enzo pulled out a copy of the main draw and set it on the table.

"Your first match is Tuesday at 3:00 p.m. against Sylvia Romero from Slovenia. Do you know anything about her?"

"Let's see," said Syd. "She's a tall lefty with a big serve. She likes to get to the net. Oh yeah, she loves to slice her backhand."

"Sounds about right. Have you played her before?"

"Never. But didn't she win a set against Sandy Willard in the Australian Open a couple of years ago?"

"Yeah, she lost the first set 6-4, won the second 7-5, but got completely obliterated in the third set, 6-0. But still a damn good showing on her part. But her ranking has dropped considerably since then, all the way to number sixty-eight."

"I wish my ranking was that high," said Syd. "Let's take a look at the entire bracket."

Syd's name was near the bottom of the draw. She faced Romero in the first round, with the winner facing number-two seed Cassandra Flores. Cassie and number-one men's player Jules Willems had been an item for the past few months. Syd sensed that Flores didn't like her, probably because of the brief fling she'd had with Willems.

"It looks like the best I can do is a second-round exit," said Syd. "Flores has been on a tear lately. She almost knocked the racquet out of my hands on Saturday. She'd love to take me to the woodshed. In fact, I think she'd revel in it. But I'd be thrilled if I beat Romero. The payoff for advancing to the second round is $43K. Wouldn't it be great to get back on speaking terms with my landlord?"

"Take it one match at a time," advised Enzo. "Or better yet, one point at a time. You never know what you can accomplish when you're completely lost in the present."

"Lost in the present is better than being lost," said Syd, thinking about Monica Rivet. "But I guess living in the present prevents me from worrying. And by the way, I've doubled-up on my antidepressants. Please don't tell my doctor."

"Syd, you know I'm here to protect you," said Enzo. "But my advice to you now is to trust no one—except me, of course."

"Well, speaking of you, I haven't seen the men's draw either. Who are you playing and when?"

"My draw's no walk in the park either. I'm playing Ramon Ramirez from Mexico at 2:00 p.m. tomorrow, an hour before you take the court."

"Isn't he the guy who made it to Round 16 at Wimbledon, losing a five-setter to Nadal?"

"Yes, that's him! He's one of the best all-court players in the world. I'm going to need a bit of magic to survive. Worst-case scenario is that we each walk away from this tournament with $24K. I'd say that's a solid investment in our future."

"Our future?" said Syd. "That's a subject that we really haven't broached."

Syd's phone buzzed, alerting her that a text message was waiting. She didn't recognize the number at first but finally realized it was from Trent.

> "I need you to come to my office this afternoon. For the record, I don't consider you a suspect, but I have a few matters we need to discuss. No lawyers, please."

"Well, I guess I know what I'm doing after lunch," Syd said to Enzo. "And it ain't practicing with you."

Syd and Enzo enjoyed lunch at Antoinette's Cafe in Silver-hill, a quaint, street-side establishment specializing in French cuisine. Syd dined on "The Veggie Crepe," featuring spinach, tomato, peppers, onion, mushroom, and swiss cheese. Enzo opted for the Croque Monsieur/Madame, which included bechamel, swiss cheese, and ham on homemade toast.

"Great recommendation," said Enzo, as he wiped his mouth with his napkin. "I was a little skeptical about French food, but this was delicious. How was your main dish?"

"Tasted like crepe," replied Syd with a smile.

There's no doubt about it: if Sydney Livingstone's in your life, you better develop a sense of humor—and quickly.

It took about 25 minutes for Syd and Enzo to drive from Antoinette's to the Franklin County prosecutor's office in downtown Columbus.

"Not many people around," said Enzo as they approached the building.

Only a handful of workers were working inside the building. Trent emerged and ushered Syd and Enzo inside his office.

"Congrats on your big win. Now that our hometown sixteen-year-old megastar is out of the tournament, I'll bet the crowd will be pulling for you."

"Everyone except the person framing me," said Syd. "You wanted to go over a few things?"

"Yes, I do," said Trent. "And Enzo, you can stay. I'm sorry that I had to ask you and Syd's beautiful mother to leave the room yesterday. It was nothing personal."

"No offense taken," said Enzo. "I want to clear Syd's name and find out who's stalking her."

"That's why you're here," said Trent. "We have fresh developments."

Trent reached into a drawer and removed a file. He pulled out a blurry picture of a woman standing in a hotel lobby. Syd recognized the lobby. A camera stationed high above the woman had taken the photo.

"Does she look familiar?" asked Trent. "I thought about the bourbon delivery and its significance. I asked hotel security to review footage of anyone coming into the hotel without checking in.

"Some shots we recovered were family members of staff, salespeople, and other visitors. But this woman stood out because she carried a package. The package was small enough to contain bourbon. She also carried a clipboard with paper."

Syd looked at the photo and squinted. The face wasn't clear, but the clothing and package were identical.

"That's definitely her," she said. "I would bet my life on it."

"I thought so," said Trent. "One of our employees recognized her but not from the hotel. It seems our employee recently had home improvements completed at her house. You know, a new vinyl floor, a sliding door installation, and a water heater. She was one of several performing the work."

"Okay," said Enzo, straightening up in his chair. "What's the name of the company?"

"It's Allstar Repair," said Trent. "They're one of those 'no job is too small' outfits. One of our detectives paid them a visit. When he showed the owner the woman's picture, he identified her as Melanie Powers."

"So we know exactly who she is," said Syd. "Does she live nearby? And does she have a criminal record?"

She works for Allstar about thirty hours a week and also runs a home handyman—or in this case, handywoman—company out of her home. On her website, she even offers miscellaneous tasks like shopping for groceries, walking the dog, and, yes, making deliveries. She is a resident of Columbus with no priors.

"Well, why isn't she here now, getting interrogated by the police?" asked Enzo.

"That's an easy one," said Trent. "Because Ms. Livingstone hasn't identified her yet. There's nothing illegal about making a delivery to a hotel. And while I'm thinking about it, I need to ask you something, Enzo. Were you present when the delivery happened?"

"I was," said Enzo.

"Does she look like the delivery woman?"

"Well, I was preoccupied," said Enzo, not wanting to reveal to Trent that he was buck naked in the bathtub with fake blood smeared over him. "I didn't get a good look."

Syd glanced toward Enzo, but he maintained eye contact with Trent.

"I'll have one of my detectives pick her up. We'll speak with her before the end of the day," said Trent.

Trent rose from his desk and walked over to the nearby coffee station, where he mixed three sugars into a large mug and poured coffee on top of it. "May I get either of you anything?" he asked.

"That depends," said Syd. "If we're done now, we'll be on our way. If there's more, I'll take coffee with Stevia and three creams."

"And I'll have a Coke," said Enzo. "And if we're finished here, I'll take it with me on the road."

Trent doctored Syd's coffee, trying his best to remember her instructions. Then he removed a soda from a small refrigerator.

"We're not quite done here," he said, handing the drinks to them. "Someone found a body in Alum Creek this morning. We received a call from an angler who saw something while unsnagging his line from a tree trunk. First, he saw a head protruding from underneath a log. On closer inspection, he saw an arm. Our guess is someone threw the body off a bridge, and it became snagged in the underbrush. We've made no identifications, but it appears the description matches Monica Rivet."

"Oh, shit!" said Syd. "She didn't leave on her own volition. Someone killed her. And what does that mean, Lieutenant Trent?"

Trent stared at the papers on his desk, avoiding eye contact. He really liked Syd, but he couldn't overlook the fact that her pendant was in the bloody car of a deceased woman. He couldn't ignore that she had an athletic boyfriend with the motive and opportunity to do away with Rivet, Syd's first opponent.

"I need to ask you something, Enzo, so please don't take offense," said Trent. "Have you had any interaction with Ms. Rivet since you arrived at the tournament?"

"None whatsoever," said Enzo. "I barely know the woman."

Trent eyed Enzo, trying to call upon his experience to determine whether he was lying. He got no feeling either way.

"Would you both be amenable to having your cars inspected by our technicians?" asked Trent. "I don't expect to find anything, but I will need your permission."

"Wait a minute!" said Enzo. "You asked Syd to come without a lawyer, and suddenly you want to search our cars? An attorney doesn't sound like a really bad idea right now!"

"If you have nothing to hide, why would you refuse?" said Trent.

"We'll go back to the hotel and talk it over, but let me assure you, Lieutenant Trent, neither of us has anything to hide!"

"Okay," said Trent. "Go talk it over. In the meantime, we'll interview Melanie Powers and try to figure out how she's mixed up in this mess. And for the record, I still feel that you're both probably innocent, for whatever that's worth."

Enzo rose from his chair, took Syd by the hand, and pulled her to her feet, a frown still on his face.

"Let's vamoose, Syd," said Enzo. "You've got a big match tomorrow and there's no need to listen to any more nonsense."

Oh yeah, thought Syd. *There is a match tomorrow, isn't there?*

CHAPTER 14

After breakfast and a pair of $150 massages at a local studio, Syd jumped into Enzo's car, and the two cruised to the tournament for a light practice session. The main draw of the tournament was in full swing, with several first-round matches kicking off at 9:00 a.m.

Victor Dan's match began at nine against Cedric Danielson, a Frenchman ranked number thirty-two in the world. Syd and Enzo took in part of the match before their eleven o'clock practice session.

When they arrived at Court 9, the bleachers were nearly full, and Victor trailed 5-3 in the first set. To Syd's surprise, Nicole was in the front row watching Victor, rubbing her hands together nervously.

"Why is Nicole here watching Victor?" asked Syd. "They barely know each other. When we talked this morning, Nicole said she was looking forward to watching my afternoon match. I never imagined she'd be here watching Victor."

A few minutes later, Victor lost the first set, 6-3. As the ushers allowed more spectators to enter, Syd and Enzo spotted a couple of seats next to Nicole and joined her.

"Hey guys!" said Nicole. "I was hoping I'd see you here. I'm a little worried about Victor. He's lost the first set, and he looks like he's stressing about it."

Syd and Enzo looked at each other, waiting for Nicole to elaborate, but she'd stopped talking.

"Soooo," said Syd, trying to diffuse the awkwardness. "What brings you out here to watch Victor? I mean, you just met him the other day, right?"

Nicole slowly pulled her eyes away from the court. Victor was trailing 1-0 now in the second set, and stress showed on her face.

"Well, yeah," said Nicole. "But during your match, I got to know him better. He was so nice. He walked me back to my car, and I introduced him to my spider friends.

"But then, I noticed Scarlet acting strangely. Her leg was straightening out and relaxing, then straightening out and relaxing again. It was happening over and over. And that wasn't normal for her. She's a pretty laid-back arachnid."

The crowd emitted a roar of approval as Danielson crushed an overhead smash past Dan for a 2-0 advantage. Nicole clapped tentatively. "C'mon Victor, honey; you can do this!"

"I'm sorry," said Syd, clearing her throat. "Did you just refer to him as 'Victor honey'? Tell me more about what's transpired lately between you two."

"Well, Victor noticed my concerns about Scarlet. He wanted to visit you in the hospital but followed me to the vet instead because I was so worried. What a sweetheart! He stayed in the waiting room with me for two hours."

Victor ripped an on-the-run backhand past Danielson to close the gap to 2-1.

"Wow!" said Nicole, jumping to her feet with both fists in the air. "Great shot, sweetheart!"

"Dang, you care more about this match than I do," said Enzo. "And Victor's my best friend!"

"You know," said Nicole, "he held my hand in the waiting room and allowed me to rest my head on his shoulder while I cried. You never meet men with so much compassion anymore. He has a heart of gold!"

Syd resisted the temptation to roll her eyes. "So where did you and Mr. Golden Heart end up after Scarlet received her clean bill of health?"

"A restaurant," said Nicole. "And then back to Victor's hotel. He treated my spiders like family. Scarlet's not totally out of the woods yet. She needs antibiotics and another blood test. The vet told her to take it easy for a couple of weeks."

"Game, Danielson," announced the head umpire. "He leads by one set to zero and four games to one in the second set."

"We have to go," said Enzo. "Our practice time is rapidly approaching."

"Oh, I'm sorry you have to leave," said Nicole. "You're going to miss Victor's great comeback. I have all the faith in the world that he'll win this match."

"Faith moves mountains," said Syd as she and Enzo rose to leave. "Please come watch me play this afternoon and help me move a few mountains."

FAULTS

"Oh, you're going to be fine," said Nicole. "Maybe tonight we can go out for drinks and celebrate both you and Victor winning your first-round matches. I'd buy, but the $400 vet bill tapped me out for a while."

Wishing Nicole luck, Syd and Enzo walked toward the players' lounge, where they would grab a can of balls for their practice session and enjoy a hydrating drink.

"Victor works his magic once again," said Enzo. "Aren't you glad you don't have a boyfriend like that?"

"Our relationship's unique," said Syd. "You never know what's waiting around the next corner."

* * * * *

Marisha Belov sat in the urgent-care waiting room on Tuesday morning while a doctor treated the long scratch on Anja's arm.

"It's definitely infected," said Dr. Michael Cullom, who had just completed his residency at a Columbus Hospital. "I'm going to give you a shot. You'll also need ten days of antibiotics. What caused this?"

"Long story," said Anja. "There was a sharp edge on my racquet string. And my arm found it."

"Fill this prescription right away," said Cullom. "The shot gets the ball rolling, but the pills eventually kill the infection."

"Are there side effects to the shot?" asked Anja as a nurse prepped the area and injected her.

"Cramps are the most common. In some cases, diarrhea appears."

When Anja emerged from the office, Belov confronted her.

"Are you going to be okay for your two o'clock match? That was some ugly stuff seeping from that cut."

"The doctor says I'll be fine, and I'm hoping he's right," she said. "But let's both pray I don't soil myself on TV, in front of the entire world."

Anja, the tournament's twenty-seventh seed, was favored to beat Hungary's Julia Silas, according to Vegas oddsmakers. But Russo wasn't taking anything for granted. When Anja arrived for the 11:30 warmup, Russo presented her with a detailed itinerary for the forty-five-minute session, including when she would take a water break and for how long.

"The difference between winning and losing this match is nineteen grand," said Russo. "You have to be firing on all cylinders."

Russo always pushed Anja just hard enough in her pre-match sessions to sharpen her game without depleting her energy. The session included dynamic stretching, serves and return-of-serves, volleys, and groundstrokes. He reserved the last ten minutes for a strategy game plan.

As the session was ending, Belov walked onto the court to speak with Anja and Russo.

"What can I do to help her?" she asked Russo.

"Make sure she eats her energy bar an hour before the match," said Russo. "And don't let her forget about staying hydrated. I'll meet her on the court at 1:45. I have to get some lunch."

"I'll take care of her," said Belov. "By the way, where do you keep the oranges—the ones you squeeze into her thermos?"

Anja and Russo glanced at each other quizzically.

"What are you talking about? said Anja. "I never squeeze juice into my drink container."

A puzzled look emerged on Belov's face.

"I'm sorry, I thought that was something you and Syd both preferred," she said. "In Syd's last match—during a restroom break—I saw that man you call 'Fitz' squeezing an orange into Syd's thermos. I assumed you both preferred that. My bad."

"Wait just a second!" said Russo. "You saw Fitz squeezing an orange into Syd's drink? No one else saw that?"

"The container's behind a courtside table," said Belov. "You know how breaks are. People are moving everywhere. Are you saying Syd never wanted orange juice in her thermos?"

"I don't know," said Russo. "But we should find out. Are you sure it was an orange?"

"Yes, well, um, no," said Belov. "It was some kind of tropical fruit. I assumed it was an orange."

Belov's revelation bothered Russo. Perhaps Sydney asked Fitz to add juice to her drink.

"It's probably nothing," he told Anja. "I'll call Syd during lunch and mention the orange. She probably requested it."

"Anja," continued Russo, "go relax before your match. Don't forget your energy bar and drink."

Russo located a chair at Columbus' world-famous Supernova Chili. After ordering two hot dogs and a Diet Mountain Dew, he dialed Syd's number. The call went directly to voicemail. Russo made a note to call again at 1:30.

★ ★ ★ ★ ★

At 12:55, Syd and Enzo concluded their practice. Putting her hands around Enzo's sweaty neck, Syd kissed him firmly on the lips. "Your match begins in an hour," she said. "Go freshen up and get mentally ready. That extra nineteen grand will be a good start toward our child's college education."

Enzo loved the way Syd put him at ease before a match. After another obnoxiously long kiss on the lips, he packed up his stuff and headed for the exit.

"Now that's financial planning!" said Enzo. "Saving for a child who hasn't even arrived."

Then he turned serious, facing Syd. "I hope we both win," he said. "But if only one of us wins, I'd hope it's you."

"Me too," said Syd with a wry smile. "Of course, you know I'm kidding, Enzo. If we're going to spend the rest of our days together, we need to focus on your tennis. I'm an injured duckling surviving on borrowed time."

She would have loved to watch the early part of Enzo's match but decided not to. Her father always advised against watching emotional matches before playing.

Syd wanted to keep things light, and she found the perfect opportunity. A comedian stood in for a local band on a fifteen-minute break. Syd grabbed a seat, pulled a salted caramel energy bar from her bag, and began chewing. She noticed two missed calls from Russo, but before she could return the call, her phone was ringing again. She didn't recognize the number but answered anyway.

The call was from Trent, who wasn't exactly at the top of her Christmas list.

The interview with Melanie Powers had gone well, in Trent's opinion. Powers claimed she'd received an email from an unknown person, requesting that she deliver a package to Room 317. She followed directions to the package, located under a remote bench in a park. The box contained a wrapped bottle of liquid (presumably bourbon), an envelope with Syd's name on it, and a clipboard and paper. They instructed her to accept no tips. Her role was to deliver the package and leave with little or no explanation. An envelope at the bottom of the box contained $150, with the following note:

If you follow my instructions well, I will use you again and pay more $$$.

"She was very forthcoming with us," said Trent. "She never laid eyes on whoever hired her. She's done nothing illegal, so she's free to leave. I wish I had more information to give you."

Syd regretted taking Trent's call. The story Powers presented to the police was not only weird; it was downright eerie. Now she had a lot on her mind with an important match bearing down.

Her phone buzzed again. This time, it was Russo. Another conversation was not appealing, but perhaps Russo would provide a scouting report.

"Hey, coach," she said. "Any last-minute advice before I take the court today?"

"I have some scouting information to give you, Sydney," said Russo. "But before that, I have a question. What was inside the drinking container you brought onto the court in your match against that young girl?"

"Energyade, the sports drink," she answered.

"What flavor do you prefer, Sydney?" said Russo. "I know these are weird questions, but please bear with me."

"My favorite flavor?" said Syd. "I think it's called 'fresh arctic' or something. I buy it in bulk and keep bottles in my refrigerator at home."

"I understand," said Russo. "Do you ever put citrus in that drink? Like, would you ever squeeze an orange into the Energyade?"

"No, that's disgusting!" said Syd. "Yuck."

"But now that you mention it, I noticed a citrus taste during that match. I thought Energyade changed its formula or something. But how would you know that?"

"All right, I have another question, Sydney. Did you give anyone permission to squeeze any fruit or fruit juice into your Energyade?"

"Of course not. I already told you; that's gross."

"What do your doctors think happened at the end of your last match?" asked Russo. "Was it fatigue? Dehydration?"

"Well, not really. They said I had an allergic reaction. But why are you asking that?"

"Syd, is there anything you're allergic to?"

"Um, dust, I believe," she said. "Ragweed in the mid-to-late fall, and maybe dog dander."

"But you're not allergic to any food or drink?"

"Now that you mention it, yes. As a kid, I had to avoid cashews and pistachios. They caused a reaction where my tongue swelled, and I had trouble breathing. I was rushed to the hospital once. And there was something else in that family I'm supposed to avoid. Oh yeah, mango."

When she heard those words come out of her mouth, Syd panicked.

"Oh, God!" she said. "How did that get into my drink?"

CHAPTER 15

The five-minute stroll from the warmup court to the players' lounge seemed like an eternity. If Belov was telling the truth, Fitz had infused her Energyade with potentially deadly juice from mango fruit.

A week earlier, she nearly withdrew from the tournament because of a shoulder injury. But after several physical-therapy sessions and a shot of cortisone, she decided to play. Syd never realized that when she crossed the state line from Kentucky to Ohio, a shit storm of epic proportion awaited her.

The situation made little sense. How did Fitz find out about her allergies? Many players on the tour knew that Syd refrained from eating cashews, pistachios, and mangoes, all members of the Anacardiaceous family. It wasn't forbidden knowledge.

So yes, players, friends, and others could have easily found out about her allergy by knowing her personally or via hearsay. Now, does this mean that Fitz also had the bourbon delivered to her room, painted "Die Bitch" on her Corvette, and kidnapped and killed Monica Rivet? Or were Fitz's actions completely separate from those other events? Or how would anyone know Belov is telling the truth? Could she have come onto the court, squeezed or slipped something into her drink during the hiatus in the match? No, she would have stood out like a sore thumb. But what about before the match, prior to Syd going onto the stadium court? Possibly, she thought, if she'd acted quickly when Syd had been speaking with Anja.

She probably should report Belov's account to Trent, but there was no time. Her first-round match with Sylvia Romero loomed. Perhaps later, she and Enzo could take another ride downtown to speak with Trent, as unappetizing as that sounded. And maybe they could take Belov along so Trent could hear her version. Entering the players' lounge, the last thing on Syd's mind was tennis.

Tournament scheduler Stuart Thornton manned the registration table inside the players' lounge. He smiled as Syd approached.

"Ms. Livingstone, I hope your visit has been pleasant so far," he said, oblivious to the overwhelming turmoil. "We're right on schedule. You're playing Ms. Romero on Court 11. The court is open, and you can begin your warmup when you arrive on the court. I believe that Ms. Romero is already on her way."

It was in times like these, Syd wished she could afford a coach. Here she was, a professional player, but she had to proceed to the court alone with no one helping or advising her. She envied Anja for having Russo by her side. A solid player-coach relationship is invaluable, especially to an inexperienced player on the tour.

Years ago, when she played junior tennis, her father accompanied her to matches, serving as her coach. He was intolerably abusive but, at other times, they bonded well. The overall experience was mixed, but Syd knew her father was there for her.

The financial hardship of divorce was more than Michael Livingstone could handle. He worked two jobs to make ends meet. He dated another woman, who became jealous of his relationship with Syd. Eventually, Syd and her father stopped communicating.

Syd wondered whether she'd actually seen her father while lying on the court or if her mind imagined it. Her father could have made the trip from Michigan to watch her play, the drive being relatively short. But why wouldn't he have approached her? Shame? Embarrassment? Regret?

Peter O'Malley had said he'd seen Syd's father, but then he backtracked and claimed he might have been mistaken. And what about O'Malley? Syd noticed he'd prevailed in his 9:00 a.m. match. She needed to come out and ask him straight up if he paid for the bourbon delivery. It had to be him since no one else knew about the brand, right? Was the delivery a macabre joke, or was he paying tribute to Milena? But what about the note? No, the delivery was no tribute. It was a mean-spirited act, meant to harass.

Checking out the giant digital scoreboard located outside Center Court, Syd was pleased to see that Enzo held a 4-2 advantage over Ramirez. Anja had already steamrolled Silas, 6-2, in the first set. She spotted Romero walking ahead of her, followed by her long-time Czech coach, Tomas Schuster.

A large, stocky gentleman, carrying a walkie-talkie, followed Romero from a distance. At first, the man terrified Syd. Then she remembered why.

The guy was Trent's goon. He was hired to protect Syd in the hospital, although Trent never bothered to inform her. That miscommunication resulted in a coffee spill, a slip-and-fall, a wild chase down the hallway, and an intrusion into an elderly man's private hospital room. Oh yeah, and a cane strike to the head. Just a run-of-the-mill evening at the hospital.

What was the man's name again? Sampson? Stevens? No, it was Samuels. Christopher Samuels! But why is he following Romero? Suddenly, it occurred to her. Samuels was guarding Romero to make sure she didn't suffer the same fate as Monica Rivet.

As Syd walked through a tunnel and onto Court 11, she saw only Chelsea and Nicole sitting in the players' box. Her entourage was significantly smaller today. Anja was battling for her life on Court 3 and was no doubt accompanied by Russo. Enzo was trying to upset a seeded player on Court 7, and Victor probably completed his match and was watching Enzo compete.

As Syd unpacked her bag prior to the warmup, she noticed another man walking onto the court. He wasn't big or intimidating like Samuels, but he scared her far more. Fitz, smiling confidently, strolled onto the court and climbed into the official's chair.

Oh great, thought Syd, *the same guy who tried to kill me now controls my destiny.* She had no one to complain to, no "unfair" button to push. She'd plow through this match and address those more complex issues another time.

"Five minutes remaining," bellowed Fitz into his microphone.

Romero was steady and hard-hitting during the warm-up, but Syd didn't feel completely overwhelmed by her strokes. It would take a grandiose effort to win, but she felt she had a puncher's chance. That is if she could block out Fitz, a stalker, and a potential grand-jury investigation.

Romero warmed up well but played even better once the match started. Down 4-3 in the first set and facing a breakpoint on her own serve, Syd ripped an inside-out forehand down the line that Romero couldn't track down. The side linesperson held her arms straight out in front of her with palms down, showing the shot landed on the line. A voice from above interrupted the crowd's applause.

"Correction," said Fitz. "The ball is out. Game Romero. She leads five games to three."

Fans stationed in the bleachers whistled in disagreement. Syd approached Fitz at the chair, her arms at her side and her racquet clutched tightly in her right hand.

"Excuse me? You're only supposed to overrule a shot if you are 100 percent sure. And you can't be sure because the ball hit squarely on the line."

"The ball was definitely out," replied Fitz, holding his thumb and forefinger about two inches apart.

The gift of wit was a blessing and a curse to Syd. She thought about saying the actual size of his appendage was irrelevant, but she knew the ramifications. Romero looked at Syd across the court and shrugged her shoulders slightly, almost apologizing for the call.

"Please!" said Syd. "You can't make that call. Your own linesman who had the perfect angle called the shot good!"

"Actually, I have the perfect angle," said Fitz, referring to his lofty position above the court. "The ball was out, and now I'm ordering you to resume play."

Syd looked over at her mother and Nicole. Chelsea shook her head in disagreement, and Nicole buried her face in her hands. The "unfair button" wouldn't even apply in this situation. She needed the "bullshit" button.

Romero won the first set, 6-3. Syd jumped out to a 3-0 lead in the second, thanks to several unforced errors from Romero and solid play on her part. Syd's lead slipped to 5-4, but a strong serving game lifted her to a 6-4 second-set win.

Enzo completed his match against Ramirez, packed his racquets and drinks into his tennis bag, and met Victor outside of the court.

"You almost pulled it out," said Victor, referring to Enzo's heartbreaking 4-6- 6-1, 7-5 loss. "If you would've made that overhead when you were ahead 5-4, I think you would've won."

"I know," responded Enzo. "I'd give my left nut to have that shot back. But overall, I played well."

"That's for sure," agreed Dan, still smarting from a 6-2, 6-2 loss in his morning match. "When you're playing well, you can hang with anyone in the world."

"Thanks," said Enzo, "but the only thing that matters is busting my ass across the complex to catch the rest of

Syd's match. I hope she pulls it out. Her psyche needs it, especially considering what's transpired."

"I'll join you," said Victor. "Although I'm sure Nicole will be there watching. She's one interesting young woman!"

"You two spent the night together, right?" said Enzo. "What was interesting about that?"

Two teenage boys approached Enzo. "Hey, Martin!" said one of them. "Sorry you lost. Would you mind signing our balls?"

The two held up oversized tennis balls—about three times larger than a human head—that they purchased at the tennis outlet within the facility.

Enzo despised disrespectful teenagers, especially ones that referred to him by last name only, not to mention the veiled body-part innuendo.

"Okay," he said, accepting their offer of a pen. "I'll sign quickly and hand your balls back to you."

The teenagers snickered and walked away without saying thank you. Enzo turned his attention back to Victor.

"Oh yeah, what made your night with Nicole so interesting?"

"Well, first, she's so damn emotional," said Victor. "She's in the vet's waiting room, crying on my shoulder because her big, hairy spider's leg is cramping. I did my best to be empathetic, but I'm a guy who squashes spiders at home without a second thought.

"But that wasn't the worst of it," he continued. "The crazy girl felt so sorry for the spider—what's its name, Charlotte or something?"

"Scarlet," replied Enzo. "It's a play on words, but I don't have time to explain."

"Okay, Scarlet then. Well, she brought Scarlet into bed with us. Luckily for me, it was after we performed the dastardly deed. She wanted to place that disgusting bug between us. Can you fucking imagine? At least I talked her into keeping it on her side of the bed. But then I kept dreaming that the spider would climb over Nicole and attack me. Have you ever seen the size of its teeth? It's nothing to mess with."

"I take it you got through the night without Scarlet sinking her fangs into your neck?" said Enzo.

"Yeah, I slept the rest of night on the fold-away after I awoke at four and saw the spider lying on its back, spread eagle. Nicole was scratching its belly, and, I swear to you, it looked like that spider was smiling, fangs hanging out and all. I think I might be going crazy."

"You're in bed with a poisonous spider straight from an African jungle, now you doubt your sanity?" said Enzo. "Man, you overreact to things, don't you?"

They entered Syd's court with the match knotted at 4-all in the third set. Syd was one point away from taking a 5-4 advantage when Romero hit an underspin drop shot from behind her own baseline. The ball barely made it over the net, with the underspin guaranteeing a low bounce. The shot was designed to be an outright winner, but Syd recognized it early and got a fast start on the ball. She arrived just before it bounced for a second time and flicked her wrist to produce another drop shot, except this one was an extreme crosscourt angle. Romero had no chance to make a play on the ball, and it appeared Syd would serve for the match while leading 5-4.

Fitz's voice boomed from above. "That was a double-bounce," he announced. "The point goes to Romeo. Deuce."

Syd's viewing box, now composed of Chelsea, Nicole, Enzo, Victor, Russo, and Anja—fresh off a 6-2, 7-5 first-round victory—erupted in protest. The crowd jeered, and Syd dropped her racket to the ground, bending over at the waist. Then she straightened up and slowly walked to Fitz's chair.

"I'm being punked, right?" she said. "Here's the part where you show me the hidden cameras, and we all start laughing."

Fitz appeared perturbed by Syd's comment. "The ball bounced twice," he said. "The point goes to Ms. Romero. Please resume play. The score is deuce."

This time, Syd wasn't going anywhere. Fitz was digging in his heels, and he would look at capitulation as a weakness.

"Isn't there a video replay you can review?" she asked. "This is the second time you've screwed me, and you are going to cost me this match!"

"No, Ms. Livingstone, there is no video review because this match isn't on Center Court or the Grandstand Stadium. However, I am taking a point away from you for the abuse of an official. The score is now Romero's advantage. One more outburst from you, Ms. Livingstone, and I will reward Ms. Romero an entire game."

It was decision time for Syd. She could accept the point penalty and return to her side of the court. Or she could gamble with Fitz, a wager that could cost her $19,000 in prize winnings if she was wrong.

Syd loved humor and fun but hated confrontation. But Fitz had already tried to incapacitate her once, and his bias could hasten the end of her career. She doubled down and moved closer to his chair.

"You really mangoed that last call," she said. Then she stopped and put her hand over her mouth. "Oh, excuse me," she continued." I said 'mangoed,' didn't I? What I meant to say was 'mangled.' You really mangled that call."

Syd prayed silently that Belov was telling the truth about what she'd witnessed. If not, she'd be on the precipice of disqualification.

Fitz's confident demeanor suddenly changed. A worried expression wiped the scowl off his face, and he crossed his arms defensively.

"Please play on, Ms. Livingstone," he said, suddenly lacking confidence in his voice.

Syd's eyes remained on Fitz. He squirmed in his seat and asked one of the line judges nearby to approach his chair for a conversation. After two minutes, he made an announcement.

"I'm going to reverse my call," he said. "The other linesman stated Ms. Livingstone did, in fact, arrive at the ball before the second bounce. I may have made an incorrect call. I'm rescinding the penalty point against Ms. Livingstone. Game to Ms. Livingstone. She leads five games to four in the second set."

After the reversal, Romero's coach sprinted toward the chair and screamed at Fitz.

"Did you just chicken out on the call?" he said. "You called it, and now you say you're not sure? This is ludicrous! I want the tournament director right now!"

Fitz leaned over to speak into his microphone.

"I am the tournament director," he said. "One of our head linesmen was involved in a fender-bender before the match, and I decided that I'd officiate it in his absence. And this tournament director says you are out of line. Please return to your post, or your player will endure the consequences."

Romero spoke with her coach. It appeared Romero agreed Syd had reached the ball on the first bounce. Whatever Romero said to her coach seemed to calm him down. He retreated to his chair, and the match resumed.

Syd used a powerful serve, along with the volley that Peter O'Malley had helped her with, to win four out of the final five points. She walked off the court a 3-6, 6-4, 6-4 winner. Nearly everyone in the players' box smothered her with hugs and high-fives.

"Great job, sweetie," said Enzo. "Let's celebrate at dinner tonight. But you're the bread-winner now, so you'll have to pay."

"I'm sorry that you lost, Enzo," said Syd. "But by the looks of it, you played a spectacular match.

"As for our dinner tonight, it might have to be Chinese takeout or something. It appears we're going to spend a few hours with our wonderful new friend, Lieutenant Gil Trent."

CHAPTER 16

With her first-round victory concluding at around five, Syd sat in Enzo's car, where they discussed their plans for the evening. Enzo's idea was to order a cocktail at the hotel, grab a shower, and find a good seafood restaurant.

"You're guaranteed $43,000," he said from his driver's side while placing his right hand on the back of Syd's neck to give her an impromptu massage. "I'm taking home 24K, and that's exciting, too. Let's savor the moment because you'll be playing tomorrow evening again."

Syd knew Enzo was truly happy for her, but she also realized he was concealing his own disappointment because of his heartbreaking loss.

"I want you to know that I'm proud of you, Enzo," she said. "You went toe-to-toe with one of the best in the business tonight. You're headed toward the top, and I want to support you every step of the way."

Enzo smiled and continued massaging Syd's neck. His grip seemed tighter than usual. She winced slightly.

"Enzo, can you lighten up?" she said. "I know you're trying to relax me, but it feels like you're strangling me. Are you okay?"

Enzo glanced to his left. Several fans peered into the car through the side window. He released his grip. Then his expression turned serious.

"I'm sorry," he said. "I guess I'm more stressed out than I realized. Of course, I'm disappointed. A win today would have been huge. But what you accomplished today makes up for everything. I've seen what you've gone through this weekend. You're a resilient fighter, and that's only part of the reason I love you," he said.

"Thanks," said Syd, placing a kiss on the side of Enzo's right cheek. "But now I'm curious. What's the other part you love about me?"

"If I said your tight ass and nice rack, would that make me a villain?"

"Not a villain, but maybe a dead man," joked Syd. "Coming from you, I'll take that as a compliment. I hope you know that you're the only person who could say that. Anyone else might end up needing stitches."

"Okay then," said Enzo. "Since it doesn't look like I'll be going to the hospital anytime soon, does that mean my plans are okay for tonight?"

"Not so fast, little buddy," said Syd. "You heard what Belov claimed. I think we need to call Trent to see how he wants to proceed. I can't enjoy the evening while sitting on that information."

The vibrating buzz in her pocket alerted Syd of an incoming call. On her flashing screen was the name "Anja R."

"Still basking in the glow of your big win?" said Anja. "You've made quite a name for yourself this weekend!"

<acc)>142</acc)>

Syd had placed the phone on speaker mode.

"Thanks, Anja, but you're not exactly Swiss cheese yourself. You won handily, while I had to fight like a cornered raccoon. Oh, and don't say anything nasty about Enzo because he's sitting right here while you're on speaker."

"Hello there, Enzo!" said Anja. "I hear you played well today. ESPN broadcast part of your match, and one announcer, I think it was Patrick Fleming, referred to you as 'a player to watch.' I know you hate to lose, but the tennis world knows who you are now."

Enzo smiled as Anja's kind words seemed to soothe him. "I appreciate it," he said. "You have such an uplifting spirit, and your words always make me feel better about myself. How can I repay you?"

"You don't owe me a thing," said Anja. "However, if you really want to give me something, it's this. I want your reassurance that you'll keep my wonderful friend Syd safe, not only for this week but in the future."

"Count on that," said Enzo. "Anyone trying to hurt Syd goes directly through me!"

Anja then changed the subject.

"Listen up, guys, this is important. I wanted to tell you that Russo called Trent and informed him about what Marisha witnessed during your qualifying match. Trent is on his way to my hotel room, where he's going to interview Marisha, coach, and me. He told Russo he wants to meet with you first thing in the morning.

"I feel so terrible that Marisha's become involved," continued Anja. "She traveled all this way, and now she'll be interrogated and videotaped. Such a shitshow!"

Checking the tournament draw on her phone, Syd noticed Anja was playing American Christine Davis, a native of Toledo, at 5:00 p.m. on Tuesday. Syd's match would begin at 9:00 p.m. under the lights on Center Court against Flores, the tournament's second seed.

"I signed out a ball machine for noon tomorrow," said Syd. "There's some stuff I need to work on so I won't embarrass myself tomorrow. Another player rented the machine from eleven to noon, and Flores has it at one. Anja, would you like to join me out there? Maybe you can give me some advice because you've played her twice."

There was a pause on the line. Then Anja spoke. "I really don't know how much help I'll be," she said. "I got toasted twice by her and never even won a set. But I'd love to go out there and hit. I'll still have plenty of time afterward to shower, grab dinner, and chill before I play at five."

"Be there by 11:50," said Syd. "Maybe I can join you for lunch afterward."

"Syd," said Anja, "I know someone who can help you develop a strategy to use against Flores, and it isn't me. It's Russo. He's offered to work with you pro bono during your next match. If you decide to employ him in the future, he'd be fine with that. Now that you're making money, Syd, it might be worth considering."

"I'd welcome that," said Syd. "I need any advantage I can get against Flores."

"She's also a world-class jerk," said Anja. "Remember how she acted like the queen of the world when she barged her way onto our practice court on Saturday? If you beat her, you'd be doing the entire world a favor."

"I'm not sure, but I think there's a decent person hiding underneath all that bravado," said Syd. "But I'm going out there to win, regardless."

"You always look for the best in people," said Anja. "That trait skipped me."

After saying goodbye to Anja, Enzo pulled his car into the lot of a bar called Pat's Place, a quaint but popular nightspot in downtown Silverhill. At 5:45, they chose a tiny booth to the left of the entrance, along the wall. Syd felt a little apprehensive as she sat down across from Enzo.

"Look, Syd," said Enzo, "I know you have a big match tomorrow night, but one drink won't hurt. In fact, I think it'll do just the opposite. I'll buy you a Southern Comfort Manhattan and me a porter. It'll relax us and stimulate our appetites . . . among other things. Then we'll grab a hot shower and enjoy a quiet dinner."

She didn't want to admit it, but Enzo was right. The mixed drink relaxed her and took her mind off the tournament and the evolving situation. Two more drinks and a couple of porters later, she and Enzo stumbled out of the bar, arm-in-arm. He opened the passenger-side door. "Your transportation awaits you, beautiful woman," he said. "I hope you're ready for your ride."

"More than you know," she said, sliding into the passenger seat.

As soon as Enzo entered the car, Syd placed her arms around his neck and kissed him intimately, her tongue thrusting deep into the back of his throat. The kiss lasted for nearly a minute, but Enzo finally pulled away to prevent choking.

"I hope there's more where that came from," he said, clearing his throat. "The hotel's right down the road. I can't wait to bathe every part of your body with that lavender body wash. And I won't stop until you tell me to."

"Please don't get a ticket," said Syd, "but will you please drive faster?"

Enzo pulled into the hotel, walked around the car, and removed Syd. He held her in the way a groom carries a bride over the threshold, her feet hanging over his arms and her head relaxed and sprawled backward. He carried her through the lobby and to the elevators, to the astonishment of check-in staff and hotel guests. When they arrived at the room, he placed Syd gently on the bed and removed her clothing, starting from top to bottom. He then completely disrobed and picked up Syd again, leading her to the shower.

"I never realized just how strong you are," said Syd. "I feel like I'm being manhandled, but I like it!"

Enzo's hands worked slowly and gently, beginning at Syd's temples, down her neck and shoulders, over her breasts, and finally to her buttocks and pelvis. Steaming water flowed down the length of her body and onto the floor.

Surrounded by the aroma of lavender, Syd imagined she was a queen bathing beneath a hot waterfall. She surrendered to the desires of her strong, young bodyguard. Her breathing turned deep and rhythmic. Desire flowed through her like an electrical current. She screamed in ecstasy, unconcerned if anyone else could hear.

* * * * *

"I hope I didn't make a mistake tonight," said Syd, after finishing the house salad and starting on her bucatini arrabbiata. "Believe me; I'm not talking about lovemaking. With over twenty-four hours to recover, I'm probably okay in that respect. But *three* Southern Comfort Manhattans? What the heck was I thinking? I have the third-best player in the world waiting to pummel me like a piñata, and I'm sucking down mixed drinks like water?"

Enzo took a bite of his whiskey roast pork shoulder and followed it with a large cut of asparagus. He wiped his mouth with a red cloth napkin.

"Sometimes, it's best not to think at all. You needed a release tonight. You'll be okay in your match. I'll be with you at practice tomorrow. If you and Anja need someone to feed tennis balls to you, I'll do it. I can also replenish the ball machine and keep the press and fans away."

Syd smiled and intertwined her fingers with Enzo's underneath the table.

"Now that you mentioned Anja," she said, "do you mind if I ask a question?"

"Of course not," said Enzo. "Ask me anything."

Syd released Enzo's grip from underneath the table and met his curious gaze.

"You mentioned tonight while speaking with Anja that she always says the right thing to lift your spirits. The conversation seemed so upbeat. I didn't know you two connected that way. Is there something I don't know?"

Enzo's expression turned serious. "Well, since you asked, I guess there's something you need to know. When I fell in love with you, I promised I would also learn to love your friends—but not romantically, of course. I've been through a lot with Anja, especially this weekend. When you were semi-conscious on the court, I panicked. Anja reassured me everything would be all right. She also has a ton of positive energy and helped me believe in myself and my game. I think she's going to be a wonderful friend to both of us."

"Do I make you feel better about yourself when I'm around?" asked Syd.

"Syd, you improve my life in every way. I already told you, I want us to be together for the rest of your life. I wasn't lying."

Before Syd could respond, a woman dressed in black spandex, and her adolescent daughter, approached their table.

"Excuse me," said the woman. "I hope I'm not interrupting, but may I ask you a question?"

The woman was looking directly at her, so Syd decided that she'd respond.

"No problem. What's your question?"

"My daughter and I drove from Indianapolis to attend the tournament. She recognized you from the Tennis Channel. Is your name Sydney?"

At first, Syd thought about fibbing so they could finish their dinner without interruption. But she indulged the woman.

"Yes, I'm Sydney Livingstone."

"Wow!" she said. "My daughter Megan was right! I

could guess you're a professional athlete by your magnificent physique, but I had no idea Megan would know who you are!"

"Well, it's nice of you to say hello. Thanks for stopping."

"May I get a picture of you with my daughter? I know she's a little oversized compared to most tennis players her age, but she actually made it to the third round of a fourteen-and-under tournament in Indianapolis. I'm hoping she stays with tennis for her self-esteem. A photo would make her day complete."

The woman's comments about her daughter surprised Syd, but she tried to hide it.

"I'd be happy to oblige. And your daughter looks absolutely ravishing," said Syd, now smiling at the girl who was now staring at the floor and hiding behind her mother. "You're going to be an outstanding tennis player. And you're beautiful, too."

After digesting Syd's words, the girl smiled shyly and reached out her hand.

"It's nice to meet you, Ms. Sydney. Thank you for letting my mom take our picture."

The flash of the camera briefly illuminated the room.

"Anytime," said Syd. "Are you going to come to my match tomorrow night? It's on Center Court at nine."

"Oh yes, we plan to come," said the mother, answering for her child. "I'm sure it will last beyond Megan's bedtime, but I'll convince her to squeeze in a nap during the day."

"Okay, well, I'll look for you there. Thanks again for stopping."

"Who will you be playing against?" asked the woman.

"Mom," said the girl, trying to disguise her embarrassment. "I told you she's playing Cassandra Flores, one of the best players in the world."

"Oh, I see," said the mother. "My daughter's a little tennis encyclopedia. I'm sorry that you must face Flores tomorrow, but at least you won your first-round match. We'll keep watching out for you on the Tennis Channel."

"That would be great," said Syd, quickly losing interest in the conversation.

"By the way," said the woman. "I've been following the story about that missing player from Canada. What's her name? Monica something? They found her floating in a lake. Weren't you scheduled to play against her before she went missing? Do the police have any leads?"

The woman's daughter pulled on her mother's shirt sleeve. "C'mon," she begged. "You've said enough. Let them eat."

"Well, I want to tell you that I hope they catch the looney who hurt that poor girl," said the woman, ignoring her daughter's intervention. "And I hope they hang him high!"

Enzo rose from the table. He slapped down a hundred and two twenties.

"Thanks for such an enlightening conversation," he said. "It's time to say goodnight."

"Thanks to you both," said the woman, failing to recognize Enzo's sarcasm. "I hope you can put up a good fight tomorrow. You know, enough to entertain the crowd."

As they walked through the lobby, Enzo addressed Syd.

"I'm so sorry I didn't end that conversation sooner. The

longer she spoke, the worse it got."

"Don't I know," said Syd. "I feel sorry for her poor daughter. You know, some people shouldn't reproduce."

As they waited for their elevator, a man in an old wool suit jacket and blue jeans approached. He was unshaven and appeared to be in his mid-to-late fifties. The man elbowed his way past Enzo and grabbed Syd's forearm.

"Hey, I know you!" he said.

Enzo was in no mood for weird fans anymore. He grabbed the man's collar with both hands, shoving him against the wall.

"Let's say I'm this woman's bodyguard. It's inappropriate to touch my client. If you don't release your grip, I'll break your wrist."

The man released his grip and stepped backward.

"I need to have a word with her," he said.

Enzo reached out and poked his finger in the man's chest.

"I think I've made it clear already that this conversation is officially over!"

"Wait!" protested Syd. "Let him talk."

"Absolutely not," Enzo responded. "Being a fan is one thing, but this guy crossed the line!"

"Enzo!" said Syd, pulling him away from the man. "He isn't a fan. He's my father."

CHAPTER 17

The sunlight streamed in from the semi-open blinds and slowly brought Enzo out of his morning slumber. Instinctively, he rolled over onto his side and reached for Syd but felt nothing. The realization of being alone jolted him into a higher state of consciousness. He sat up in the bed, realizing Syd was working on her computer across the room.

"You're already surfing the net at 7:30 in the morning?" he asked. "Are you checking out the stock market or cattle futures?"

"Cattle have no future," quipped Syd without breaking eye-contact from the screen. "But if you must know, honey, I'm on YouTube watching past videos of Flores' matches."

"Have you noticed a fly in the ointment or a chink in the armor? Every player has one, you know."

"Definitely," said Syd. "She's terrible at shaking hands. She's also lousy at hoisting championship trophies. Let's hope I can capitalize on those weaknesses."

"That's what I love about you, Syd!" said Enzo, rising out of bed and heading for the shower. "You're an eternal optimist."

"You know I only use humor to ease tension," said Syd. "Sometimes, it's the only coping mechanism that keeps me sane."

If there was a glaring weakness in Flores' game, Syd couldn't find it. Because she's a player and not a coach, most of her energy went into striking the ball, conditioning, and movement, not searching for opponents' flaws. Her father always told her the best way to find another player's weakness was to improve her own game.

Syd didn't sleep well the previous night. She spent hours hydrating and visiting the bathroom, trying to negate the effects of three Southern Comfort Manhattans. The surprise meeting with her father didn't pave the way for a good night's sleep either.

Years earlier, Syd accepted the fact that her father no longer wanted to see her. Now he was suddenly back. Were his intentions as pure as he claimed? Was he feeling bad for abandoning her after the divorce? Did he really want to repair their relationship? Or perhaps he wanted something more. Money? Justification for his actions? Her forgiveness?

Or could it possibly be something sinister? Did he blame her for the breakup of his marriage? She remembered overhearing her parents' angry conversations about the way he had treated his daughter both on and off the court. Perhaps her father felt she wasn't loyal when she continued her career without consulting him or asking for advice? Was he concealing his hatred and now pretending to care?

The more Syd ruminated over her father's intentions, the less threatened she felt by him. He was definitely a strange and troubled man, but she couldn't imagine that he would ever target and stalk his own daughter. After forty-five contentious minutes of conversation, which included resentment and accusations of abandonment, she'd ended up hugging him. Then she surprised herself. She told her father she loved him. She believed he was here for the right reasons. If she was wrong, she'd find out soon.

Another factor that affected her sleep was a phone call from Trent. He'd scheduled a 10:00 a.m. visit to Syd's hotel room and requested that Enzo accompany her. What would that impending meeting be about? Would Trent announce he was arresting Fitz after yesterday's interrogation of Belov? Would he state that he intended to bring charges against her, based on the discovery of her pendant at the murder scene? Or did he know something else, possibly gleaned from the autopsy or other evidence? After breakfast with Enzo, she would know the answers to those questions.

* * * * *

"I'm not in the mood for small talk," said Trent, sitting on the foldout couch of Syd's room. "We've got plenty to discuss, and I don't have much time."

Enzo and Syd sat across from Trent in wooden chairs. Enzo reached over and grabbed Syd's hand, squeezing tightly. Syd meditated silently to avert a panic attack.

"Jamie Pendleton, Rivet's companion, is no longer a person of interest," said Trent. "Cameras recorded her working out in the gym and going for a swim during the time of Rivet's murder. Pendleton didn't shower between the workout and pool, but poor hygiene is no reason to file charges. So Pendleton is out."

"What about Fitz?" asked Enzo. "You heard Belov's story. If he was crazy enough to send Syd into a deadly allergic reaction, then he may have killed Rivet."

"I agree with you," said Trent. "At least in principle. But besides Belov's word, we have no proof Fitz infused Syd's drink with any kind of citrus fruit. No other witnesses have come forward to corroborate the story. And since Syd was playing in what's considered a qualifying match, there were no cameras at courtside. He also vehemently denies the accusation and claims that Syd may have coerced Belov into making a false statement.

"And now that brings me to Belov. She's sticking by her story and says she's 100 percent sure of what she saw. She pulled me aside after our meeting and said she's afraid of Fitz and what he might do to her as retribution. I don't know whether I believe Belov. My intuition tells me not to trust her completely, but that may be because of her introverted way of communicating."

"What does your intuition tell you about Fitz?" asked Syd. "Do you have a problem because Belov is predisposed differently than you, or are you protecting Fitz because he's part of the good-ol'-boy network?"

"Just a minute there, Ms. Livingstone," said Trent. "I don't judge anyone by how they live or who they sleep with. My job is to enforce the law, period. And as far as the 'good-ol'-boy network' you're referring to, Fitz doesn't mean diddly squat to me, especially if he tried to kill you.

"For the time being, however, I cannot prove who's lying between Belov and Fitz. So whether you want me to arrest either Fitz or Belov, my hands are tied right now."

"I'm sorry," said Syd. "I probably shouldn't have said that. You can understand the amount of stress I'm under. At least I hope so."

"Noted," said Trent. "But I want to discuss your father. You mentioned when I arrived that he approached you near the elevators last night. What hotel is he staying in?"

Syd thought about Trent's question. In all of her surprise and emotion, her father's choice of hotel may not have come up.

"Enzo?" she asked. "Do you remember? Where is my father staying?"

Enzo shook his head. "I know he said he was staying across town, but I can't remember where. He promised, though, that he'd be at Syd's match. He said he needed to stay away from Syd's mother because of a restraining order."

"Hopefully, I can talk to him before or after your match tonight," said Trent. "I'll be in attendance, but not as a fan. I'll make sure our stalker isn't up to any shenanigans."

"My father isn't responsible for what's happened here," said Syd. "If you're considering him a suspect, you're definitely barking up the wrong tree."

Trent looked down at his notes. He searched for the right way to phrase his response in order not to offend Syd or Enzo.

"You're probably correct," he said. "But doesn't it seem odd that he finally came back into your life at the exact time when all hell's breaking loose? Something seems amiss. At least for the time being, he remains a person of interest."

"Who else are you interested in speaking with?" asked Syd.

"I need to talk with Peter O'Malley. Your deceased doubles partner received a delivery of Crystal 10 from him and then turned up dead. If we find he sent a bottle to your room anonymously, then we'll have another person of interest."

Enzo squirmed in his chair, releasing his grip from Syd's hand. He obviously wanted to interrupt, but he was hesitant to do so. Both Trent and Syd noticed Enzo's strange reaction.

"Is there something you'd like to add, Mr. Martin?" asked Trent.

"Yes," said Enzo. "I need to apologize to Syd. I spoke with O'Malley in the treatment center at the tennis facility yesterday. He was being treated for a calf muscle injury, and I was getting stimulation therapy on my shoulder."

"Wait," said Syd. "Why didn't you tell me about this conversation?"

"You've seemed stressed, and I didn't want to throw another iron into the fire. But nothing earth-shattering happened. It was just a conversation."

Syd stood and walked across the room.

"Enzo, you need to tell me what's going on. My life's in danger."

"I didn't lie to you, Syd!" said Enzo. "I'm only trying to protect you from your racing mind. But now that it's in the open, I'll tell you what we discussed. I straight-out asked O'Malley if he had sent the bourbon to your room. I told him if he had, we'd find a private location—perhaps behind a building—to settle things.

"But he denied everything, saying he had no idea about the delivery. He said he had sent that brand of bourbon to Milena before she died but denied having anything to do with her death or the murder of Monica Rivet."

Trent looked at Syd, sitting on the opposite side of the room, her hands crossed in a defensive posture.

"It's nice to know that information, Enzo," said Trent. "But let's make a rule. No more secrets from either Ms. Livingstone or me."

"Noted," Enzo said, remembering Trent's reply to one of Syd's statements.

"Ms. Livingstone, I don't think your boyfriend had nefarious motives for not telling you about his conversation with O'Malley," said Trent. "He probably didn't want to stress you out more than you already are."

Syd returned to her seat next to Enzo, still slightly perplexed about why he'd failed to reveal the conversation.

"Unfortunately," said Trent, "because of my job description, I have to tell it like it is."

Now it was Syd squirming in her chair.

"Go ahead, lieutenant. I'm a big girl. Tell me."

"You are still a major person of interest," said Trent. "My opinion aside, you could have hired someone to paint that message on your own car. I mean, who in their right mind would think someone would deface their own rental car?"

"Yeah," said Syd. "Especially when I declined the insurance."

Enzo started to speak, but Trent motioned for him to remain silent.

"In addition, you could have had the whiskey delivered, and you could have killed Monica Rivet."

"But wait," said Syd. "If I would have been busy murdering that girl late at night, then wouldn't Enzo have noticed my absence? We were together the whole time!"

"You could have left the room quietly while he slept," said Trent. "Or, you could've worked together to oust Rivet from the tournament. You both benefited if Rivet couldn't compete. You would have been one step closer to a substantial payout."

"I can't believe I'm even hearing this!" said Enzo. "You're calling us murderers?"

"No, I'm not," said Trent. "For the record, I truly don't believe either of you committed a crime. But when a prosecutor sees the evidence and turns the case over to a grand jury, no one will give a rat's ass about my opinion.

"So for now, Syd's a person of interest, and you're knocking on the door, Mr. Martin."

Trent stood up and gathered his things. "Have a pleasant morning," he said. "I hope you win your match. I watch a lot of tennis myself, you know. I've never liked Cassandra Flores. On TV, she seems like a real bitch."

"That's an excellent description of my life now," said Syd. "A real bitch."

* * * * *

The end is near. I feel it. Sydney will pay for her turning her back on a wonderful friend. I'm certain she's not enjoying what I've done: sending bourbon to her room, painting that message on her car, and killing her opponent. And that makes me happy because I've spoiled some positive things in her life, including qualifying for a Master 1000 tournament, earning a substantial payday, and improving her ranking. Local reporters are referring to her as "indestructible." They'll soon eat their words. She'll bankroll $43K, even if she loses this next match, which is probably inevitable. But you know what? I'm not concerned about the amount of money she earns. I'll make sure she never spends it. I've sacrificed so much. The training, the diet, my elbow pain, and even getting scratched by the player I killed! But I've heard that nothing worthwhile comes easy. And now it's time to put my plan into action.

Overall, my breakfast was pretty good this morning. The hash browns were crisp, the pancakes were light and fluffy, and the coffee was fresh. The sunny-side-up eggs weren't quite runny enough, though, and that prevented me from mixing the yolk with my bacon. But I'm not complaining. My plan is coming to its fruition. An overcooked egg won't spoil my plans.

Geez, it's 9:30 already. I've got to hurry. Has my package arrived yet? I ordered it from Amazon as a rush-shipment. My email stated they would send it to the hotel before ten. I'll check with this guy at the registration desk.

Hell yes, it's here thirty minutes earlier than promised! And I don't even have to sign for it; just show the guy my ID. Even if a camera caught me receiving this package, what would that prove? I could muster a myriad of excuses about what was inside. Stop being so damn paranoid!

Nobody's inside the business center, so I'm free to go in there and open it. The package feels heavier than I expected, but maybe that's because of the shipping material. I'll use these scissors in the tray next to the printer to cut the tape. I'm reaching inside the box now. I can feel it. The surface is cold, smooth, and metallic. What a beautiful, shiny little globe-shaped treasure! Damn, I hope this works!

CHAPTER 18

The forty-five-minute meeting with Trent left Syd with less than an hour to be on her practice court. She was disappointed at Enzo for failing to inform her about his interaction with O'Malley. She loved the way she and Enzo shared everything about themselves. Why did he conceal the discussion with Peter?

Michael Livingstone offered to drive his daughter to her practice session, but Syd felt she needed the time to talk and strategize with Anja. The 9:00 p.m. match would be broadcast for the entire world. A major beat-down administered by Flores was a genuine possibility. The last thing she desired was to embarrass herself on national television.

While waiting for Anja in the lobby of her hotel, Syd's mind wandered back to her conversation with her father the previous evening.

"I've made a lot of mistakes in my life," he said. "But my biggest was allowing our relationship to fizzle. I want you to know it was 100 percent my fault and not yours. I hope that you can find it in your heart to forgive me."

"Why did you come to Columbus?" she'd asked him. "Why this tournament and why now?"

"You know, I had a real brush with death," said Michael. "I was careless and came into contact with someone who had COVID-19. While in the intensive care unit for twenty-eight days, I reflected on my life.

"Syd, I was sure that I was dying. No matter what medicine or how much oxygen they gave me, I couldn't get enough air. I asked God to take me during the third week. The pain and discomfort were too much.

"When you're sure that you're going to die, you think about your life and what's important," he continued. "While I loved your mother, I knew our relationship was irreconcilable. But I felt the relationship between us was salvageable, despite my egregious behavior. I love you, Syd, and I'd like to be a part of your life. But if you want me to go away, I'll understand. And I'll accept 100 percent of the blame."

"I saw you in the stadium when I was lying on the court, gasping for air," she'd said. "I know how that feels. Why did you keep your presence a secret until last night?"

"Just scared, I guess," said Michael. "Every time I mustered enough courage to approach you, it seemed like your mother was nearby. As you know, our relationship is contentious. She even filed a restraining order."

"I'm glad you survived that awful virus," said Syd. "I won't lie, there were times I needed you, and you weren't there. But I've never stopped loving you. And I want you in my life."

The sound of Anja's voice surprised Syd.

"Hey daydream girl, let's get a move on! We don't want to lose our court. You were in quite a trance. I hope I didn't startle you."

"No, I was just thinking," said Syd. "Thanks for picking me up."

Normally, Enzo would have given Syd a ride, especially since he was no longer competing. But their conversation had turned chippy after Trent's interview, and the two decided they both needed a few hours to chill. She would meet him for dinner at around five.

Anja and Syd kept the conversation light on their way to the match. They avoided contentious topics such as murder investigations, mysterious deliveries, missing pendants, and newly relevant fathers. As Anja's car pulled into the parking lot of the complex, Syd's phone displayed the name of Victor Dan.

"What's up, Victor?" said Syd. "Or is this my friend Nicole using Victor's phone to reach me?"

"Syd," said a male voice. "This is Victor. Nicole's gone. She left my hotel room in a huff at about one this morning. I haven't seen her since. Has she contacted you?"

"Oh shit, yeah," said Syd. "I had two missed calls from her while I met with Enzo and a police investigator. I forgot to call her back. Have you tried calling her lately?"

"I called her three times after eleven this morning, and they went to voicemail. I hope nothing's wrong."

"If she stormed out at one in the morning, why did you wait until eleven to call her?"

"I don't know. I guess I was pissed. We had a fight over that damn spider. What's its name, Starlite or something.

"Scarlet."

"Yeah, that's right. Anyway, she placed Scarlet on my chest without my permission while I was watching TV. I felt its hairy legs walking through my chest hair, and I freaked. I flinched so hard that the spider flew off me and onto the floor. Nicole accused me of trying to murder her best friend. Have you ever heard anything so ridiculous?"

"I'd say that's pretty run-of-the-mill for Nicole," said Syd. "But I'm surprised she would leave in the middle of the night."

Syd took a deep breath, waiting for Victor to respond. After an awkward silence, she continued. "Why don't you relax? She's probably just ticked off. I'll call her after my practice session. I'm sure she's fine."

* * * * *

Anja and Syd jogged through the players' entrance, flashing their IDs to an elderly man who was manning the gate. Before they could get to Court 9 for their practice session, they needed to go into the lounge to retrieve several baskets of practice balls.

Monitoring the table in the players' lounge was none other than Al "Fitz" Fitzgerald.

"Welcome, ladies," he said. "Your baskets are sitting there in the corner. Please return them when you're finished. The eleven o'clock players finished about fifteen minutes ago, and they've placed your ball machine behind the wall in the back of your court."

"I think you'll love our new machine. We ordered five of them for this tournament," continued Fitz. "They're called Pivot 360. Not a cheap date, but experts refer to them as 'petite powerhouses.' They perform better than any competitor's brand and have a five-year warranty. It also has a remote control feature to activate the unit up to 150 feet away. I'd love to get your feedback after you try it."

Syd looked at Fitz for some kind of reaction. If her presence stressed him, he was doing an excellent job of concealing it.

At 11:59, Anja and Syd arrived at the court, where they met Peter.

"Excuse me," said O'Malley to Anja. "Do you mind if I speak with Syd alone for a second?"

"No problem," said Syd to Anja. "Why don't you go on the court and stretch? I'll join you in a couple of minutes."

Syd didn't expect to see O'Malley at her practice court.

"Do you need something, or can this wait?"

Peter grabbed Syd by the arm and pulled her to the side.

"Listen, I need to tell you something. Enzo practically attacked me in the treatment room yesterday before his match. He accused me of sending a bottle of bourbon to your hotel room. I told him I had no clue what he was talking about, but he became incensed. He grabbed me by the collar. I thought he was going to throw a punch."

Syd looked into Peter's eyes. He looked concerned and afraid.

"I'm sorry if Enzo scared you. He really is a good guy. I'll make sure he doesn't bother you again."

"It's not that I fear Enzo or anything," said Peter. "I can take care of myself. I'm worried about you, Syd, especially with that temper of his."

"Thanks for your concern," said Syd, "but I know Enzo well. He'd never hurt me."

Then Syd remembered the advice Peter provided to her on the court.

"Your impromptu lesson helped me," she said. "I've been volleying like a champ all week. I hope we remain friends in the future."

Peter smiled and looked into Syd's eyes. "Good Lord, you're beautiful," he muttered under his breath. He'd always been astonished by her beauty, and his feelings hadn't diminished over the years. "I'm always glad to help good people like you," said Peter. "We're kind of in the same boat. I'm playing Flores' boyfriend, Jules Willems, at 2:30 on Center Court. He's number one in the world. No one is even giving me a chance. Wouldn't it be magical if we both shocked the world?"

"Not only magical but awesome," said Syd. "I need to get to practice. Good luck."

The mention of Willems reminded her of their brief affair. He'd come onto her strongly that night. She was younger, unattached, and a little awestruck. They ended up spending a couple of nights together, a physical relationship with no strings attached.

By the time Syd appeared on court, Russo was already feeding balls to Anja. Several hundred spectators hung around the court, eager to get a glimpse of Flores' next opponent.

"We love you, Syd!" hollered a man's voice as she walked onto the court. Cameras flashed as she removed five identical rackets from her bag and tested out their strings by striking her palms against them. WBUS in Columbus was conducting a live feed. One of its reporters approached Syd.

"It's been a turbulent time for you. How do you put distractions aside and focus on tonight's match?"

Syd stared at the microphone, just four inches below her chin. When she'd arrived at the tournament as a qualifier, she couldn't pay someone to request her autograph. But now she was the media's primary focus. Her fifteen minutes of fame had finally arrived.

CHAPTER 19

Despite not being a grand-slam event, the MMO carries nearly as much clout as any non-major event in the world. Hundreds of participants, interviewed anonymously, felt the tournament was run as efficiently as the prestigious US Open.

The MMO had the feel of a grand slam event on Wednesday morning. Vendors operated in high-gear mode, pedaling fast food, club memberships, instructional videos, keychains, racquets, souvenirs, and apparel. Temperatures were in the upper-eighties with a 10 percent chance of rain. The average wait for food and drinks was about fifteen minutes. The side courts burst at the seams with spectators. The day's marquee matches on Center and Grandstand courts were scheduled two hours apart, all the way to the final matches held at 9:00 p.m. and 10:00 p.m., respectively. Syd's nine o'clock match against Flores provided maximum exposure, with the potential to make her a household name.

After her media interview, Russo approached Syd. He'd smeared an inordinate amount of sunscreen on his face, neck, and arms, giving him a ghostlike appearance.

"Anja spoke with you about my offer to coach you during the Flores match. Does that interest you, Sydney? It will cost you nothing."

"That's a generous offer, coach," said Syd, wiping a drop of sweat running down the side of her face. "I would love it if you worked with me tonight. It's a steep hill to climb thinking I could beat Flores, but if you're not afraid, I'm all in!"

The noontime sun was bright, and Russo adjusted his sunglasses to keep the rays out of his eyes.

"Sydney, she's a fantastic player. But I can help you devise a strategy. I'm not guaranteeing you'll win, but I promise I can give you a fighting chance."

A fighting chance, thought Syd. Most players crumble when they see their names next to Flores' in the draw. They're defeated before they walk onto the court. A fighting chance sounded like the deal of the century.

"Let's make it happen," said Syd. "When can we devise our strategy?"

"Anja's playing at five tonight against a player from Toledo," said Russo. "I'll need an hour with Anja after this session. Anja already has a game plan. I need to meet her at 4:15 for a pre-match warmup. Could we discuss our strategy over a Gatorade between two and three?"

"That would be fantastic," said Syd. "I'll meet you in front of the Midwestern Sports tent."

Russo spent the next hour on the court with Syd and Anja. For the first forty minutes, Syd and Enzo drilled vigorously under Russo's supervision—forehands and backhands, both down-the-line and crosscourt; serves and returns; overheads and lobs; and a "rally-in-the-alley" drill.

Syd told Chelsea that her father was in town to watch her play. With a restraining order in effect, she didn't want her mother to panic at the sight of her ex-husband. Both showed up at today's practice session but sat on opposite ends of the court. Chelsea told Syd she wasn't bothered by Michael's presence.

"You only get one father in your lifetime," said Chelsea. "I hope you can work it out."

* * * * *

The sight of Enzo surprised Syd. He arrived at her court while she was in the heat of a mock battle with Anja. He stood in the corner, smiling and watching with his arms crossed.

With twenty minutes remaining in the session, Syd decided it was time to put Fitz's Pivot 360 into action. The machine housed two hundred balls in its holding compartment. The Pivot 360 could send them at various speeds, angles, and spin. With one turn of a dial, the unit could generate ball speeds up to 75 mph.

The previous users, a female player from Bucharest and her coach, placed the machine behind the wall of Court 9. Syd and Anja wheeled the machine onto the court. Fitz had said they would find a hand-held remote magnetically attached to the unit, but neither Syd nor Anja could find it.

"We'll operate the controls on the unit itself," said Syd. "But remember to tell Fitz the remote wasn't on the machine. That tight-ass would probably send us a bill for it."

Syd grabbed both baskets of balls, the ones provided by Fitz in the players' lounge. They carried them to the machine and loaded them into the holding tank.

"Both of you need to practice inside-out forehands," shouted Russo from the opposite end of the court. "Make the machine fire the ball to the left side of the court."

"I'll try," said Syd.

Russo and Anja watched Syd as she squinted her eyes to read the directions on the back of the machine. She turned one dial in a clockwise manner and another in the opposite direction. She also flipped a couple of levers up and others down.

"I'm ready when you're ready," shouted Anja, hopping up and down on her toes, anticipating a ball.

"Here we go!" said Syd, flipping the switch to the "on" position. The unit's motor fired up with a whirring sound but then stopped running as quickly as it started.

"That was weird," said Syd. "Let me try again."

Same result. The machine fired up and stopped.

Three more tries; three more identical reactions.

"That's great," said Syd. "This new machine Fitz bragged about is ready for the repair shop already. I hope he got a great deal."

"Syd, let me try for a second," shouted Enzo, emerging from his corner and walking onto her side of the court. "I'm pretty good at these types of things."

"She's all yours," said Syd, walking around the machine and standing next to Anja, who had ventured over.

If Enzo was a great technical mind, Syd hadn't seen evidence of it in the past. She remembered that he once required help while changing a defective windshield wiper. But maybe he was better with electronics.

Enzo flipped a few switches up and down, rotated a few dials, and opened the door to the battery compartment. "Let's try it again," he said.

As the machine fired up, it lost power once again.

Syd noticed a typed note taped to the front of the ball machine under the long nozzle.

"Hold on a minute, Enzo," she said. "There's something on the front I need to read."

The headline of the note read:

Please read before operating.

The type underneath the headline was tiny, like something printed out in eight-point font. Syd moved closer and squinted her eyes. The first sentence read:

Sometimes the machine will lose power after it starts. If that's the case . . .

There was an even smaller type underneath:

Then . . . you're FUCKED!

FAULTS

Syd stood motionless, perplexed by what she'd read. Were her eyes deceiving her?

A whirring sound interrupted Syd's thoughts. Instinctively, Syd ducked as an object flew out of the machine's nozzle. It whizzed over her head, traveling at a high rate of speed. The object flew above her head, missing her by a centimeter.

She looked up at Enzo. On his face was a look of either complete bewilderment or borderline craziness.

"What just happened?" she said to Enzo. "Why did you turn on the machine when I was standing in front of it? Are you trying to kill me?"

Enzo pointed in Syd's direction, but no words came out of his mouth.

"Why did you activate the machine?" asked Syd. "Please say something!"

A weak voice finally emerged from Enzo.

"Syd," he said. "Turn around and look behind you."

CHAPTER 20

Syd glared at Enzo for a few seconds longer before turning around. Shock and horror replaced her bewilderment. Crumpled on the court behind her was an unconscious Anja, her face bloody and legs twitching.

For a few seconds, the silence around Court 9 was deafening. Syd sprinted to Anja and knelt by her side.

"Someone, please do something!" she yelled. "Call 911 and notify the doctor on call. And please hurry!"

Fitz, who was also in the vicinity, ran to the court to assist Anja.

"Anja, please don't die!" screamed Syd, elevating her head to prevent her choking on her own blood. "I'm not strong enough to lose another friend!"

Fitz removed his hat and scratched the top of his head. "This whole thing just makes no sense," he said. "A tennis ball can't do this kind of damage. Something's not right."

Russo approached Syd and Fitz, his hands quivering uncontrollably. "No tennis ball caused this," he said. "I found this on the court. It flew out of that machine."

Russo held a steel ball that was smaller in diameter than a tennis ball. It weighed more than a pound.

Belov pushed her way through the myriad of gawking spectators at Court 9. She nudged Syd out of the way and wrapped her arms around Anja's neck.

"I don't think she's even breathing. Oh, God! Please stay with us, Anja!"

By the time the ambulance arrived, a doctor on call had already performed CPR. Anja breathed sporadically. Word of the accident spread throughout the complex. Hundreds gathered around the court, making it difficult for paramedics to attend to her. By the time they reached Anja, her breathing had become shallow, and her vital signs were weakening.

A helicopter landed in a vacant area cleared out by security. Paramedics loaded Anja onto a stretcher and carried her to the aircraft. Syd leaned inside to speak to the pilot.

"I'm going with her," she said. "She's my best friend, and I can't leave her."

"State laws prohibit you from riding with us," he said. "She's in excellent hands, but you must clear the area."

Syd backed away slowly with tears in her eyes. She offered a silent prayer to whoever might be listening.

Once Anja was inside, the chopper rose above the throng of people and headed westward, en route to the nearest hospital.

Belov rushed toward Syd. "Where are they taking her?" she asked. "I need to be by her side."

"I don't know which hospital they're taking her to, but we'll find out," said Syd. "Try to remain calm until we know more. Believe me, Marisha, I'm struggling, too."

* * * * *

Trent emerged from a public restroom located a few hundred yards from the court. He sported a light blue dress shirt with a red-and-white-striped tie and black suit pants. Spectators jumped out of the way as his stout 250-pound frame moved quickly through the crowd. He was almost to Court 9 when he noticed he was being followed by a sandy-haired, toned, six-foot-eight man who was carrying a Yonex tennis bag over his shoulder. Trent, trained to be aware of people following him, assumed he was one of the tournament's competitors.

"Excuse me, sir," said Peter O'Malley, who assumed by Trent's attire and reaction that he was a member of law enforcement. "What just happened?"

"Who am I talking to right now?" said Trent, failing to break stride.

"My name's Peter O'Malley. I'm a player and a friend of Sydney. I heard the commotion, and I came running over."

"Stay back," he said to O'Malley. "But don't leave. I've wanted to speak with you for a while now."

Trent located Russo, sitting on a courtside chair with his head in his hands. Lying on the ground next to his feet was the round steel projectile. Russo looked up, recognizing Trent from their previous meeting.

"Lieutenant," he said, reaching down to pick up the sphere. "I believe this object flew from the ball machine and struck my player," he said. "I spotted it along the fence. It doesn't belong on a tennis court."

"Place it down on one of those chairs beside you," said Trent. "We don't want anyone else handling it."

Trent spotted several ushers and tournament employees watching nearby.

"Listen, please!" he shouted in their direction. "Cordon off this entire area. Make a large circle around all spectators in the vicinity. No one comes, and no one goes."

As Trent sat down next to Russo, the older man spoke. "Tell me where they're taking Anja," he said. "I'm like a father figure to her. She needs me by her side."

Tears streamed down Russo's face. His sunglasses were on the ground, and he was sobbing uncontrollably. Trent removed an unused handkerchief from his pocket and handed it to Russo.

"I'm sorry," said Russo. "Anja and I are so close. I'd never forgive myself if she doesn't make it."

"It was so sudden," said Trent. "I don't think anyone could have prevented it, including you. Did you see what happened?"

"Yes," said Russo, rubbing Trent's handkerchief in circles over his left eye. "Anja was struck by–I don't know what to call it–that projectile. The machine wasn't working properly, and Enzo attempted to fix it by operating the manual controls. There should have been a remote control, but none of us could locate it."

"So why was the machine pointed at Anja?" asked Trent. "Shouldn't players know better than to stand in front of a ball launcher?"

"Anja knows better," replied Russo. "Sydney Livingstone was there, but the machine was shut off. She was reading instructions when it suddenly turned on. The actual target was Sydney. She ducked at the last second, and Anja was standing behind her."

Sydney was in earshot of the conversation between Trent and Russo. She walked to the machine and removed the printed instructions.

"Here is the bait, lieutenant," she said, handing the paper to Trent. "Someone designed this note to lure the victim to the front of the machine. It worked like a charm."

Trent perused the note, shaking his head in disbelief. He placed it in a plastic bag.

Sirens wailed in the background. Within minutes, six police officers and four investigators were on the scene. Trent instructed four officers to collect the names of everyone in the vicinity and to move them to a vacant court. He asked a pair of officers to assist employees in securing the marked-off area. The remaining two plain-clothes detectives stayed with him. One collected the metal ball and placed it inside of a plastic bag.

Trent recognized Fitz standing nearby and approached him.

"Mr. Fitzgerald," he said. "Nice seeing you, despite the unfortunate circumstances. I've been here since noon watching Ms. Livingstone practice," said Trent. "I'm going to her match tonight, so I took the afternoon off and made a day of it.

"Anyway, nature calls, and I take a five-minute break to use the pisser. By the time I get back, all hell's breaking loose. Can you give me your version of the events? Were you close enough to observe what happened?"

"Yes, I was in the vicinity," said Fitz. "I was walking around the complex, and I passed by Syd's court. I was among the hundreds watching her practice. Someone screamed, and people rushed the court. That's when I muscled through everyone to see what was happening."

"Did you notice anything odd? Or did you notice anyone acting strangely?" asked Trent.

"Not really. It looked like a run-of-the-mill practice session until everything exploded. Now I hear that something flew out of that machine and struck Ms. Radonovic. This can't happen at one of the world's most prestigious tournaments!"

"Mr. Fitzgerald, we're detaining everyone near this court until we can sort out what happened," said Trent. "More officers will arrive soon. It's an inconvenience, but we have no choice at this point."

"Okay, lieutenant, do what you must. I'll check with tournament headquarters. I may have to make an unpopular decision soon. If you need me, call my cell. My number is here on my business card."

"I'll have a detective accompany you," said Trent, motioning toward Edward Gonzalez, a short, overweight man in his late forties. "Everyone near Court 9 is a person of interest in this case, Mr. Fitzgerald, including you. I'll give you ten minutes to take care of business and be back on this court. Mr. Gonzalez has a stopwatch on his phone, and you're already down to nine minutes and fifty-five seconds."

Members of law enforcement were already photographing spectators' IDs and interviewing them.

"We need everyone to empty their pockets," said Trent. "We're trying to locate a remote control device. We will transfer anyone refusing to cooperate to headquarters for additional questioning."

The first person Trent wanted to interview was Enzo, who hadn't stopped pacing since the object struck Anja.

"Mr. Martin, come take a seat," said Trent. "I'm sure this rocked your world, but I need a statement. It'll take five minutes. Then you can start ruminating or pacing, or whatever else you need to do."

Trent sat down in an individual chair on the north side of the court, between the singles and doubles lines. Enzo grabbed a chair and pulled it across from Trent. Both of his hands were shaking, his feet sat firmly on the ground, and he tried to restrain his legs from pumping up and down.

"I'm sorry, lieutenant," said Enzo. "I'm having a heck of a time settling down after watching my girlfriend almost get killed and then seeing what happened to Anja."

"Do you have any idea how it happened, Mr. Martin? You were at the controls when the incident occurred. With no remote in sight, it appears you were in the ideal position to activate the unit."

Enzo wriggled in his seat. He longed to return to his pacing as his heartbeat quickened, but he resisted the urge.

"Yes, I could turn the machine on. But why would I, when my girlfriend was staring down the muzzle? And besides, when I tried to turn it on previously, it would start up and then peter out."

"It didn't peter out the last time," said Trent. "Would you mind emptying your pockets? I think whoever has the remote might be our culprit."

Enzo reached into his pockets and placed several items on the court: car keys, a cell phone, $60 in cash, a few quarters and dimes, and a knife. At Trent's request, he extended the knife's blade. It measured four inches.

"We're going to confiscate that knife so we can analyze it, Mr. Martin. Why are you carrying such a long blade, anyway?"

"Have you seen what's been happening around this tournament, Trent? You've already discovered a body in the river, and it's obvious that Syd is in the killer's sights. I'm not like one of your detectives who can bench press a Tesla. I need to protect both Syd and myself."

"Well, your little knife didn't prevent this incident today, did it, Mr. Martin? Is there any reason you'd try to injure your girlfriend?"

"Of course not. That's a stupid question. All you have to do is ask Syd, and she'll tell you I'd never hurt her."

"I already did, Mr. Martin. But I'm not completely sold on that. You were standing in front of the ball machine's control panel."

Trent reached beneath his seat and pulled out the see-through bag that contained the circular metal object, "Have you ever seen this before today?" he asked. "Do you know why anyone would insert this into a device that propels a tennis ball seventy-five miles per hour?"

"I've never seen it before today, but I know why some-one would load it into a ball machine—to kill my girlfriend.

"And I think you should get off your ass and investi-gate Fitz, the tournament director. According to Belov, he squeezed a fucking mango into Syd's hydration drink. And you know what happened after that. It's obvious that he's behind all of this."

As if on cue, Fitz returned to the court with Gonzalez.

"I'm suspending play, once in-progress matches con-clude," said Fitz. "This is going to piss off our fans in atten-dance. And what about our TV audience? Our ratings will nosedive. I'm canceling all activities for tomorrow, too. We need to sort this out and return to action on Thursday."

Trent emerged from his chair and motioned for Fitz to follow him behind the wall where the ball machine had stood waiting earlier in the day. Trent placed his right hand on Fitz's shoulder, his lower lip quivering.

"Sir, the last thing you should worry about is the image of this fine tournament or your coveted TV ratings. If I were going to arrest one person pertaining to events of the past few days, it would be you."

Fitz bristled at Trent's words and voiced an objection.

"Just shut the fuck up," said Trent. "I don't like you, and I don't want to listen to your drivel. First, I think you tam-pered with Ms. Livingstone's drink. Second, your previous history doesn't give me the warm-and-fuzzies. And finally, the ball machine is yours, and the damn remote control is still missing. You're lucky we didn't find it on you, or you'd be under arrest for murder."

Fitz looked at the ground and mumbled. By the time he looked back up, Trent's anger hadn't subsided.

"Okay, detective, I may have squeezed a little juice into her drink," he said. "But I never dreamed it would almost kill her. Sydney Livingstone dropped a dime on me at another tournament. I was a flea's pubic hair away from permanently losing my officiating license.

"I'd heard about her cashew allergy, and I researched the subject. Mangoes are in the same family as cashews and pistachios. I figured mango juice might make her a little queasy. Then, she'd lose to Lovejoy, our hometown sweetheart, and attendance would skyrocket.

"It was a harmless prank, not attempted murder. But that's all I'm guilty of, lieutenant. I didn't murder Monica Rivet, and I did not place a metal ball in the machine and activate it!"

The commotion on a nearby court interrupted Trent's response. Several police officers wrestled a tall, young man to the ground.

"Lieutenant Trent, a man stepped out of line and attempted to exit the court," said officer Philip Davis. "We told him to halt, but he made a run for it. Lucky for us, another spectator made a diving tackle."

Syd sprinted to the other court, running side-by-side with Trent. By the time she arrived, several security guards and police officers restrained the man. When they stood him up, she could see the man's face.

"Oh my God!" she gasped. "That's Peter O'Malley!"

Chapter 21

The original plan was to slice Sydney's throat with my knife. The entire process lasts fifteen to twenty minutes. There was no need to kidnap her because I've gained her trust. I needed a reason to slip away with her—a lunch perhaps, a relaxing hike in the woods, or a visit to a local park or bookstore. Remove her far from the hotel, where screaming would be futile.

Once I had her alone and away from others, I could spend the first five minutes incapacitating her. With the element of surprise as my ally, it wouldn't be difficult.

Once in captivity, she'd understand what was happening. But it wouldn't matter anymore. Her screams, moans, and apologies would fall on deaf ears.

I'd spend a few minutes talking to Sydney. We'd discuss the pain she caused. We'd talk about how she placed her own selfish needs ahead of others. I'd explain how actions come with repercussions, especially when dealing with people important to you or the people important to them.

By the time we finished, she would understand. Maybe she wouldn't blame me for killing her. She could die knowing justice had been served. Maybe we could hug before I ended her life. That would be nice.

Cutting her throat would be easy, at least for me. I would be administering justice, like a firing squad shooter or an electric chair operator. Nothing personal, just the ultimate phase of due process.

I'd attempt to make it less painful once she understood my reasoning. I'd ease her as gently as possible into the next world, where wrongdoings are forgotten, and grudges are forgiven. Hopefully, my lust for vengeance and appetite for justice will expire along with Sydney. Then I could live a normal life without being tormented by voices instructing me to kill.

Everything would have been fine if it weren't for that asshole, Al Fitzgerald. Is he screwing with me or what? Sydney exposed Fitz after she spotted him enjoying an intimate dinner with a player. I get it. But Fitz knew the rules and violated them. He has no one to blame but himself.

I still can't believe Fitz squeezed a tropical fruit into Sydney's drink! What a dope! Obviously, he's not careful like me. He didn't kill Sydney, but he ruined my plans for the time being. Trent has security positioned everywhere, protecting Sydney and her opponents, and monitoring everyone else in the suspect pool.

For a while, I considered putting my plan on hold, at least for this tournament. I didn't think anyone would find the body of Monica Rivet so quickly. A miscalculation on my part. I should have released the car into the river. It would have submerged, leaving no evidence of murder. And I should have anchored the body before I threw it over the bridge.

Everyone would have assumed Rivet left town for personal reasons. No big deal. No news coverage. No internet pandemonium.

I feel a little regret over killing Monica, although I resent her for scratching my arm. That was uncalled for. I'd talked to her at some other tournaments, and we enjoyed pleasant conversations. We weren't friends but close enough to be friendly acquaintances. She did nothing bad to me. She didn't deserve to die, but it was essential for me to keep Sydney around a little longer. I couldn't get to that young upstart from Columbus, but Sydney took care of her on the tennis court.

Since the entire city of Columbus has become a fishbowl to the rest of America, I have to proceed with caution. It's not like I can walk on the court with a concealed knife and attack Sydney in front of the entire crowd. The last person who committed such an act was an unemployed German lathe operator named Gunter Parche, back in 1993. From what I understand, he attacked the world's top player in a tournament in Hamburg because he was a fan of her rival. But that guy was a complete loser, unlike me.

If I tried such an act today, security would stop me. They do an outstanding job of guarding players at courtside now, at least during the main draw of a tournament. To his credit, Fitz had the wherewithal to strike during a less-conspicuous qualifying match. Kudos to him for that.

When I was a youngster, my mother always told me to keep my eyes and ears open. "There's always another opportunity waiting around the corner," she'd say. "Watch and wait, and you'll discover it right in front of you."

So I waited. And I watched. And then I waited a little longer.

While I was walking by one court, I overheard a conversation that Sydney had signed out a ball machine for noon on the following day. I never thought twice about the conversation until a couple of hours later. Then, as my mother had promised, I discovered my opportunity standing right in front of me. I'd like to think my mother was helping me from beyond the grave, but I don't know if that's true. She was a person who spoke about forgiveness and reconciliation, not revenge. Maybe the double espresso was talking to me instead. Yes, let's accept that explanation and leave my mother out of it.

Anyway, what if something else rocketed out of that ball machine, something far more deadly than a tennis ball? I rushed back to my hotel and searched the internet. I found just the product I was looking for at National Steel Ball and Roller Company. It was a two-inch, solid, hot-stamped steel ball, weighing 1.13 pounds. It sold for just $4.49, plus shipping. But I needed it in twenty-four hours. I had to pay an extra forty-five dollars to receive it by the next morning, before Sydney's practice. Greedy bastards.

At around 11:40, another coach left the machine behind the wall of Court 9. That was a break. Anyone could have tampered with that machine. That leaves about five thousand potential suspects, including me.

I waited for the area to clear. Once I saw my opportunity, I removed the weapon ball from my pocket and placed it into the final launching hole in the machine, guaranteeing that it would be the first projectile to fly out of there. I left no other tennis balls in the unit. Someone else would load the hopper with balls, and there was no way they'd notice the sphere already loaded. I spotted the remote control attached magnetically to the side of the unit. That device would come in handy, allowing me to start and stop the machine anytime and to wait for the perfect opportunity to let my creativity fly. I placed it in my pocket.

I visited the business center at the hotel and printed off a bogus list of instructions, which I taped beneath the ball-launching nozzle. The headline was in a decent-sized font, but the words below were smaller. The plan was to catch the victim's attention and lure her in closer. Then I would spring my trap! Boom!

Realistically, I felt my plan had a 10 percent chance of succeeding. What were the odds the stars would align? Minuscule, at best. I hoped no one would see the weapon loaded in the machine. And what about Sydney? How did I know my bogus instructions would lure her in? Then there was the remote control itself. I'd have to rely on pressing the "start" and "stop" buttons from inside of my pocket in order to remain inconspicuous. Could I pull that off? And even if everything worked beautifully, how did I know the machine was capable of sending a 1.13-pound projectile through the air? I was like a basketball player heaving a shot the length of the floor, hoping for a miracle ending.

Do those shots usually go in? No. Do they find their destinations on rare occasions? Certainly. It was worth a try.

So you can imagine my surprise when the plan cut through several obstacles like a hot knife into butter. Someone loaded the balls without noticing the Trojan horse. I managed the remote control from my pocket. And here was Sydney, squinting in the sunlight, attempting to read the fine print, one foot in front of the launcher! I was in shock. My plan came to fruition!

When she reads, "You're fucked!" she'll know, for a brief second, that she was suckered in—like a large-mouth bass realizing there was a hook inside that juicy nightcrawler.

But I need to quit thinking and act! Reach into your pocket and press the button. If you freeze now, you'll regret it for the rest of your life! She's standing in the cross-hairs. Just press the damn button!

Okay, done! The machine is firing up. Stay there for two more seconds, and that's it. Two little seconds. I wish the crowd would shut up so I could hear the motor starting. Yes, I hear it now. What a wonderful sound! And my plan has been nothing short of brilliant. Good thing for society that I'm not using my talent for evil.

It's happening now. Soon, I'll relax and return to normal with no more hatred and no more revenge.

Holy shit, it fired! Wait, did she just duck? What the f—?

CHAPTER 22

By the time Syd and Enzo reached the hospital, Marisha Belov was in the waiting room, pacing nervously. She greeted Enzo with a warm embrace but only nodded at Syd.

"Thank you for coming to see Anja," said Marisha. "I broke several driving laws on the way here, but I arrived without any sirens following me."

It was clear to Syd that Marisha was trying to remain upbeat, but her red and puffy eyes and haltering voice made it obvious that she'd been crying.

"It can't end this way!" said Belov, turning her attention more toward Enzo than Syd. "We had an awful argument this morning. I wasn't even planning to attend the practice afterward, but I reconsidered later. I don't think she was thinking clearly when she walked out onto that practice court today."

"Please sit down for a second," said Enzo, easing Marisha down into one of the waiting room chairs. "It's not your fault what happened out there today. There's a crazy person among us, and it has nothing to do with any disagreement between you and Anja."

Syd had noticed Trent approaching, but Marisha and Enzo hadn't looked up yet.

"Excuse me for eavesdropping," said Trent unconvincingly. "But I understand what happened today in your hotel was more than a 'disagreement.' In fact, we sent two cars to your hotel room after other guests had contacted us, but nobody was there when we arrived. I ordered the hotel maintenance person to open your door to determine if anyone was injured in there."

Syd and Enzo glanced at each other.

"Trent, are you saying the confrontation turned violent?" asked Syd as Marisha hung her head, embarrassed by the question.

"Well, I think that's something Ms. Belov can answer," he said. "Would you like to discuss it now or tomorrow in my downtown office?"

"I prefer not to discuss it here," said Marisha.

Syd interrupted.

"Marisha, just because you two had a disagreement doesn't mean you're responsible for what happened to Anja. I know you care for each other. She's my best friend, too."

Tears welled in Marisha's eyes. She seemed to stare into space.

"I will only discuss it privately," she said. "With the lieutenant."

Enzo rose from his chair and took a lap around the waiting room. Then he returned to Trent.

"I told you who's doing all of this," he said. "Fitz tried to kill Syd by juicing her to death. And now, his brand new ball machine, the one he bragged about, almost took Syd's head off. Luckily, her reactions are world-class, like her tennis game, and she ducked in the nick of time. But you know the guilty party. Remove him from the equation, and you'll see everything stop happening."

Trent stared at Enzo, attempting to determine the sincerity of his statement.

"Your wish is my command, Mr. Martin," he said. "We approached the ATP and the MMO staff about our findings pertaining to Mr. Fitzgerald. He's suspended until we complete our investigation. They've taken away his credentials, and he no longer has access to this tournament."

Enzo returned to his seat, his anger subsiding.

"None of us are safe until you lock him up. It all makes sense now. Fitz had a grievance against Syd, and he's been trying to murder her since this tournament started. And I hope you can nail him for killing that Canadian girl."

"We've confiscated Mr. Fitzgerald's car," said Trent. "We can hold him for seventy-two hours, but there's no doubt he'll make bail. Our initial examination of his car showed no blood or other evidence, but we are waiting for forensics to go over the vehicle more carefully."

A man dressed in scrubs and a blue mask emerged from the ICU. The nametag on his chest read, "Dr. David Johnson, ICU."

"Lieutenant Trent, Ms. Radanovic is able to speak with you now," said Johnson. "She's heavily medicated, so I would recommend talking to her while she's still somewhat lucid."

"Dr. Johnson," said Syd, cutting off Trent's reply. "Please tell us about Anja's condition. Is she going to be okay?"

"Yes," he said, ignoring the annoyed look Trent cast toward Syd. "But please, call me Max. There's no need to be formal. Anyway, Anja's nose broke in two places, but that's not the concerning part. Blows to the nose seldom result in life-threatening injuries, as the nose acts as a buffer to cushion a blow.

"Our concern is that Ms. Radonovic crashed the back of her head on the asphalt as she hit the ground. It appears she's suffering from a subdural hematoma, which is a swelling of the brain. We're managing it, but her prognosis is unclear."

Russo entered the waiting area and was now sitting on the left of Enzo.

"When can I see her?" he asked. "I'm like a father to her, and she needs me."

Trent regained control of the conversation.

"Everyone needs to relax," he said. "I'm going to meet with her first. If she's up to seeing visitors afterward, then Dr. Johnson—I mean, Max—will tell you if and when you can see her. But right now, it's my turn."

Trent followed the doctor toward the ICU, and they soon disappeared behind swinging doors.

* * * * *

Syd and Enzo combined their individual bills, and she approached the nearest vending machine with six ones, barely enough for a couple of Diet Cokes. Syd felt a vibration in her pocket. The name on the screen read "Nicole."

"Oh, shit!" exclaimed Syd, quickly accepting the call. "Nicole? Is that you? I've been worried sick! Where have you been?"

The sound of Nicole's voice was reassuring.

"Syd, I'm so sorry I haven't tried to call you earlier," she said. "Victor and I got into an argument, and I stormed out. I didn't get a hotel room until 5:30 in the morning. I was halfway back to Savannah. I didn't want to call you because I knew you needed sleep."

"I'm thrilled you're okay, Nicole," said Syd. "Are you back in Savannah now?"

"Well, no, actually," she said. "Victor got through on his cell, and we patched things up. You know, I have a terrible temper when someone disparages anyone that I love. And Victor said some horrible things about the relationship between Scarlet and me. But he's apologized, and now I'm driving back to Columbus to watch you play. I'm three hours out right now. I heard on the radio what happened at the tournament today," continued Nicole. "Are you okay, Syd? The report insinuated that you might have been the target."

Syd took a deep sigh.

"I'll tell you more when you arrive. It wasn't fun. Did you know Anja was injured?"

"Yes, I heard that," said Nicole. "I'm praying for her right now as I drive. Is she going to make it?"

"I think so," said Syd, "but I'll know more soon. Please don't stop praying!"

While bringing the soft drinks back to her seat, a pair of men carrying microphones and another holding a camera blocked Syd's path.

"Here's some breaking news," said a man holding a microphone. "We're live at North Columbus Health Center, where we've spotted tennis player Sydney Livingstone, who may have been the target in today's ball machine attack. Sydney, can you tell us how you avoided the attack?"

Syd looked to see if Enzo was available to intervene, but he was no longer in his waiting room area. She hadn't seen him use the restroom since they'd arrived, and she assumed he'd made a trip there.

"One quick statement, Ms. Livingstone," said the other man, thrusting his microphone forward until it bounced off her chin. "Please share with our viewers what's going on."

The only time she'd remembered being accosted by reporters was after she completed a doubles match with her former partner, Milena, who had just been suspended by the World Tennis Organization.

Reporters swarmed Milena and peppered her with questions like: "How did that banned substance get into your system?" and, "Why did you feel the need to cheat?"

Milena's father stepped in to shield his daughter. He grabbed a male reporter by the upper arm and squeezed it with a vise-like grip, causing the man to squeal in capitulating horror. He shoved another reporter, causing the man to fall backward onto the ground. The reporters scattered, threatening to sue as they exited. She'd met Milena's father once, but he left quite an impression.

Unfortunately, Milena's father was probably overseas, thousands of miles away, while Enzo was taking care of business behind a partition. The only person left to assist her seemed to be Russo, who, despite his diminutive 150-pound frame, emerged from his seat and tried to get between Syd and the reporters.

"Excuse me, sir," said a reporter, grabbing Russo by the shoulders and pulling him out of the camera's view. "You're going to wait off camera until we're finished shooting."

With that, the man shoved Russo back down in his seat and warned him not to get up.

"Do you have any idea who's doing this to you?" another reporter asked.

"Why are you the target?" asked another.

Emerging from between the ICU doors, Trent sensed Syd's dilemma. He confronted the four reporters on the scene.

"I'm going to ask you to clear the area," he said. "And you're going to be the first, Hawthorne," he said, pointing a finger at the reporter who had bullied Russo. "It's time for you to leave. I'm in no mood to play games."

Hawthorne shook his head in defiance but gathered his equipment and headed for the door. The remainder of his staff followed.

"Thanks for the break, lieutenant," said Syd.

"I wouldn't worry about thanking me," said Trent. "You're dead-smack in the middle of this investigation. I would spend more time thinking about how you're going to defend yourself. Once again, I don't think you're responsible for what's going on, but remember that I'm not the grand jury. At some point, you'll have to clear your name."

Enzo returned from the restroom and was standing next to Syd now, wiping his freshly washed hands on his khaki shorts. *Obviously, there were no towels in the restroom,* thought Syd, *because Enzo has a major germ issue with hot air dryers.*

"Are we allowed to visit Anja?" he asked Trent. "Or did you sap the life out of her?"

"I think the nurses are attending to her," said Trent. "Give her fifteen minutes. Why don't the three of us sit down and have a chat?"

Syd and Enzo sat back down next to Russo, who appeared humiliated after being manhandled by the reporter.

"I've done a little digging over the past day," said Trent, "and I found something that may be important. Let me ask you, Ms. Livingstone, were you around Milena when they suspended her for using an illegal substance?"

"Yes, of course," said Syd. "She was my doubles partner. I remember how the entire thing went down. Why are you asking?"

"I researched the details behind her suspension," said Trent. "Did you know she passed a drug test a few weeks before she failed a second one? That scenario made little sense to me. If they cleared her after the first one, why was she asked to take another so soon? And then the answer hit me. Someone must have reported her, spurring another test. Do you have any idea who that was, Ms. Livingstone?"

"No, of course not," said Sydney. "I know that it wasn't me. It was a complete surprise to Milena when a World

Tennis Organization official approached her after a match. Milena thought someone had gotten their wires crossed because she'd already taken a test. But they insisted and handed her a vial."

"So she finally agreed to take the test?" asked Trent.

"She had no choice. I was using one of the public restrooms when she entered and told me. She begged me to pee in that container, but I refused. If they had traced that sample back to me, my career would have been over."

"So what happened next?" asked Trent.

"She placed her mouth under the faucet and sucked in cold water for what seemed like a minute. She almost vomited when she finished drinking. I guess she hoped the water would dilute the sample."

"Obviously, that tactic didn't work," said Trent.

"No, it didn't work," said Syd. "That test led to her suspension and ultimately damaged our friendship. Then she acted erratically after that, blaming me because Peter O'Malley found me attractive. But believe me, lieutenant, I had no interest in O'Malley, and I told her that."

"And what happened to your friendship at the end?"

"It all but eroded," said Syd. "The situation broke my heart, but I had to go on with my playing career. I found another doubles partner. By the time I received word that she ended her life, her funeral was over. I still feel terrible about not attending."

Enzo and Russo both hung their heads as Syd continued.

"There are no do-overs in life. I miss her every day. I need her in my life, but she's gone forever."

"My reason for bringing up your relationship with Ms. Lombardi is that it's germane to the investigation. I needed to find out who reported Milena, making it necessary for her to take two tests in a three-week period. The WTO initially resisted my request, citing confidentiality," said Trent. "But once they understood that this was a murder investigation, they revealed the informant's name."

"It was O'Malley, wasn't it?" said Enzo. "I'll bet he wanted Milena banished from the tour so he could pursue Syd. He's always wanted her."

"That's not the name we were given," said Trent.

"Whose name did they give you?" asked Syd.

"That name provided," said Trent, "was Cassandra Flores."

CHAPTER 23

The digital clock above his desk read 6:55. Trent usually started work at eight, but this Thursday was no ordinary day. An unsolved murder stared him squarely in the eye, and everything revolved around the MMO. He informed his wife, Bridget, that he wouldn't be home for their 6:00 p.m. dinner, knowing that he had at least six interviews on tap. Whatever information he gathered would determine today's course of action.

Al Fitzgerald, one of his prime suspects, was in custody for now. Trent disliked Fitz in a primal sort of way. He sensed nothing sincere about the man. Fitz suspended play for today in his last official duty as tournament director. Trent knew he had a narrow window of time to squeeze Fitz for information.

Trent felt that Fitz didn't fit the profile of a killer. Was he self-centered? Certainly. Boisterous? A pain-in-the-ass? No doubt. But could he slash a woman's throat and dump her body into a river? Probably not. But he'd been wrong before.

He approached the Keurig coffee machine, searching for a flavor. They were out of hazelnut. His second choice, vanilla cream, was also missing. Someone should be monitoring the inventory. Once he solved this case, he'd launch a massive investigation into this coffee nonsense. He chose a flavor called "Pacific Bold" and programmed the machine to "extra strong."

Frequent interruptions broke the flow of Trent's hospital interview with Anja. Her semi-lucid comments were difficult to decipher. She claimed Belov's jealousy instigated their physical confrontation.

He scheduled Belov to be his first interview. She seemed close to the center of the action when a disturbing event occurred. She had as much opportunity as anyone to commit these crimes. He could say the same for Anja's coach, Paul Russo. He was a frail man with a lot of energy. Russo was obsessed with his Fitbit, constantly checking his steps while strolling through the facility or walking in place. He seemed protective toward Anja, but now he befriended Syd. Perhaps he was a good businessman looking for opportunities to enhance his coaching resume. Or maybe, he and Anja were plotting against Syd. If he could break down one, the other would follow.

Trent was eager to speak with Cassandra Flores. When he contacted her, she'd seemed incredulous and perturbed. Despite her objections, Trent insisted she visit his office at noon.

"There are tens of thousands of dollars on the line," she said. "How dare you distract me and jeopardize my career!"

Trent wondered why Flores dropped a dime on Milena. Perhaps her answer would lead him in a different direction.

And what about Peter O'Malley? Trent was aware of the bourbon connection but didn't think it was relevant.

But why did O'Malley try to escape while being detained temporarily? What was he running from? Was he trying to hide evidence? Did he still care for Syd? At 3:00 p.m. today, he would try to find those answers.

Trent reserved the 5:00 p.m. slot for Syd's father, Michael Livingstone. Is it coincidental that he walked back into Syd's life while all hell was breaking loose? Why did he sneak around the facility for days without announcing his presence? Perhaps he didn't want to violate his restraining order. Or possibly, he preferred to fly below the radar before striking. But why try to hurt his daughter? They were estranged, but was that enough reason to stalk and kill? Something wasn't adding up.

Also in the equation was Nicole Hase, the spider-lady who was a best friend to Syd. They grew up in the same town and attended the same schools. She was a decent tennis player in high school, qualifying for district championships twice. Syd overshadowed her from a tennis point of view. Could there be underlying resentment? Like other suspects, Nicole had opportunity. But did she fit Trent's profile of a killer?

Enzo's buddy, Victor Dan, remained a viable suspect. Victor recently conjured up a relationship with Nicole. He's a rangy, agile young man who could easily carry out any crime. He had access to the ball machine, but so did everyone at the tournament. The machine was parked behind the wall for at least twenty minutes. He could've pocketed the remote and hid among the crowd. If he left the area immediately after the strike, he could have avoided detection.

Enzo and Syd appeared happy, although Trent knew Syd was upset with Enzo for concealing his conversation with O'Malley. Enzo was directly in front of the machine when it fired the projectile. But wouldn't that be too obvious? Did he want to end their relationship? Wouldn't a breakup be simpler?

Trent's twenty-plus years of experience told him Syd was not behind any of this nonsense, although her locket was found at the murder scene. An obvious setup, right? Syd may have been the target of the ball-machine attack. Did she duck at the perfect time, or was she tipped off by an accomplice? Syd and Enzo would be his final interview of the day.

Fitz would soon go before a grand jury since he admitted to tainting Syd's drink. More charges could follow, especially if the interview revealed Fitz stalked Syd or caused Monica Rivet's death.

Wouldn't it be convenient if Fitz admitted to everything: sending the bourbon to Syd's room, painting the message on her car, loading the ball machine, and killing Rivet? All loose ends tied up in one tidy knot and the investigation closed. How convenient. His fishing trip with his buddies next week would go on as planned, and he'd receive kudos from his bosses for solving a case that garnered national attention.

A man can dream, but Trent was a realist. There was something that he didn't see, either obvious or obscure. He'd review notes of his interviews to glean a tidbit or two of overlooked data. Maybe then, everything would fall into place.

Trent barely downed his second cup of morning coffee when detective Ray Norton knocked and entered his office, all at the same time. Norton was in his early fifties, mostly thin in the upper body and limbs, although a soft belly emerged slightly over his waistline. He had blond, curly hair that flowed almost to his shoulders and a large protruding nose below a set of thick glasses. Trent thought Norton looked like a sixties protester, although the math didn't add up. Perhaps he was raised by flower children.

"Damn, Norton!" said Trent. "I appreciate you knocking, but could you wait for my response before barging in?"

"I'm sorry, chief," said Norton, with no remorse in his voice. "You're in early, but I'm glad I caught you!"

"I didn't know you'd be working so early since I assigned you to the night shift," said Trent. "But you've gotta make it quick. I have a ton of interviews, and I'm not fully prepared yet."

"You're right, chief," said Norton. "I was working at night, basically a security detail."

"Weren't you supposed to monitor some of the suspects in the tennis case?" asked Trent. "The way you barged in, I assume you found something important?"

"I definitely found something important," said Norton. "I visited the hotel where Syd and Enzo are staying. They shared a drink in the bar and returned to their room at nine. I don't think they noticed me, but who cares if they did?

"Then, I checked out the hotel where Anja and Belov were staying. Nothing abnormal. Appetizers and drinks at the bar, then eventually back to their room. Spider girl and Victor are staying at the same hotel but in different rooms. Victor exercised in the fitness center for about forty-five minutes while the girl drove away for a short time before returning alone. No sign they spent any time together last night."

"And O'Malley spent the evening with us," said Trent. "We can't hold him for much longer. But our doctor administered a sedative. Seems like the young man can't tolerate closed-in places. So that leaves us with Michael Livingstone. You must have uncovered something because there's no one else you were assigned to."

"Game on!" said Norton. "He farted around in the pool and later went inside the sauna area. I didn't see him eating anything, so I checked with the hotel staff. They said he ordered room service—a turkey and bacon club, potato salad, and a fruit bowl. They mentioned he ordered a bottle of bourbon delivered to his room."

"That's interesting," said Trent, "but that only proves that he likes bourbon. So you're here at seven in the morning to tell me Michael Livingstone enjoys drinking a little hooch?"

"No, of course not," said Norton. "You interrupted me before I finished. I meant that very respectfully, chief.

"Upon leaving the hotel, I examined Michael's car in the parking lot," said Norton. "It's a Volkswagen Passat sedan, twelve years old, and not in good condition."

"Norton, would you please—"

"Okay, chief, I'm getting to it," said Norton. "I shined my flashlight on the driver's side of his car and found nothing. But then I walked around to the rear bumper. I found this attached to the bumper, just out of plain view."

Norton placed a small black device on Trent's desk.

"All right, enlighten me, Norton; what the hell is that?"

"Chief, take a closer look."

Trent picked up the device and examined it. Buttons were labeled "on/off," "pause," and "resume."

"Shit the bed!" said Trent. "This is a fucking remote control! And you found it on Michael Livingstone's car?"

"Damn tootin'," said Norton.

Trent shook his head and grinned. "Once again, I underestimated you, Norton. You've done one helluva job!"

CHAPTER 24

"Just doing my job, chief," said Norton, trying to conceal a slight smile. "Do you want me to pick up Michael Livingstone at his hotel?"

"No, hold up on that," said Trent. "He's scheduled to arrive at five today. Hopefully, he won't notice the remote is missing and end up skipping town."

"If you're sure," said Norton. "But so you know, I'd be happy to bring him in. I'd hate to see him slip through our fingers, especially now that I've—I mean we've—discovered important evidence against him."

"I could be wrong, but I don't see him making a run for it. Why don't you get some rest, Norton? I'll keep you posted if anything else develops."

Norton nodded his head affirmatively and exited Trent's office, disappointed that Trent didn't give him the green light to corral Livingstone.

Trent turned back toward his computer and opened the file labeled "Michael Livingstone." He entered a couple of paragraphs on Norton's findings, including time, date, and location. He took a snapshot of the remote and included it as an attachment. One of his technicians arrived, placed the remote in a plastic bag, and entered it as evidence. Trent needed about thirty minutes to come up with a detailed list of questions for Belov, but first, he needed to call Victor Dan.

* * * * *

Seated for breakfast at Cracker Barrel restaurant were Syd, Enzo, Nicole, and Michael Livingstone. Syd invited her mother to join them, but she declined after realizing Michael would be there.

"I don't hate your father," said Chelsea to Syd. "I just don't know exactly what he's capable of anymore. It's best we stay apart for the time being."

Syd suggested that her mother join her and Enzo for a 2:00 p.m. brunch at the hotel and perhaps an outside pool visit. She could take a three-mile run at noon and still enjoy a waterside chat with her mom. The rest of her day would comprise a 4:30 hitting session with Enzo and a 6:30 encounter with Trent.

"So, Nicole," asked Enzo, "wasn't Victor supposed to join us for breakfast? Everything's still okay, isn't it?"

Nicole smiled and blushed slightly. "Oh, yes, everything's fine. We're over that little misunderstanding about Scarlet. He needed to take an important call, but I'm expecting him any minute. I've already ordered orange juice, pancakes, and bacon for him, with a side of hash browns. Isn't it funny how quickly you get to know someone?"

Syd quickly glanced underneath the table to see if Nicole brought her furry friends to breakfast. No eight-leggers present.

"Scarlet accepts Victor now," she said. "At first, she could feel his tension. But since he's relaxed, she's relaxing along with him."

Enzo's discussion with Nicole did little to break the tension surrounding the table. No one seemed interested in Nicole's attempts to anthropomorphize Scarlet.

Syd flinched in her chair when it was Michael who broke the ice.

"I hope I'm not speaking out of turn," said her father. "But I feel that you should withdraw from the tournament, Syd. The media, investigators, and everyone else believes you were the target of whoever jerry-rigged that ball machine. You were one millisecond away from disaster. Is it worth risking your life, especially with a match against Cassandra Flores looming?"

Syd remained motionless in her seat. Should she appreciate her father's concern, or should she be pissed over the assumption that Flores was going to pistol-whip her? She gave her father the benefit of the doubt.

"I know, Dad. Enzo and I have talked about this, ad nauseam," said Syd. "We feel that I need to stay here and finish what I've started. If I go home, the lunatic wins. I don't know if you realize this, Dad, but I have physical issues. My tennis career will end sooner than anyone realizes."

"Syd," her father said, in a stern but concerned voice, "I need you in my life. I've wasted so many years being a self-centered, uncompromising bastard. But thanks to counseling, I know now who and what's important. And that's you. You must remain safe."

Syd stared at her father, mouth open, but with no words. Enzo had reached under the table and was squeezing Syd's hand to offer support. Nicole continued to stare at her menu, which she held in front of her face with both hands.

Finally, Nicole spoke out.

"Someone told me the biscuits and gravy are out of this world. Does anyone want to split an order?"

* * * * *

Victor Dan had answered the phone on the third ring, unaware that Trent was calling. "It's probably a robocall or something," he told Nicole. "Let me shitcan this person, and we'll head down to breakfast."

Once Victor realized that Trent was on the line, his demeanor changed. "I need to take this," he said. "Get my order started, and I'll be down in a few minutes."

The conversation lasted for twenty minutes. Trent asked if Victor was at the MMO during the ball-machine attack. He told Trent he was at Center Court stadium watching number-two seed Novak Djokovic defeat unseeded German player Benjamin Roeser. Victor said he didn't know if anyone could corroborate his story, noting he was sitting alone near the top of the stadium. He spoke to Nicole during the event while she drove back to Silverhill.

"Don't even think about leaving town for the next few days," Trent instructed. "I know you're out of the singles draw, but I need you to stay close until I give you the okay."

By the time Victor had made it down to breakfast, his pancakes and bacon were cold, but the tension at the table had subsided.

"We're out of doubles now," said Enzo, overjoyed to see Victor arrive. "The tournament's backed up because of the delay. The new director considered canceling the tournament for security reasons but dropped the doubles instead. But we'll get to keep our first-round earnings, so at least we won't leave empty-handed."

Victor raised his thumb and forefinger to his already squinting eyes as he tried to process the recent information provided by Enzo.

"Wait, they canceled the doubles? That means we're done playing. Let's leave and start practicing for the US Open."

Then, Victor looked over at Syd. "Oh, I almost forgot. Enzo needs to stay for support. I get it. I guess we'll all be here for you, Syd. Your own little cheering section. And besides, Trent told me not to leave anyway, so I guess it's all good."

Enzo straightened up in his chair. "Whoa! Trent ordered you to remain in town? Why?"

"I guess he looks at me as a person of interest," said Victor. "For some reason, I'm in the middle of this gigantic mess."

"Personally, I'm glad you're staying," said Nicole. "I'm here to support Syd. But I don't like what Trent's cooking up in that little pot of his. I can't believe he would even fathom that you're involved."

"To be fair, he really didn't accuse me of anything," said Victor. "He wants me to stay in town for the time being."

The server arrived at the table and cleared the empty dishes. Victor directed her away from his plate because he was still navigating his way through soggy pancakes. After accepting a coffee warm-up, Syd spoke.

"Nicole, it's interesting what you just said about Trent," said Syd. "When I spoke to Anja in the hospital, she told me we shouldn't trust Trent. She feels he has a hidden agenda."

Enzo interrupted. "I agree with Anja," he said. "In my book, it's open and shut. It's obvious that Fitz is the driving force behind this shit. I don't see why this investigation isn't closed."

* * * * *

It was almost nine, and Trent's thoughts turned toward Marisha Belov. She and Anja were an item, no doubt. But was it possible she resented Syd for taking time away from Anja? She was well-muscled and capable of killing someone and tossing them over a railing. But crimes of jealousy are passion-related. No evidence existed that Anja and Syd were lovers. But maybe she was working with someone who wanted Sydney dead.

The interview progressed as Trent had expected. Marisha said the recent turn of events horrified her. She told Trent that she agreed that Syd was the intended target of the ball-machine attack.

"Anja would never hurt anyone, especially not Sydney," she said. "She adores that woman."

Marisha said she had no idea who may have been taunting Syd but remained steadfast that Fitz altered Syd's drink.

"He's the one who's committed these crimes," she said. "I mean, if you're crazy enough to poison a player, wouldn't you be crazy enough to kill someone?"

Trent avoided confronting Belov early in the meeting. To him, she exhibited a naturally defensive nature, releasing small amounts of information at a time. He wondered if she was hiding something. As long as she was cooperating, he'd keep things status quo.

"Have you heard anyone say anything inappropriate when referring to Ms. Livingstone?" he asked.

"I associate little with Sydney's friends," she said. "I only overhear what Anja tells me. Sydney and Enzo play some kind of weird game together. The thing makes no sense to me. One of them will create a fake murder scene, making it appear like they have been murdered. The other discovers the scene and totally freaks out. In my opinion, that is abnormal behavior."

"Hold on!" said Trent. "I've never heard this. Which one of them pretends they've been murdered?"

"I believe they take turns," said Belov. "I only know this second-hand from Anja. You know, kind of like pillow-talk. Please don't mention I told you any of this. Anja has sworn me to silence."

"But these murder scenes you're talking about, they're consensual?"

"Yes. It's a strange little game they play. Do you think it's relevant to the case?"

Trent didn't answer. He was still trying to process the data provided by Marisha. "Ms. Belov," he said, "you mentioned you had an altercation or argument with Ms. Radonovic yesterday morning, before the accident with the ball machine. Is that correct?"

Marisha looked down into her lap, clearly embarrassed by the question. She nodded affirmatively.

"You also mentioned the confrontation turned physical. Do these events often happen between you and Anja?"

"Rarely, if ever!" replied Marisha, moving uncomfortably in her seat. "Lieutenant, our relationship is wonderful. I think you're getting the wrong impression."

"I realize all couples have disagreements," said Trent. "Sometimes, my wife pisses me off. But who got physical first?"

"I made the mistake of telling Anja she was overreacting about something," she said. "I knew that was a mistake when I said it. I should've been more subtle."

Trent turned his rotating chair to face Belov. "How did she react?"

"She pushed me. My head snapped back, and it bumped the wall. The noise was worse than the impact. But I became infuriated and started yelling. I'm sure that's what people in the adjoining rooms heard.

"Once I finished screaming at Anja, she broke down," she continued. "Lieutenant, she has a temper, I'll admit.

But I can't see her trying to injure someone permanently. She's not wired that way."

"I understand," said Trent. "Can you tell me exactly what precipitated the disagreement between the two of you?" asked Trent.

"I'm not at liberty to discuss personal matters like this," said Marisha. "Everything we discuss remains in the strictest of confidence."

Trent rose from his seat and walked behind his desk toward a curtain that disguised the contents of a whiteboard. He pulled the curtain open. Handwritten notes containing the names of suspects, along with their motives, were scrawled all over the board. Syd's name was circled in the middle of everything.

He removed a marker from the base of the board and tapped it next to the name of Monica Rivet. "I'm sure you've heard of Ms. Rivet," he said. "Do you realize she's no longer with us? She was probably murdered by the same person who almost killed your lover with that flying circle from hell. Nobody likes to kiss-and-tell, but this is a damn murder investigation!"

At first, Belov seemed taken aback, but then she nodded in agreement. "All right," she said. "I will tell what started the whole thing."

CHAPTER 25

Marisha placed her elbows on Trent's desk with the palms of her hands supporting her forehead. She shut her eyes and took deep breaths with her mouth open.

"I feel like I'm betraying Anja," she said. "I want you to know that I love her. She's my soulmate, and I feel like I'm betraying her."

Trent leaned back in his chair and tilted his head toward the ceiling, and his eyes focused on Marisha.

"Ms. Belov," he said. "Just because you're telling the truth about someone doesn't mean that you don't love them. By being honest, you can help Anja."

"Yes, that's true," replied Marisha. "But I feel terrible. Please, assure me that you won't reveal me as your source."

Trent grimaced slightly. At this pace, he might end up delaying his noon appointment with Cassandra Flores.

"You have my word," he said. "Now tell me what precipitated the argument between you and Ms. Radonovic."

"Coach Russo and his role with Sydney," she said. "Anja looks at Russo as more than a coach. He is like a surrogate father figure. Anja never had much of a relationship with her father. He left when she was seven and made infrequent appearances after that.

"Don't get me wrong," Belov continued. "She wanted Russo to help Sydney. But she felt Russo was also taking on a fatherly role with Sydney. That's what bothered her. It wasn't about the coaching."

Trent took a gulp of his coffee, only to realize that it had become cold over the past thirty minutes. He walked to his trash can and spit out its contents.

"I'm sorry," he said. "I'm going to get another. May I offer you a bottle of water, coffee, soda, or anything?"

"Maybe a ginger ale," said Belov. "I am parched, given the circumstances."

Trent opened the small refrigerator and pulled the remaining can of Sprite from the bottom shelf. He returned with his own steaming coffee and handed the soft drink to Belov.

"So did Ms. Livingstone know your companion was angry over her coach's emerging role?"

"No," said Belov. "But Anja didn't want to lose Russo the same way she lost her father. But she suggested the coaching arrangement. Her anger made little sense, and I told her that."

Detective Megan Guthrie knocked on Trent's door and cracked it open. Trent beckoned her to enter.

"I don't mean to interrupt, lieutenant, but there's something you need to know. Peter O'Malley is going crazy in his holding cell, hyperventilating and everything. He says he's going to have a heart attack. He's demanding to speak with you immediately."

"Okay," said Trent. "I know he has issues with confinement. Bring him into the waiting room. I'll move his three o'clock interview up. I don't think he's a flight risk."

Guthrie nodded and closed the door.

Trent turned his attention back to Marisha.

"Do you think Anja is capable of taking out her anger on Ms. Livingstone? You mentioned that she has a temper."

"Absolutely not," said Marisha. "Deep down, she knew she was irrational. But she would never hurt Sydney."

Trent asked Marisha if there was anything else she'd like to add. She shook her head.

"Thank you for your time today, Ms. Belov," said Trent. "You're free to go now. Please stay in town until further notice."

"Believe me," said Belov. "I'd never leave Anja in her condition, regardless of the circumstances."

* * * * *

While Trent was contemplating the interview with Marisha, the screen on his desk phone flashed. Trent picked up the phone, expecting it to be Guthrie with an update on Peter O'Malley. Instead, his secretary informed him that the call was from Dr. David Johnson at the hospital.

"Yes, Dr. Johnson," said Trent. "How may I help you?"

"Hello, Lieutenant Trent," said the doctor. "But please call me Max. I wanted to give you an update on one of our patients, Anja Radonovic. We've seemed to stem the internal bleeding in her head. All indications are she's going to make a complete recovery. We will release her within the next day or two, barring any unforeseen circumstances."

"That's great," said Trent. "Her companion, Marisha Belov, just left my office. I wish I could have informed her of the good news."

"No need," said Dr. Johnson. "I called her right before I reached you. She was elated. In fact, she's on her way to the hospital now."

Trent thanked the doctor and walked to the waiting area. Peter was shivering with a blanket around him, surrounded by staff members ready to administer aid.

"Mr. O'Malley, I'm so sorry you're having such a hard time in our holding cell," said Trent. "Your lawyer was going to have you released after our scheduled interview. So why don't we proceed so we can send you on your way?"

O'Malley jumped out of his chair, his eyes filled with hope.

"Yes, let's talk now then. I requested a sedative, but the doctor said I couldn't take one for another hour. It's torture inside that cell. I can't go back there!"

O'Malley followed Trent into his office, where he offered him a seat on the couch.

"How about a nice cold soft drink, Mr. O'Malley? I have Coke and Diet Coke, but I'm out of ginger ale."

"Diet Coke, please," said O'Malley. "The tournament didn't default me because I was detained. They said, given the circumstances, that if I showed up for my four o'clock match, I could play."

"Shouldn't be a problem," said Trent. "Unless you confess right now. But based on my experience, I don't think that's the case."

O'Malley snickered and sank into the couch a little deeper. It was the first time he'd relaxed since his detainment.

"The reason we're holding you, Mr. O'Malley, is because you tried to run from our officers after we ordered everyone to stay. Obviously, that behavior was suspicious. Why did you try to escape?"

O'Malley opened his Diet Coke and took a big gulp. He muffled a burp before he spoke.

"It was pure panic, lieutenant," he said. "When I was a kid, my mother and I were trapped in an elevator for five hours. It was during the summer, and the power went out. The temperature kept rising and rising. I thought we were about to be cooked alive. By the time they freed us, I was in shock. Now, the thought of being confined causes me to panic."

"But you weren't trapped inside anything," said Trent. "You were outside, under the blue sky on a beautiful summer day."

"I know," replied O'Malley. "That's the rational response. But with claustrophobia, there's nothing rational about it. The fact that I couldn't leave made it imperative for me to flee. It's a mental disease."

Trent believed O'Malley suffered from claustrophobia. But was his fear of confinement enough of a deterrent to keep him from murdering someone?

"If you have nothing to hide, Mr. O'Malley, then I expect you'll be a free man soon," said Trent. "My first question is about the late Milena Lombardi. What was your relationship to her?"

"We dated for a year, off and on," he said. "I would describe the relationship as tumultuous. You know, week to week. I loved her, but sometimes we didn't get along. It was one argument after another."

"So when did your relationship end?"

"Funny," said O'Malley. "It never officially ended. We never said, 'today is the day we're calling it quits.' But toward the end of her life, they forbid me to see her. Can you imagine that?"

"Did she tell you not to come around anymore?" asked Trent.

"Oh, hell no," said O'Malley. "It was that psycho father of hers. I never met him, but whenever Milena said anything bad about me, he'd call and tell me to stay away. I don't scare easily, lieutenant, but that dude freaked me out."

"Did you comply with his so-called orders?" asked Trent.

"Not usually. But I looked over my shoulder constantly. Milena claimed he was all-bark-no-bite, but I wasn't so sure. She told me he was one stocky dude."

"Were you aware Ms. Livingstone possessed a pendant containing pictures of herself and Milena?"

"Yes, I've seen Syd wear that. But that was long after Milena died."

"Did you see anyone take the pendant from Ms. Livingstone's bag?"

ley. "I've heard the rumors. There's no way Syd would've
killed anyone. If that pendant was at the scene, then someone planted it. Syd has a mischievous personality, I'll admit.
But she's a wonderful person with a soft heart."

Trent looked up at his whiteboard and noticed it was
visible to O'Malley. He closed the curtain.

"Did you admire her so much that you sent a bottle of
bourbon to her hotel room?"

"Hell no!" said O'Malley, with panic in his eyes. "I sent
a bottle of Crystal 10, my favorite stuff, to Milena a few
weeks before she ended her life. We enjoyed drinking together, and she was going through a rough time. But here
in Silverhill, Ohio? Of course not."

Trent sensed that he was getting under O'Malley's skin.

"You loved her, didn't you?" said Trent. "And I'm speaking of Ms. Livingstone now. And Milena knew, didn't she?"

"Um, no, I mean yes. You're asking me two questions,"
said O'Malley. "Milena knew I was attracted to Syd. But I
don't love Syd. It's more like infatuation. But she's stuck on
that ass-wipe, Enzo Martin. If I were you, I'd investigate
him. He doesn't have both oars in the water."

"Thanks for the advice, Mr. O'Malley, but it's my investigation. Did Milena resent your fascination with Sydney
Livingstone?"

"Of course! She was pissed as hell, but I wanted her to
know the truth. I think she resented Syd over it. But you
know what, Syd never had any romantic interest in me. I
told Milena that she shouldn't blame Syd, but she couldn't

227

forgive her. I guess I'm guilty of being a jerk, or maybe of being brutally honest. But I've committed no crime."

Trent smiled at O'Malley.

"You know, there's nothing unlawful about being a jerk. If that were the case, half of my department would be incarcerated."

O'Malley stood up and walked to the door of Trent's office.

"Are we finished now, lieutenant?" he asked. "I need to return to my hotel and calm down. After that, I need to practice for my second-round match. There are a lot of dead presidents on the line for me."

"And hopefully, no more dead victims," said Trent. "One more question. Did you have access to the ball machine on Ms. Radonvic's court yesterday?"

"I guess anyone at the tournament could've had access," said O'Malley. "There was a sign-up sheet inside the players' lounge. But if you're asking me if I messed with a ball machine, the answer is no. I prefer practicing with human beings, not mechanical ones."

O'Malley exited the office and returned to the waiting room. Trent signed a release and handed it to a petite brunette secretary behind a window. Within ten minutes, O'Malley was walking out of the building and through the parking lot, breathing in a cool gust of air that represented freedom.

Trent walked back to his whiteboard and opened the curtains. After staring at it for several minutes, he dialed Norton's number. The voice that answered sounded groggy.

"What's up, chief?" said Norton.

"I'm sorry to bother you, especially after I encouraged you to take some time off," said Trent. "But I need a favor. Go to Russo's hotel at around four and see if he's there. If he is, bring him in for questioning. I'd want to speak with him before I meet with Michael Livingstone."

CHAPTER 26

Before his noon appointment with Flores, Trent had just enough time to slip away for a quick lunch at the world-famous Three Star Chili, with its headquarters in Columbus. It would take him about ten minutes to wolf down three chili dogs covered with cheese and onions and chase them with a large Diet Coke.

Bridget, Trent's wife, became concerned about her husband's weight over the past year. The once hard-nosed college fullback was now in his mid-forties, and his body showed the effects of a high-stress lifestyle. Trent promised Bridget he would eat sensibly and avoid snacking. In two months, he'd lost fifteen pounds, but his goal was to drop another fifteen by Christmas.

At 11:55, Trent rolled back into the parking lot of his office. As he exited the driver's side door, at least ten reporters with microphones surrounded him. Several camerapeople filmed him walking toward his office.

WCIN reporter Bill Hawthorne was the first to approach. Hawthorne reminded Trent of a younger version of John Goodman—tall, overweight, and somewhat intimidating.

"Is Cassandra Flores a suspect in Monica Rivet's murder?" asked Hawthorne.

"Has the autopsy yielded any clues?" shouted a short-haired blonde in a red jumpsuit. "Are arrests imminent?"

"Everyone, back away," said Trent. "Ms. Flores is not a suspect."

"Then why is she here, lieutenant?" shouted Hawthorne, pushing his way through the smaller statured reporters, mostly women.

"We're gathering information," said Trent. "That's all I have to say. And Hawthorne, quit bullying people!"

Trent reached for the door handle and entered the building, leaving the reporters shouting futile questions.

Flores and Jules Willems were waiting for Trent outside of his office. Neither appeared happy.

"We've been here since 11:40," said Flores. "Can we get this interview done quickly? You're interrupting training. We're two of the best players in the world."

Trent perused Willems, whom he'd only seen on television previously. Willems was tall, strong, and rangy—everything you'd expect in a world-class athlete. He was also exceptionally handsome for a jock, with a thick head of black hair and a rugged jaw bone.

"Well, Ms. Flores, now that you mention it, I didn't expect to see *two* of the world's top tennis players here today, only you. Mr. Willems, I've watched you for years, and you are a stupendous player."

If Willems was moved by Trent's comment, he did an excellent job of concealing it.

"But since you're here anyway," continued Trent, "why don't you come in and join us? You may find the conversation somewhat pertinent."

Willems looked toward Flores with surprise. He never expected to be a part of the interview process.

"I'd gladly sit and relax in your waiting room," said Willems. "I'm here to support Cassandra, although I don't understand why she's here."

Trent opened the door to his office and motioned them inside. "We're following every lead. Neither of you is a suspect."

"Take a seat," said Trent. "We'll move quickly so you can get back to training."

"That ship has already sailed," said Flores, tossing her keys onto Trent's desk. "I'm wasting my time in this pathetic office, not to mention Jules' time. So how may we help you?"

"Ms. Flores, have you noticed you've been under surveillance?"

"Yes," said Flores. "I have noticed people hanging around. Why am I being watched?"

"We're not spying. You're being protected. One of Ms. Livingstone's opponents was Monica Rivet. You understand what happened to her, right?"

"I am aware," she said. "Monica worked diligently at her game, but she was never a threat to anyone in the top twenty. But I'm sad about what happened."

Trent saw Willems roll his eyes over Flores' last remark.

"We're trying to avoid another tragedy," said Trent. "If there's an inconvenience associated with that, I apologize.

"However," continued Trent, "I stumbled over a tidbit of information we should discuss. And I don't know if Mr. Willems can help, but I may as well ask."

Flores and Willems appeared to be puzzled. Neither understood where the conversation was going.

"Ms. Flores, how well did you know Milena Lombardi?" he asked.

"I knew her. She was younger than me, and we played in some of the same tournaments. After they suspended her, I never heard much from her again. I know she committed suicide. Unless you're going tell me she did not."

"No, we believe it was a suicide," said Trent. "But I'm more interested in what triggered her suspension. She passed one drug test with flying colors. But they asked her to take another test two weeks later. Do you know why they tested her a second time?"

Willems took a deep breath in his chair and interrupted Trent.

"Lieutenant, we knew Monica, but so did hundreds of other players. Why are you asking Cassandra these questions?"

Trent looked over to Flores, now staring at the wall behind him.

"Maybe Ms. Flores can provide us with an answer, Mr. Willems."

Flores stared into space for a few more seconds and then closed her eyes. Then she sobbed.

"It was because of me," she said. "I was the one who reported her."

ORION GREGORY

Willems turned his chair at a ninety-degree angle to face Flores. "Cassandra," he said, "why did you blow the whistle? How did you know she was doing something illegal?"

Flores faced Willems and chewed softly on her lower lip. Then she spoke.

"You don't remember, do you? Milena was the new girl on the tour, and she was constantly flirting. Back then, you and I were doubles partners and friends, but I wanted more. You spend a lot of time with her. She told you she was taking an illegal substance to improve her game. I couldn't allow an unfair advantage, so I made the call."

"Cassandra, you reported her based on what I told you? And now, she's dead?"

"I know that!" said Flores. "But it was illegal. And I despised her for taking your attention away from me. I loved you then like I do now."

Silence dominated the room—first sixty seconds, then ninety. Finally, Flores spoke again.

"I never knew she'd kill herself over it. And besides, they assured me they would never mention my name. How is it, lieutenant, that you got a hold of that information?"

Trent walked to the undersized refrigerator on the other side of his office. He pulled out a bottle of water, failing to offer anything to Flores or Willems.

"I need to ask you an important question, Ms. Flores. Did your resentment toward Milena Lombardi carry over to Sydney Livingstone, her former doubles partner? Do you despise her as well?"

235

Flores pulled her head back quickly, the base of her skull bumping against the back of her chair.

"If you're asking me if I like Sydney Livingstone, the answer is no. She is one of Jules' many past lovers. But do I hate her? I wouldn't say that. I've received counseling for my anger and my resentment. Hating only hurts the hater. Hate is like an acid that eats away at the container that houses it."

"Enough of the psychobabble!" shouted Willems. "Milena Lombardi is dead, and there's a reasonable possibility she'd be alive today if you hadn't dropped a dime on her.

"But with that being said, lieutenant, you can't prove Cassandra did anything illegal. Milena took the prohibited drug and ended her own life. How did she break the law?"

"As far as I know, she didn't break the law," said Trent. "Someone's out to get Ms. Livingstone, and I'm trying to find out who. Like I said earlier, I have to run down every lead."

"Well, you have run this one down, and it led you to a dead-end, Lieutenant Trent. It's game over as far as Cassandra and I are concerned. And just because I've slept with several young players, that doesn't make me a bad person or a criminal."

Willems realized that he might have overstepped his boundaries during the outburst. He looked over at Cassandra, who stared at the floor.

"Cassandra, my love," he said, "I shouldn't have said that. You're not like the others. I love you, and we have a future together. Just think about our kids someday, what dominant players they will be."

Flores emerged from her seat, energized by Willems' apology. Then she turned her attention toward Trent.

"Let me say something right now, sir. You have drudged up the past for no reason and nearly harmed our wonderful relationship. But as you can see, genuine love prevails in the end. My conscience is clear. And if the situation presented itself again, I'd probably act in the same manner. And regarding Jules' brief fling with Sydney Livingstone, that's water under the bridge.

"I appreciate that you've hired a bodyguard for me. But you should have saved your biggest, baddest bodyguard for Sydney Livingstone. Because tonight, when I face her, there will be a bloody massacre. But I'm speaking in a tennis sense, of course."

CHAPTER 27

Cab driver? Yes. Philosophy professor? Certainly. Computer programmer? Possibly. Professional tennis coach? Not in a million years.

Trent sized up Russo as he walked into his office at precisely 4:15. He seemed fidgety, like a hyperactive child, nervously scanning the room for a chair. He wore a white Adidas cap pulled down almost to his eyebrows while his salt and pepper hair and scraggly beard reminded Trent of a notorious American villain—the Unabomber.

Trent motioned for Russo to sit. Russo turned his left wrist clockwise so he could check his Fitbit wrist. Then he took a seat.

Russo appeared frail and undernourished, his six-foot frame carrying a maximum of 150 pounds. Trent guessed him to be around fifty-five, but the lines on his face and meek stature made him appear considerably older.

"Thanks for coming in today, coach," said Trent. "First, I want to offer my condolences about Ms. Radonovic's accident. You seemed broken up over it."

Russo nodded and hung his head, pulling nervously at the sleeve of his white sweatshirt.

"I failed her, lieutenant," said Russo. "I should have protected her, and I did not."

"It's not your fault," said Trent. "Who could guess something that bizarre would happen? But I understand she's doing a miraculous job of recovering. We were concerned, but she's out of the woods now."

"I believe Anja's incredible fitness helped her recover," said Russo. "Sometimes she complains that I work her too hard, but I take fitness very seriously."

Trent studied Russo's face. He sensed a genuine concern for Anja and a sense of pride for developing her into a world-class player.

"May I offer you a Gatorade or soft drink?" said Trent. "I know it's blazing hot outside. Sometimes I forget to offer refreshments."

"I would like a cold drink, sir," said Russo. "But nothing with calories, please. Maybe a Powerade Zero or Diet Coke?"

Fumbling through the cooler, Trent located a can of Diet Pepsi and showed it to Russo, who nodded his head.

"I'm surprised that you're concerned about calories," said Trent. "I watch calories too, but I'm not skinny like you."

Russo smiled slightly.

"It's a slippery slope, lieutenant. You stop paying attention one day, then three, and then one hundred. Before you know it, you're out of shape."

"My wife would love you," said Trent. "I can't steal a cookie anymore. She's on me like a panther."

Trent snuck in a quick feel to his own midsection. It felt more flabby than usual.

"I admire your discipline, coach. I'm sure you pass the same work ethic onto your players. How many players do you have under your umbrella?"

"I have two other players, besides Anja," said Russo. "Both are female, and each one is ranked among the top 150. One is seventeen and the other nineteen. They are from Yugoslavia, my native country."

"What about Sydney Livingstone?" asked Trent. "Is she paying you?"

Russo straightened up in his chair. He ran his hand through his beard before answering.

"Not yet," he said. "But Anja suggested I work with Sydney on a trial basis. She's made more money already, so I hope she will retain me after this tournament."

Trent smiled and leaned back in his chair. "So you plan on coaching her against Flores. Can she win that match?"

A strange question, thought Russo.

"Yes, I offered my services. But it will be a challenge. We haven't had much time together."

"What is your relationship with Anja, especially off the court?"

"Pardon me?" asked Russo. "I'm not sure what you're asking."

"I apologize," said Trent. "I didn't mean to be confrontational. You said you felt responsible for the ball-machine accident. Do you feel like her guardian?"

"Now I understand," said Russo. "If she told me today that she couldn't afford my services, then I would offer to coach her for free. She is like a daughter."

"She thinks of you as a father figure?"

"Of course," said Russo. "She knows I love her unconditionally, no matter what happens on the court."

"What do you know about Marisha Belov?" asked Trent. "Is she a positive influence on Anja?"

Trent's question seemed to surprise Russo.

"I don't know how to answer that, lieutenant. If Anja is happy in the relationship, then I am fine."

"So there's no tension or jealousy between you and Ms. Belov?"

Russo leaned over in his seat and placed his palms on his forehead. A frown appeared on his face.

"There's nothing to be jealous about. I am her coach and a father figure. Marisha is Anja's lover. We are both in Anja's life."

Trent believed Russo to be sincere but wondered about Belov's perspective.

"Are you aware there was an altercation between Anja and Marisha?"

"Yes, I knew that something happened. I'm staying at the same hotel. When I arrived at their room, the police were there. Anja said it was a misunderstanding."

Trent paused for a moment, waiting for Russo to offer more information. When he didn't, Trent continued to probe.

"Did you get Ms. Belov's side of the story? How did she react?"

Russo took a deep breath.

"I'm not a psychologist, lieutenant. But I will say she was in tears while the police talked to her. She didn't mention to the police that Anja pushed her, but she revealed that to me afterward."

"Would you say it's out of the ordinary for your player to react violently?"

"Anja is a wonderful person," said Russo. "I can't imagine her hurting anyone. If you're asking if she has a temper, I would say yes. She's destroyed a few racquets. But until the incident with Marisha, I've never heard of her being violent."

"Do you know what caused the altercation?"

"I don't. I figured that it was a lover's quarrel that got out of hand."

Trent stared into Russo's eyes, searching for evidence of deceit. He couldn't detect anything, so he changed his line of questioning.

"Sydney collapsed after her qualifying match. Were you coaching her then?"

"No," said Russo. "But I gave her advice before the match, as a mentor. I watched from her players' box."

"And I saw you and Anja in the hospital that night, visiting Ms. Livingstone. Would you say that you and Sydney have become close in the short time you've known her?"

Russo took a moment to think.

"I'd say we bonded well, especially after she pulled out that match in a dramatic fashion. I was proud of her, and I told her that."

Trent noticed that Russo downed the soft drink he'd provided a few minutes earlier.

"Another?" said Trent, pointing to the soda. "I can get it for you?"

To his surprise, Russo nodded affirmatively. He walked to the cooler, pulled out another can, and handed it to Russo.

"Could Anja have been jealous of your burgeoning relationship with Ms. Livingstone?"

Russo placed his can of Diet Pepsi on Trent's desk and walked to the window to gaze at the traffic in the distance. Then he turned and faced Trent.

"It was Anja's idea for me to coach Sydney. But on the ride back from the hospital, she grew distant. She admitted that she was bothered by my new role."

Trent walked over to Russo, who was still standing by the window. He placed his left hand around Russo's shoulders. "Have you ever met Michael Livingstone before?" asked Trent. "He is Sydney's father."

"No, I don't know him," said Russo. "But Anja pointed him out. He was in the stands watching us practice when the object struck Anja. Given the circumstances, I never officially met him."

Trent reached into his drawer and pulled out a device covered in flimsy plastic.

"Coach Russo, we found this remote control device in the possession of Michael Livingstone," said Trent. "Do you know how he could have acquired it?"

"I have no idea," said Russo. "By the time the machine arrived on our court, there was no remote control. Did you ask the previous user if there was a remote with the machine?"

"The previous users were Doris McKeon and her coach. They provided written statements that the remote was with the machine when they left it," said Trent. "There was probably a fifteen-to-thirty minute span when it was unattended."

Russo's eyes grew wide. He turned toward Trent.

"Wait! Sydney's father was at that practice session! Are you saying he activated the control from where he was sitting? But that would mean that his daughter was the intended target."

"Possibly," said Trent. "But sometimes, things aren't always how they seem."

"I can't imagine a father trying to kill his daughter," said Russo. "Did Sydney wait until Anja was behind her? She could have signaled her father to activate the machine before ducking out of the way."

Trent walked back to his chair and sat down. Russo eventually followed suit.

"I've considered that. It's definitely possible. Since we're talking about theories, do you have any others you'd like to share?"

"Before I arrived today, the rumor was Fitz caused all this, especially after what Marisha witnessed. But now that you've mentioned the discovery of the remote, I have no idea. I need time to think."

"Don't think too hard," said Trent. "You've got to be ready to coach Ms. Livingstone to victory tonight. If that bitch Cassandra Flores wins, it'll ruin my entire week."

There was a tapping sound on Trent's door. Detective Megan Guthrie peeked cautiously behind the door until Trent gave her a manual cue to enter.

"Lieutenant, your five o'clock appointment is here. I told him to wait in the lobby."

Glancing at his cell phone, the time read 4:47.

"He's here early," said Trent. "Guthrie, tell him I'll be ready in ten minutes. I'm hoping he can provide some useful information."

"He appears extremely nervous," said Guthrie. "I hope Norton didn't jazz him up too much on the ride here."

"Let's hope not," said Trent. "But thanks for letting me know. You can leave the door open a crack on your way out."

Trent turned his attention back to Russo.

"I guess we're done here. Thank you for your time today. Oh, please do me a favor on your way out. Say hello to Michael Livingstone. He should meet the man who'll be coaching his daughter."

CHAPTER 28

The weather forecast for Thursday evening was for partly cloudy skies, temperatures in the high seventies, and light winds coming from the southwest. Showers were expected after midnight, with rain continuing through the early morning hours.

Trent arrived at the facility at 7:00 p.m. He planned to sit courtside with detective Christopher Samuels for Syd's televised 9:00 p.m. match against Flores. Samuels' task was to guard Syd at the hotel and accompany her to the stadium when she arrived at 7:30.

Physically, Trent felt fine, but he was mentally tired from conducting interviews. He secured a table at an outdoor eatery, dining on garlic hummus and bagel chips. He'd already sucked down a large Diet Mountain Dew and was looking to order another. Trent liked caffeine because it energized him and suppressed his appetite.

From where he was sitting, Trent could see the ESPN announcers interviewing a smiling Peter O'Malley, who had just survived a 2-½ match against Argentinian Oscar Deuer. The claustrophobic jail cell had no long-term effect on O'Malley, who would probably face number-one seed

Jules Willems in the third round tomorrow. Willems was beating George Hagan of the Netherlands, 6-2, 3-1, in a match that began at 5:30.

Trent made the difficult decision to cancel his interviews with Syd and Enzo. He felt it would be unfair to Syd on the eve of her big match against Flores. They'd speak again soon.

Trent was concerned about the data he gathered from Michael Livingstone. He wanted to remove Livingstone from his suspect list, but lingering doubts prevailed due to his evasiveness.

Why had Michael come back into his daughter's life? Perhaps he sought to repair the relationship with his daughter. The timing, however, just didn't seem right. Why was the remote attached to his car? Was someone setting him up? And what about the restraining order? Is Michael a ticking time bomb? Or is he simply going through a rough period? Why isn't Chelsea panicking now that Michael's in town? Is he really dangerous?

Normally, Trent would have detained Michael for forty-eight hours after their interview, but he cut him a break because his daughter was playing the biggest match of her life. He'd detain Michael after the match.

* * * * *

Sydney arrived with Enzo at the tennis center, a few minutes shy of 7:30. Samuels' gold Buick Enclave pulled in behind Enzo. A bodyguard also tailed Flores.

Enzo didn't speak much on the drive, like his demeanor at lunch earlier in the day.

Enzo's appetite was normally ravenous, especially when he wasn't scheduled to play. But today was different. He'd only pawed at his burger and sucked on a few of his over-salted fries. When he wasn't hungry, there were usually two explanations. He was sick, or something was bothering him.

"I don't think you should play," Enzo had said before the others joined them at the table. "The faster we leave town, the better. There's a strange aura hanging over this tournament."

"I know," said Syd. "Murder and flying metal balls are ruining the entire experience."

Syd looked at Enzo, and a grin emerged.

"But at least I've gotten a few leads as a nutrition guru," she said. "The 'Diet Bitch' website is growing in popularity."

Enzo usually appreciated Syd's humor, but he didn't even break a smile.

"Someone's out to get you, Syd. And they're probably still around. Fitz is in jail, but there could be someone working with him. Let's eat our lunch and get the hell out of Columbus."

Syd's answer was interrupted by the arrival of Nicole and Chelsea. Before she knew it, lunch ended, and Enzo's objections were never addressed.

Syd wanted to tell Enzo that she was eager to compete against Flores, especially after her strategy session with Russo, who'd devised an amazingly detailed battle plan.

Anja had also attended the strategy session held at Syd's quarters over a room-service breakfast.

Anja glowed at the meeting. She appeared positive and upbeat.

"I'm done acting immaturely," she said. "I want Russo to help you win the biggest match of your life!"

Russo had also given Anja a peek at the game plan he'd prepared. "He's a genius," said Anja. "Absorb what he's saying. You might accomplish the impossible tonight."

Russo's plans were elaborate. He provided a complete description of Flores' tendencies—where she liked to place her first serves and which type of spin she preferred on second serves. Russo also compiled a flowchart showing where Flores positioned the ball on groundstrokes and service returns.

"This is why I'm not married," said Russo. "I lived with a woman for twenty years, but she refused to walk down the aisle with me. She said I was overly compulsive or something. I think she referred to it as OCD."

As Syd looked over the plans, the level of detail astounded her.

"If I had a week to digest this information, I could implement your plan," she said. "But I hope you do not think I can absorb this stuff by match time."

Russo placed his hand on her shoulder. "I know Flores like the back of my hand. If you listen to me, you'll know exactly what to expect. And you will have an advantage."

Enzo's advice to pack up her car and head back to Savannah was distressing to Syd. If she lost to Flores, she would head home with a fantastic payday, one that could lift her out of her current financial crisis. But what if she prevailed somehow, on worldwide television? She loved Enzo for caring, but she wished he could understand her perspective.

Syd and Enzo left the hotel at 7:15 and headed toward the tournament. Syd sensed that Enzo was deep in thought.

"Tell me what you're thinking," said Syd. "I need to know."

Enzo's car passed Queen's Domain, one of the preeminent theme parks in the Midwest. They were within a mile of the tennis facility.

"I know how much this match means to you," said Enzo. "But nothing's worth your safety or your life. It's not too late. We can leave now."

As they entered the players' lot, Syd turned to face Enzo. "Tonight is probably the end of the road for me," she said. "I practiced with Flores, and she almost knocked the racquet out of my hands.

"I truly love you," said Syd. "But if I leave now, I'll never know if I could've won. That's more painful than any defeat. But if it means that much to you, I can withdraw. You're more important to me than tennis."

Enzo faced Syd, a slight smile appearing on his face. He emerged from his driver's side, opened the passenger door for her, and placed a kiss on her cheek.

"It's your road," he said. "It's your decision. I'm in your corner."

* * * * *

"I'm so excited for you!" said Chelsea, wrapping her arms around Syd as she entered the facility. "Your stepfather Brian called this morning. He wanted you to know he's pulling for you tonight. He wishes he could be here, but he's too busy at work."

"Tell him I appreciate that," said Syd, wishing she had developed a closer relationship with Brian. "Mom, I hope we can spend more time together soon. Maybe Enzo and I can meet you and Brian for dinner sometime. We have so much to talk about."

Syd looked over at Nicole.

"Where's Victor?" she said. "Did you two spend the night together?"

"We certainly did!" said a grinning Nicole. "Victor will arrive around match time. He said he needed a nap. I hope I'm not wearing him out!"

"TMI," laughed Syd. "A little too much information!"

"You know what I mean," said Nicole. "I can't believe how he's warmed up to Scarlet. He's not afraid to hold her anymore. She doesn't like to show it outwardly, but I think Scarlet is fond of him."

"A match made in heaven," quipped Syd. "It was bound to happen."

* * * * *

After a visit to the players' lounge, Syd hustled to the area outside Center Court, where she would meet Russo for ten minutes of dynamic stretching. Samuels followed Syd wherever she went, trying to remain transparent. Enzo remained close by for good measure.

"Listen to me while you warm up," said Russo. "It's imperative you get off to a fast start against Flores. She plays less confidently when trailing."

"Easy for you to say," joked Syd. "I don't think she's trailed anybody all year."

The two continued discussing strategy while Syd performed a routine that included high-knee running, butt kicks, shuffling, and karaoke/crossover maneuvers.

Once the reporters realized who Syd was, they rushed at her to secure a pre-match interview.

"Not now, please," she said, trying to be polite despite their interference. "I'm in the middle of a warm-up."

One of the reporters shouted over Syd's words.

"Vegas has Flores as an 11-1 favorite. Can you be competitive considering what's happened?"

Syd continued loosening up, hoping her lack of response would discourage them.

Hawthorne, the same reporter who had bullied Russo in the hospital, confidently pushed his way forward.

"Is it true your father is a suspect in the disappearance of Monica Rivet?"

Russo attempted to stand in Hawthorne's way, but Hawthorne pushed him aside with the thrust of a forearm. As Hawthorne moved even closer to Syd, he stood between her and a scowling Samuels.

"Maybe you didn't hear what she said," said Samuels. "Get the fucking bananas out of your ears. If you don't walk away within five seconds, I will move you. And it won't be gently."

Hawthorne scanned Samuels. He was well-built, but Hawthorne felt he could sustain himself in a confrontation. He smiled wryly and tried to lift his microphone over Samuels' shoulder, closer to Syd's face. Samuels grabbed Hawthorne with both hands and spun him violently to the left. Hawthorne lost his balance and tumbled to the ground.

"I want you to come toward me again," said Samuels. "At that point, I'm acting in self-defense."

Hawthorne jumped to his feet, but his desire to fight Samuels was diminishing by the second.

"Screw you in the ass," he said. "I didn't know people with IQs lower than thirty were permitted."

Samuels feigned a movement toward Hawthorne, causing the reporter to backpedal quickly away. Samuels wheeled around and faced the remaining reporters. They scattered like buffalo at a crocodile sighting.

Samuels appeared so menacing, Enzo asked permission before approaching Syd.

"Of course you can," scowled Samuels. "I'm trying to keep these termites away. As far as I know, she doesn't consider you a destructive insect."

"I wouldn't be so sure," said Syd, smiling at Samuels. Then she turned her attention to Enzo.

"Behold, oh ye of six legs! Her highness has giveth permission for thouest to approach!"

Several spectators watched their interaction, and a burst of laughter ensued.

"I'm going to let you finish the warmup in peace, your hiney," replied Enzo, hoping to seize on the momentum. "I'm meeting Victor for a beer."

"Yes, be merry, frolic, and enjoy good cheer," said Syd, in her best English accent. "But if thou art a latecomer, beware the witching hour of which no good will come!"

"Call me if you need anything," said Enzo. "And cool it with the Shakespearean lingo. It's much ado about nothing."

Several of the more literary fans in the crowd let out a collective moan, but Russo either didn't get Enzo's joke, or he was not amused by it.

"Sydney, please concentrate on the task at hand," whispered Russo. "I saw Flores a few minutes ago. She has that killer look in her eyes, and she doesn't seem happy I'm coaching you."

"That makes two of us," said a straight-faced Syd. Then she broke into a smile.

"Lighten up, coach. I'm only teasing. I play better when the mood's a little lighter."

Although it seemed counterintuitive, Syd took a hot shower before every match, even in sweltering conditions. She'd allow the hot water to stimulate blood flow and loosen muscles. The entire process took about ten minutes.

She jogged by the players' locker room, nodding at Samuels, who stood outside the entrance.

"I'm right here if you need me," said Samuels. "Once you're finished showering, I'll escort you to your court."

Inside the locker room, Syd undressed, placed her clothes on a bench, and headed to a shower stall surrounded by translucent glass. A few minutes earlier, Syd had noticed a couple of players in the shower area. But to the best of her knowledge, they had cleared out.

A few minutes into her shower, Syd heard an exit door slamming shut. She ignored the sound and continued to bathe. Then she thought about the sound again. No one is permitted to leave the shower area through those exits, except during an emergency. But what if the sound meant someone had *entered* the area instead of exiting? Those doors were normally locked from the outside, but what if someone propped an exit door open? Had someone entered from the back of the building?

Syd tried to convince herself that her imagination was running wild, but she couldn't stop the pounding in her chest. If an intruder was inside, Samuels couldn't help. He was still guarding the entrance, not the exit. By the time he noticed something amiss, it would be too late.

Syd saw a figure moving past her shower door. She couldn't determine if the silhouette was a man or woman, but it was definitely not a child. The steaming water flowing down the length of her body no longer soothed her. Instead, an icy chill ran up her back. She didn't want to turn the water off abruptly, in fear of creating attention.

But she didn't want to emerge from the shower either. She waited in the shower for a few more strenuous minutes, hoping the intruder would leave.

Seconds seemed like minutes, and minutes seemed like hours. This wasn't her imagination. She was sure of it. Someone was there with her.

She considered bursting out of the stall buck naked, letting out a kamikaze yell, and smacking the intruder with a bottle of conditioner. Unless it was a player. Oh, God!

What if this was Enzo up to his old tricks? He'd promised no more pranks, but was he wacky enough to attempt one more? She doubted it.

In one motion, Syd turned both faucet handles in opposite directions. Much to her distress, the running water squeaked to a halt like an SUV slamming on its brakes. So much for subtlety.

Syd leaned out of the shower stall. "Enzo," she said hoarsely. "Is that you?"

Nothing.

Running out of options, Syd attempted a full-court basketball shot with no time left.

"Okay, Samuels," she yelled, trying to sound self-assured. "Our trap worked! Come out and arrest him!"

Five seconds passed. Then, suddenly, she heard the exit door open and then immediately slam shut. She crept out of the stall, the conditioner bottle ready to strike. Not exactly her weapon of choice, but she was in no position to be picky. She walked the corridor leading back to the dressing area, peered around a gray-tiled wall on her left, and located her bag, which was open and lying on the floor. Clothes were scattered on the floor and over lockers.

Somewhere inside her bag, Syd placed her Tiger Claw weapon. Her eyes scanned the room as she reached into her bag, trying to locate it. She felt a piercing sensation on the ring finger of her right hand. She pulled her hand back instinctively. Had she left the Tiger Claw in striking position? That was unlikely.

Syd opened the inside of the bag to allow more light inside. She noticed something glistening back at her. She turned her bag over and shook it. A large brown and tan spider, its body size nearly an inch-and-a-half in diameter, dropped to the floor. Its legs were long and hairy, and all three rows of eyes glared at her, including two large ones in the middle. Syd looked down at her hand and saw a small circle of blood forming.

Syd could feel the pulse throbbing in her head, and the room slowly blurred. She placed her hand on a locker for support and let out a guttural scream that reverberated off the walls.

"Samuels!"

CHAPTER 29

By the time Samuels entered the locker room, Syd had pulled her body off the floor and onto the bench. Samuels' white dress shirt perspired at the pits, and his red-and-white tie slung over his shoulder.

"I heard you screaming from outside the door," said Samuels. "Are you okay?"

"Just another shower in paradise," said Syd, pulling clothes over her semi-exposed body. "Someone entered through the exit door while I was showering. I think I scared them away."

"Why are you grabbing your finger?" asked Samuels.

"That's the part I forgot to tell you," said Syd. "Whoever visited me while I was showering left a little souvenir behind—a poisonous spider. It welcomed me by taking a chunk out of my finger."

"Where's the spider now?" said Samuels. "Is it in the shower?"

"I think it's still hanging around my tennis bag," said Syd. "Believe me; you can't miss him."

Samuels moved his hand toward the bag and slowly flipped it over. The spider, now exposed, stood frozen and crouched on the bench, anticipating Samuels' next move.

"That thing's bigger than shit," said Samuels. "I've met smaller bus drivers."

"Hold the line," said Syd. "I'm not sure, but that might be Scar—"

A slamming sound interrupted her comment. While she was studying the spider, Samuels had removed one of his brown loafers. The impact from the blow sent the insect scattering into four or five separate locations.

Samuels stepped back and inspected the carnage.

"Damn, I guess that was a bit of overkill," he said. "I despise spiders. You'd never guess that from a guy of my stature, would you?"

Trent and two other detectives suddenly burst into the room.

"Is everyone all right in here?" he said. "I received an alert that there was some kind of commotion."

Samuels looked over at Trent nervously, hoping he wouldn't be chastised for not protecting Syd.

"Someone tried to sneak up on her in the shower," said Samuels. "She scared the stalker away, but she got attacked by an enormous spider."

First an intruder, and then a potentially deadly spider bite. Trent appeared puzzled, like he wasn't buying any of it.

"Excuse me," said Syd. "I'm not sure if the intruder was male or female. The figure moved quickly past the shower door."

Trent asked his detectives to scan the room. The search revealed no intruders.

"So the human didn't hurt you, but the spider did?" asked Trent. "You have some strange things happening to you, Ms. Livingstone!"

"Isn't that why your staff is here to protect me?" said Syd, purging blood from her small wound.

"We need to get a doctor here, stat," said Trent, examining Syd's finger. "She has a match in thirty minutes. And where's the spider? Maybe we can use it for identification purposes."

"Part of it's over there," said Samuels, pointing in one direction. "And the other parts are there, and there. Sir, I may have been a little harsh in my reaction."

"You've got the right to protect yourself, Samuels," said Trent sarcastically. "Now, if we can put together this eight-legged Humpty Dumpty, everything will be fine."

"Wait a second," said Syd. "I know someone who can identify that spider. I think it might be Scarlet."

"So this Scarlet person is an expert on spiders?" asked Samuels.

Trent shook his head.

"Samuels, drop the subject," he said. "I know all about this spider issue. We'll put the pieces into a bag to determine whether it's poisonous."

Syd examined her ring finger once again. The blood had stopped, and the prick mark was small.

"I'm going to play," said Syd. "No web-spinning creepy-crawly will ruin my big moment. Someone may want to notify Nicole, though. She's next of kin."

* * * * *

At around 8:40, Syd met Russo in the players' lounge for a few last-minute instructions.

"I hope you are okay," said Russo. "I understand there was some type of altercation in the locker room."

"A stalker here, a spider there," said Syd. "Nothing out of the ordinary. But let's focus on the present. I think Flores is prepared to take me to the woodshed."

Russo frowned. "Lieutenant Trent tells me a spider bit you, possibly a poisonous one," said Russo. "You can pull out of the match. You've already made enough money. It's not worth risking your health."

"I'll be fine," said Syd. "It's a scratch, maybe not even a bite. The damn thing probably tried to push me away with its claw."

Russo glared at Syd. Excess skin hung down from his chin, and several veins protruded from his neck. Russo's beard seemed even more scruffy than before. Syd wondered if he ever took a brush to it.

"Listen to me, Sydney," he said. "You cannot execute my plan unless you are 100 percent healthy. Do you understand?"

Syd nodded.

"I'm fine. But we're running out of time. Tell me how I can win this match."

"Let's walk to the stadium," said Russo. "I'll brief you along the way."

The stroll to the stadium normally took five minutes, but the capacity crowd made Syd and Russo weave in a serpentine manner, with Trent and Samuels following.

As they walked through the tunnel and entered the court, the crowd roared in approval. Syd was now Columbus' favorite daughter. The partisan fans desired a competitive showing against Flores.

Syd's players' box—comprising of Chelsea, Anja, Victor, Nicole, and Enzo—rose to their feet, applauding excitedly. A doctor waited at courtside, preparing to examine the wound. Syd sat next to the doctor and opened her hand.

"I don't know if I was bitten," said Syd, as the petite female African-American doctor examined her finger. "Something sharp inside my bag might have jabbed me."

"I doubt it," said the doctor. "From what I can tell, an insect definitely bit you."

Syd glanced toward the top of the stadium, which was filling quickly. The sun was setting, and the arena's lights glistened brilliantly off the reflective glass, which encased a section reserved for dignitaries and the press.

"Okay, it's a spider bite," said Syd. "Can't you apply some anti-fungal cream and wrap the finger?"

The doctor looked at Syd and paused before answering.

"I can do that," she said. "Most spiders in the Midwest are relatively harmless. I was informed this spider could be exotic. Is that possible?"

"I'm not sure," said Syd, trying to block out Nicole's eventual reaction to Scarlet's dismantling. "Why don't we assume it was born and bred in Columbus? I need to play."

"It's your call," said the doctor. "But if the spider is venomous, then strenuous exercise will worsen your condition."

Syd tried to remain optimistic.

"I'll be fine," she said, noticing Flores limbering up on her side of the court. "I can't afford to worry now."

"As I said, it's your decision," said the doctor. "We've taken a picture of the spider's remains and sent it to our lab. If we find out more, I'll let you know."

With that, the doctor placed a small bandage on Syd's right ring finger and exited the court.

Syd turned her attention toward Russo. "See that gentleman standing high up in the corner of the stadium?" she said. "That's my father. He's come back into my life. I believe his intentions are good."

"Sydney, that's nice," said Russo, pulling his chair closer. "But there's someone over there who doesn't have good intentions. Cassandra Flores is preparing to destroy you. Focus and prepare for battle."

Flores' winning streak ballooned to twenty-nine consecutive matches with her first-round win. Her last loss was to Natalie Odessa in February, a nail-biting, three-set affair in which Flores held three match points.

"Two minutes until warmup!" announced the head linesperson, a stout middle-aged woman with a rugged, weathered face.

"You have to implement our plan with no deviations," said Russo. "Are you ready and willing?"

Syd nodded her head, not entirely sure what she agreed to.

"Tell me which groundstroke is Flores' best," said Russo. "The forehand or backhand?"

Syd paused. "I would say that she's tremendous on both sides, but her forehand may be the best in tennis."

"I agree," said Russo. "So, during the ten-minute warmup, you are going to direct every shot to her forehand side. Only give her shots to her backhand if she requests them. And if I know her, she won't request anything."

"Okay," said Syd. "But you're talking about warmups. What about during the match?"

"Bear with me," said Russo. "Just direct all shots to her forehand for the entire first set."

"Why would I do that?" asked Syd. "We agreed that's her strength."

"I have done my research," groaned Russo. "Direct the damn ball to her forehand until I tell you differently. Trust me!"

Ironic statement, thought Syd. Someone asking for trust when she couldn't trust anyone. But if Russo were crazy enough to instruct her to drive off of a cliff, she'd press the accelerator.

"You're the boss, coach," she said.

The more Syd hit the ball to Flores' forehand during warmups, the more her opponent became grooved with the shot. Russo's strategy contradicted the advice that her father had given her as a youngster: Find a weakness and exploit it.

Flores held serve easily in the first game and broke Syd's serve in the next. Syd continued to play to Flores' forehand in the third game, and Flores continued to dominate with her forehand, hitting two crosscourt and two down-the-line winners.

As they crossed paths on the way to their chairs at 3-0, Flores mumbled under her breath.

"I'm humiliating you in front of the entire world."

"What did she say?" asked Russo.

"She asked for my address," said Syd. "She wants to send me a Christmas card."

Russo tried to remain stoic, but he couldn't suppress a smile.

"I like how you keep things in perspective," he said. "Now, stay with our plan."

As she leaned over to take a sip of her drink mix, Syd began feeling queasy.

Syd thought about her finger. It had started to swell, although the bandage was still covering the puncture wound.

"I'm going to get sick," she said, sprinting off the court, down the tunnel, and into the women's restroom.

And as she vomited into the mouth of the commode, all she could think about was Nicole's smiling face.

"Don't you just love my little Scarlet O'Hairy!"

Perhaps Nicole was behind all of this.

CHAPTER 30

"So much for Syd getting off to a fast start," said Enzo to Victor. "And where the hell did she go? Maybe I should sneak down there and ask Russo for an update."

Nicole held on tightly to Victor's arm and looked up at him, expecting him to respond to Enzo. But no reply was forthcoming.

"Victor, honey!" said Nicole. "Enzo spoke to you. Didn't you hear what he said?"

Victor appeared startled and turned to face Enzo. "I'm sorry there, buddy," he said. "I was thinking about this match. What did you say?"

"I asked you if I should talk to Russo about Syd?" said Enzo. "Look at her. She's disintegrating."

Victor put his left fist up to his mouth and paused before answering.

"Why don't you hold off?" he said. "Maybe Russo is cooking up something. Anja's told me he's a borderline genius."

Anja, sitting in the row behind them, responded. "Syd isn't acting right. I know her. And it's not about tennis. She's sick or stressed."

"After all you've been through, you're concerned about Syd's welfare," said Nicole. "You're a special friend."

"Syd is like family," said Anja. "When one of us wins, the other wins. And vice-versa."

Enzo noticed that the swelling on Anja's forehead had disappeared. Her bruise was barely noticeable.

"Where's your friend, Marisha?" he asked. "Will she join us in the box tonight?"

Anja took in a deep sigh before responding.

"Marisha will not be joining us," she said. "As you know, we had a slight altercation. She decided it would be better to leave. She left the country on the red-eye last night."

The abruptness of Anja's statement left everyone speechless. Thankfully, the awkwardness was interrupted by the sound of the crowd applauding as Syd jogged back on the court, clutching a towel close to her mouth. She sat down next to Russo, removed three liquid energy packets from her bag, and sucked each one down.

"C'mon, Sydney, put on a good show for us!" yelled someone from the upper deck.

Flores looked annoyed at the pause in the action. She approached the umpire in her chair.

"How many restroom breaks is a player allowed?" she asked. "It seems interesting how nature seems to call right when she's getting steamrolled."

The umpire looked at Flores, who was leaning back in her chair, arms folded.

"Players may take multiple restroom breaks as long as they are within reason," said the umpire. "And I'm the one who determines what is within reason."

Flores rolled her eyes in disbelief, let out a sigh, and turned away to speak with her coach.

Shaking, weak, and slumped over her chair, Syd felt defeated. She'd won just two individual points so far. The scoreboard lights, displaying the 3-0 tally, seemed to burn a hole through the center of her brain.

"Should we call it a day?" she asked Russo. "I'm getting pistol-whipped, and I may have spider venom coursing through my body as we speak."

Russo was grimacing, but she was not sure if it was because of the score or concern over her health. Then his expression turned into a smile.

"Sydney, the courtside doctor approached me while you were in the restroom," he said. "They sent a picture of the spider's body parts to an exotic insect specialist. The spider that bit you was not a poisonous tarantula. It's a common wolf spider that's bountiful in the Midwest. Its venom is harmless to humans."

Syd shifted in her chair and sucked down another energy gel.

"But then why was I feeling sick? Why did I run off the court and lose my lunch?"

"It's amazing how stress affects our bodies," said Russo, shaking his head. "The mind can make or break us."

For a moment, Syd felt relieved she wouldn't perish from the spider bite. But she glanced at the scoreboard. She was getting her butt kicked in front of the entire world, and Flores had no intention of letting up.

"This focus-on-the-forehand thing isn't working," she said. "Can't I hit the ball to her backhand side once in a while? I may not win, but at least I won't get humiliated."

Russo wanted to grab Syd by the collar and shake her, but he resisted.

"Do not stray from our plan until I give you the go-ahead," he said. "Scrap for every point and stay with our plan."

Commentating from the announcer's booth, Jack Mc-Duff was questioning Sydney's strategy.

"I don't know what Livingstone's doing right now," he said, "but she better change something, or this match will be over very soon."

Flores won her next service game by complementing her 110-mph serve with forehand winners. Syd finally broke her own serve to make it 4-1. The crowd briefly came alive, but Flores extinguished any remaining momentum by closing out the first set, 6-1.

"She's out of my league," said Syd during the court-side change." My goal now is to keep from embarrassing myself."

Russo pulled out his notebook and pointed to a page he'd written on.

"Do you see this, Sydney?" he asked. "In the first set, she has hit only thirteen backhands. She's sliced ten and hit topspin on three. Do you see what I'm getting at?"

"I don't know," said Syd. "Maybe that ten plus three equals thirteen?"

"No," said Russo. "Topspin is aggressive, while the slice is defensive. Since she's in a defensive mode with her backhand, it's going to be difficult for her to change that mindset. Our plan is working!"

Syd glanced up at the big screen located high above her on the opposite side of the court.

"That scoreboard doesn't agree," she said. "That big fat six is kicking the ass of that skinny little one!"

"I know that," said Russo, hoping Syd didn't notice that a significant number of fans were exiting in search of a more competitive match. "But we need to maintain our course for a little longer. Continue directing everything to her forehand. When we change our strategy, she'll never see it coming. Try to stay competitive for now."

For a fleeting moment, Syd considered the fact that Russo was plotting against her. *Paranoid thinking*, she thought. She'd sink or swim with Russo's strategy, with no regrets or what-ifs.

The spectators in Syd's box, and the rest of the crowd, were eerily quiet. Anja rubbed her temples as if she was fending off a migraine. Enzo moved uncomfortably in his seat while Nicole and Victor tried futilely to comfort him. Chelsea was still clapping and yelling toward Syd, encouraging her to fight on. Michael Livingstone was standing near the top row of the stadium, pacing like a caged tiger.

Flores jumped all over Syd in the first game of the second set. She blasted crushing forehands from corner to corner, forcing weak responses. Flores dominated the net now, crushing Syd's floaters away with ease.

Syd held serve while trailing 2-0 to pull within a game

in the second set. At the court change, she looked at Russo for the go-ahead.

"It's time to make our move!" he said. "She's thinking ahead to her next match. Start attacking that backhand and following your shot to the net. She's stuck in her defensive mindset."

Relieved that Russo had lifted the restraints, Syd prepared to attack Flores' backhand. Clawing back from a 6-1, 2-1 deficit would be difficult, if not impossible.

While Syd directed many of her shots to Flores' backhand, she seemed unphased, increasing her lead to 3-1. Syd hung tough during the next game but eventually succumbed and trailed 4-1. Most of the fans had cleared out.

"It's not too late," said Russo. "You need to move to the net sooner. She won't be able to hit the ball past you with her backhand. She's on autopilot right now, and it's your job to disrupt her."

"Disrupt" is an interesting word choice, thought Syd. Whoever was tormenting her was disrupting her life. Maybe she could dish out a little disruption herself.

Neither she nor Russo needed to verbalize it was essential for Syd to break Flores' serve. If Flores pulled ahead 5-1, the improbable journey would become an impossible one.

Flores won the first two points and appeared on her way to 5-1, but Syd fought back. She ripped her own forehand to Flores' backhand and attacked the net. Flores responded with a backhand slice, which floated into Syd's target area. She volleyed the shot away for a winner.

After a Flores double-fault, Syd attacked the backhand again, and Flores responded with another weak slice backhand return. After a twenty-shot rally, Syd again approached the net to Flores' backhand side. Flores blasted a hard topspin shot, but the ball landed over a foot beyond the baseline. A minor victory for Syd, but 4-2 sounded a lot better than 5-1.

The trend continued in the following game. The favored player either sliced a wounded duck into Syd's power zone or missed an attempt at a topspin passing shot. Syd held serve for 4-3.

"Let's go, Syd!" screamed Enzo, standing with both feet on his chair as the players changed sides. "You can do this!"

Flores regained her form and held serve, taking a 5-3 lead. With Flores one game away from winning, Syd figured that she had nothing to lose. She had already avoided a total embarrassment. ESPN announcers were complimenting her on her refusal to quit.

The next game consisted of several grueling points. Finally, Flores held an advantage after winning a crucial deuce point on a forehand winner. One point away from winning the match, Flores strutted back to her side of the court. Fire raged in her eyes like a falcon, ready to swoop down on a fieldmouse.

As Syd walked back to serve, Russo caught her attention from the side of the court.

"Remember your friend, Milena!" he shouted. "Her fighting spirit is within you!"

Flores seemed unnerved by Russo's interruption and appealed to the head umpire.

"I'm giving you a warning for coaching during the match," boomed a voice from above. "Please refrain from communicating with your player until the court change."

Russo acknowledged the umpire. "I am sorry, ma'am," he said. "It will not happen again."

On match point, Syd missed her first serve. The second serve struck the top of her frame. As the ball climbed unusually high into the air, Syd was resigned to her fate. *It's been a good run*, she thought—definitely better than expected. But whether it was because of unintended topspin, a gust of wind, or the guiding hand of Milena, the ball took a downward turn and plunged toward the service box. It struck the back edge of the service line and bounced awkwardly high. The only person more surprised than Syd was Flores, who had relaxed, expecting a double-fault and her ultimate victory.

Too stunned to swing at the ball, Flores looked to the head umpire, hoping the unwieldy serve was out. No such luck. Deuce.

A muffed Flores forehand, followed by a service ace, gave Syd the game. But Flores still led 5-4 and was prepared to serve out the match.

"Remain focused," said Russo, during the change. "Move to the net and attack her backhand. She's still in hibernation mode."

On four straight points, Syd, aided by two double-faults, broke the serve of an unnerved Flores, tying the set at 5-5.

Flores looked at her coach, searching for an answer. Now the commentators in the booth were also taking notice.

"I'm not sure how this happened, but she's back in this match," bellowed McDuff. "I never saw this coming."

Cassandra Flores' game continued to collapse, her backhand either flying hopelessly long or wide or setting up Syd with an easy volley. On set point, she flailed at the backhand, sending the ball three feet wide.

"The second set goes to Ms. Livingstone, seven games to five," said the umpire into her microphone.

Spectators who stayed were about to witness a three-set affair. The ESPN announcers swooned over Syd.

"If Livingstone pulls off this upset," said celebrity announcer Patty Shurmur, "this will be the biggest comeback of the year."

"It won't happen," said former women's number-one player Kendra Paige. "Flores won't play two poor sets in a row."

During the ten-minute break between the second and third sets, Syd's eyes met those of Jules Willems, one of many spectators in Cassandra's box. An ever-so-slight smile appeared on his face, and he nodded at Syd. Her incredible comeback had surprised the world's number-one player and the boyfriend of Flores.

"Sydney, this is where we have to be careful," said Russo. "Flores has ten minutes to compose herself and re-establish her game. We'll continue with our current strategy until she solves our riddle."

If Flores was going to come up with an answer to Syd's strategy, it would not happen in the early part of the third set. Syd came out smoking, teeing off on forehands and backhands from the baseline, and attacking her opponent's backhand. Her 3-0 lead advanced to 4-1, and then to 5-2. Now Flores needed to break serve to stay in the match.

After a long game that included seven deuces, Flores played well enough on a few key points to win the game and close the gap to 5-3.

But as much as she wanted to secure the victory, Syd couldn't overcome several big passing shot winners from Flores. Her backhand was rounding into form, and the element of surprise was no longer working. Suddenly, the score was 5-4 and with Flores serving to tie the match.

"She's figured out what we've been doing," Syd told Russo. "She's hitting her backhand with confidence again. What should I do?"

"In terms of strategy, I cannot help you anymore," said Russo, pulling on his wiry beard. "Plan A worked as I had planned. But I don't have a Plan B. She's solved the riddle."

"Then how can I win?" asked Syd. "She's better than me. I need your guidance, and I need it now!"

Russo took a deep breath and placed his hand on Syd's shoulder. "I don't have the answer," he said. "But I know someone who does."

"If not you, then who knows the answer?" asked Syd.

Russo smiled softly at her.

"It's you, Sydney. If you're going to win, it absolutely must come from here," said Russo, putting his hand gently over his heart. "Now fight for each point, as if your life depends on it."

CHAPTER 31

Trent kept a keen eye on Michael Livingstone during the match.

Michael's impromptu appearance during the most tumultuous time of Syd's life seemed like more than coincidence. But what father wants to kill his daughter? And why? Trent searched for answers as he watched Michael pace at the upper deck of the stadium.

With Syd leading 5-2, Michael returned to his seat. But once Flores had closed the gap to 5-4, the back-and-forth ritual resumed.

O'Malley was in the heat of battle with Jules Willems. Trent used his cell to check the score. O'Malley won the first set, but Willems had retaken control, winning the second set and leading 4-2 in the third.

Most of Trent's other suspects were accounted for. Nicole and Victor were morphing into one person in Syd's players' box. Anja, Enzo, and Chelsea were present as well. But had Belov really left the country? She'd been a fixture at Anja's side. It seemed strange that she left so abruptly.

Trent would charge Fitz with a crime for his interference in Syd's match, but he didn't fit the profile of a killer. And besides, strange occurrences continued after he was incarcerated. But is it possible he was working with someone? He was a strange, insecure, narcissistic little man.

Trent refrained from becoming emotionally involved in Syd's match. Samuels gave in to the temptation, cheering wildly whenever Syd won a big point. Trent viewed Samuels as hardworking and blue-collar, but not someone who'd climb the management ladder.

With the game knotted at deuce, Flores drove an explosive backhand down the line and approached the net. Syd barely reached the ball. Instead of trying to execute a weak passing shot, she flicked her wrist, launching the ball upward. Flores moved backward quickly to attempt an overhead smash. But Syd's shot floated a little higher than Flores expected. Letting out a groan, she jumped and took a full swing. The ball clipped the top of her racquet frame and floated harmlessly out of bounds.

Flores uttered an expletive and fired a ball to the back of the court, narrowly missing an aging official. She received a warning from the head umpire.

Match point.

Syd was one shot, one error, one inch from pulling off the biggest upset of her life.

But she'd learned the hard way; one point is equal to one thousand miles away. She didn't want to repeat mistakes of the past, retreating into a defensive shell and hoping her opponent would make a mistake. She vowed to play aggressively.

On match point, Syd's first serve, aimed at Flores' backhand, landed four inches wide. Flores moved into the court, preparing to pound Syd's slower second serve.

As she prepared to serve, all Syd could see was Milena's face. She smiled sweetly, serene and at peace, a look rarely exhibited from Milena in actual life.

"You know you're my hero, right?" whispered Milena in a soothing voice.

Syd bounced the ball three more times, trying to gather her wits. *Go away, imagination! This is not the time.*

The crowd hummed, eagerly anticipating matchpoint. But to Syd's chagrin, Milena's smile returned, blocking out everything, including her peripheral vision.

"Don't think," said the image. "Act!"

Holy shit! thought Syd. *All my life, someone's coached me—my dad, various local pros, and Russo. But never someone from the afterlife.*

The smile evaporated from Milena's face. A tear streamed down her cheek.

"Someone's trying to hurt you," she whispered. "Don't trust—"

The umpire's voice boomed over the loudspeaker, erasing the image in her head.

"Time violation," she said. "Please adhere to the thirty-second clock."

Russo was standing up now, staring at Syd quizzically. Flores rocked back and forth, preparing to pounce on Syd's second serve.

She bounced the ball three times, and then three more. Two seconds showed on the serving clock. Another violation would cost her the point. Syd hurriedly lifted the ball into the air and struck a flat serve—forsaking the safety of spin, which she always used for second serves.

Syd contacted the ball at the highest point she could reach, aiming for the center service line. For a second, she thought the ball would strike the net. A double-fault would erase the match point and put the contest back in limbo. But the ball narrowly crossed over the net. It landed just inside the center line and the service line. The ball's speed caused it to explode upward upon bouncing.

Flores, surprised by the fearlessness of Syd's second serve, lunged for the ball. The result was a high, looping return, landing close to the net. Syd moved forward to hit an overhead smash, which, if executed correctly, would give her the greatest victory of her life.

It would have been easy to choke. She could hesitate and arrive at the ball late. She could attempt to guide the ball safely, causing either a miss or a winning return from Flores.

Syd remembered her father's advice as she executed the shot.

"Keep your head up and pull the trigger."

As the ball bounced in front of her, Syd turned sideways and crushed her overhead smash toward her right side, near Flores' backhand. Flores took one step toward the ball and stopped. The shot landed five inches inside the sideline and was past Flores in what seemed like a millisecond.

Game. Set. Match.

The crowd erupted. Russo rushed onto the court, picked up Syd, and twirled her around in his arms. Enzo sunk to his knees in the players' box as the rest of her supporting staff celebrated wildly.

By the time Syd reached the net, Flores was there waiting for her, arms on her hips. Syd extended her hand.

"Congratulations," whispered Flores, as if she was unwilling to show the world her decent side. "You deserved it today."

"Thank you," responded Syd graciously. "It's an honor to compete against the best."

Michael, still stationed at the top of the stadium, collapsed into his chair, unable to disguise his emotion.

ESPN sent its on-court announcer, Bob Bradley, to the court to interview Syd. She wanted to talk about the match but couldn't stop crying. Syd thought about Milena. She longed to share this moment with her.

But Milena had been there, right? She guided Syd right up to the end. But what was she saying before Syd's final serve? Or was Milena a byproduct of dehydration and imagination?

After launching a few autographed balls into the stands, Syd gave a brief courtside interview. Then she walked to the sideline and sat next to Russo.

"I owe this victory to you, coach," she said, trying to avoid getting emotional. "Without your strategy, I would've been just another victim of Flores.

"I know that you've offered to work pro-bono, but I'm having none of it," she said. "I'm paying you from now on, as long as we're working together."

Syd didn't see Enzo and Anja, who exited the players' box and stood on the court behind her.

Enzo had pulled out his cell phone, which was in its calculator setting.

"You're now guaranteed $73K," he said. "My guess is that Russo receives over fourteen thousand. Not bad for a couple of day's work, is it, coach?"

"Not shabby at all," said Russo. "But I won't accept money from Sydney, especially now. She should give it to charity, purchase a home, or maybe spend more time with her parents. Always remember, a parent's love never dies."

"You're going to be compensated!" said Syd. "You are truly a genius."

"What did I tell you!" exclaimed Anja while hugging Syd tightly. "I knew he could help you. But I never dreamed that he could help you *this* much!"

The hour was approaching midnight, and sprinkles of rain fell onto the court as the remaining fans rushed toward the exits.

"The rain came a few minutes late for Flores," said Enzo. "But I'm sure she's in a shower of her own right now, licking her high-and-mighty wounds."

"She's not that bad of a person," replied Syd. "She's just a fierce competitor. This may sound weird, but I think she could become a friend someday."

Samuels, bloated from three hotdogs and two boxes of popcorn, was nearly hoarse after voraciously rooting for Syd.

"That was fun!" he said to Trent. "But I guess this is where the fun ends. Are you ready to climb up into the nosebleeds and arrest Michael Livingstone?"

"We probably should," said Trent. "He can't explain how he acquired the remote control. He also seemed vague about why he attended this tournament. But you know what? I think I'm going to punt for now."

"Whoa, chief," said Samuels. "Why would you wait?"

"Just a hunch, but I can't picture him sneaking into the dressing room to kill his own daughter. Something doesn't fit."

Samuels looked at Trent skeptically..., using a napkin to wipe the last evidence of mustard from the corner of his mouth.

"You're not going to arrest him because of a hunch?" he said. "Are you being straight with me, chief?"

"Yes, Samuels, I am." said Trent. "I'm going to leave him alone for now. Once Syd loses, we'll put him in 'cuffs. But until then, why don't we enjoy the show?"

CHAPTER 32

It would've been easy to celebrate and party all night long. Many players probably would, after such a monumental victory. But every match was vital for Syd, considering physical issues would soon end her career. As long as she continued to win, they'd schedule her to play the next evening again. She was running out of matches, and each deserved 100 percent focus.

When she arrived back at her hotel room at one in the morning, Enzo's bouquet of lilacs awaited her in the lobby. A card accompanying the flowers read: *"Congratulations, Sydney! US Open Qualifier."* Syd held the flowers close to her chest. Then she read the attached card.

"Wait a minute," said Syd. "Do you know something I don't know?"

Anja, Chelsea, Victor, and Nicole emerged from around a corner.

"Surprise!" they all yelled in unison, each taking a turn at hugging Syd.

Enzo was acting like a kid, unable to rein in his excitement.

"With your amazing victory tonight," he said, "you've earned enough points to qualify for the US Open next week! I knew you'd qualify if you won, but I didn't want to tell you. And now, we're both scheduled to play in the Big Apple next week!"

As the group danced wildly, Syd couldn't help but notice a man in a suit, sitting in the lounge nearby, taking in the celebration. The man caught Syd's gaze, although no one else had noticed him. He reached into the pocket of his jacket and flashed a police badge. Syd nodded silently and turned her attention back to the group.

"Nicole and I are going too," said Victor. "We'll all have a great time there."

"Unfortunately, I won't be playing," said Anja, with a smile fading from her face. "It's doctor's orders. They want me to take it easy for a couple of weeks. No practicing and definitely no competing."

"But you look so much better," said Nicole. "Are you sure you can't play?"

"Just this morning, I bench-pressed two hundred pounds in the workout room," said Anja. "I thought I'd be cleared, but the doctors say it's too early."

Victor walked over to Anja and squeezed one of her biceps.

"Anja, just because you're as strong as a bull doesn't mean you're ready to play a three-hour match," said Victor. "Your focus should be to live to fight another day."

"I hope you'll join us in New York, anyway," added Syd. "Enzo and I would love to spend some time with you and Marisha."

Anja attempted to smile, but her face turned serious.

"I'm traveling to New York alone," she said. "I don't know if Marisha is ever coming back. And Russo, he'll probably be spending most of his time with you, Syd. But I understand."

Syd set down the flowers and took Anja into her arms.

"I know life isn't fair right now," she said. "I was the target of whoever operated that ball machine. I had no idea you were standing behind me."

Syd hoped Anja was truthful about harboring no animosity. She would drop Russo in a second if it meant preserving their relationship.

The gathering lasted about an hour. Everyone eventually found their way back to their rooms. Syd and Enzo, buoyed by a couple of glasses of red wine, took a hot shower together and enjoyed an intense but comparatively brief night of lovemaking. Russo probably wouldn't have taken that well, with another match looming. But what he didn't know wouldn't hurt him.

* * * * *

Friday, 9:00 a.m.

I'm sitting here, looking back on an unsuccessful day. Why? Because Sydney is still breathing and taking up valuable space on this planet, oblivious to the pain she's caused.

Sure, she won her match, and I guess I should receive kudos for that. I was one of the people here for her, offering my support.

My mission's success or failure, however, is not determined by wins or losses. Anything short of her demise is a failure.

I'm not a perfectionist, though. I realize there is no perfect plan and no perfect execution. But the prospect of Sydney surviving and returning home to Savannah is completely unacceptable. She must perish. Hopefully, more slowly and painfully than Monica Rivet. I really had nothing against Monica, the poor soul. She was at the wrong place at the wrong time. How tragic!

No one noticed when I had tossed my knife over the fence and into the high grass in a deserted corner of the tennis facility. It was the same weapon that had taken care of Rivet. I entered the legal way, passing through the metal scanners. Luckily, the knife was waiting for me, like a hidden jewel.

Finding that spider was a stroke of luck. It was a sign that I shouldn't abandon my quest to vanquish the dreams of that girl, the one who's caused me so much anguish and pain. Spiders don't scare me, but keeping it alive inside a paper cup wasn't easy. By the time I placed it inside of her tennis bag, it was really pissed.

The spider was meant to be a diversion. With Syd's full attention focused on the insect, I'd have time to sneak behind her and cut her throat. And while she was bleeding out, I'd calmly and patiently explained my reasoning to her. She would've understood everything before she passed into the next world. Perhaps God would judge her more harshly than me once she arrived. Or maybe I'd face the harshest judgment one day. I don't know. Not my call.

I had just enough time to jam that pen inside the exit door without anyone noticing. Luckily, the pen remained in place because no one exited through that door. And no one noticed me entering.

In the end, my gullibility cost me. Sydney hollered out to Samuels, telling him that their stakeout had worked. My first thought was about being taken into custody and placed inside of a confining cell with no way out. It caused me to panic. I ran out the door like a scared seven-year-old. Truly pathetic.

Sydney's victory over Flores bought me a little more time to execute my plan. No more near-misses and no more chickening out. I may not get another shot. I've got to make it work when the time is right.

* * * * *

"Juliana Rabot, from Czechoslovakia," said Enzo, staring at the updated women's draw, while enjoying an expensive room-service breakfast. "She's ranked thirty-fifth in the world. She upset the number-fourteen seed in straight sets. If I were to categorize this match, I would say difficult-but-winnable."

"I remember her playing in the Big Ten," said Syd. "Where was it? Michigan, I think."

"Exactly," said Enzo. "She was the Big Ten runner up. She also made it to the Final 8 in the NCAA Singles Championships. She's a grinding baseliner, but don't take my word for it. I'm sure Russo has a special chapter in his tennis encyclopedia reserved for her."

"I'll be talking to him in a couple of hours," said Syd. "He's really pumped. He thinks I have a shot at winning the whole thing. What a poor, misguided soul!"

* * * * *

By the time evening rolled around, Trent had placed eight security people on duty, two females monitoring the women's locker room and six others scattered throughout the park. The media coverage surpassed any of the major tournaments. A relatively unknown American had cracked the top sixteen of the women's draw, and there was still possibly a killer at large. No player was safe, whether it be at the end of a knife, flying metal sphere, or spider's bite.

As expected, Russo spent two hours with Syd over lunch, dissecting every part of Rabot's game and devising a strategy. Syd was no longer in any mood to question Russo's methods, especially after the Flores match.

Rabot was nothing like Flores, however. She seemed courteous but somewhat reserved. She was the type of player who would make an opponent hit thousands of balls over the course of a match. Russo had structured a plan he referred to as "first strike." The idea was to play consistently with Rabot until Syd had the opportunity to attack.

Early in the match, Syd realized Rabot was not powerful or flashy. She was a consistent, high-percentage player who was willing to grind out points from the baseline.

"She feeds on impatience," Russo said to Syd after Rabot posted a 6-4 win in the first set. "You're attacking a little prematurely. Wait for the right time, and then pull the trigger."

Once Syd settled into the long points and stopped rushing, Rabot eventually provided a ball that Russo termed "attackable." That's when she'd implement Russo's first-strike strategy. Syd eventually broke Rabot's serve and maintained her advantage throughout the second set for a 6-3 win.

The crowd, relatively silent in the first set, became a bigger factor in the match, raucously cheering for Columbus' new "Cinderella Girl." After Syd held serve to go up 1-0 in the third set, Rabot requested an injury timeout because of leg cramps. After the three-minute hiatus, Rabot emerged tentative and sluggish. She abandoned her patient and consistent style, attempting to hit winners on low-percentage shots early in the points. As more of her shots landed away from their intended destinations, Syd's confidence and concentration soared. In what seemed like a flash, Syd was through to the final eight with a 4-6, 6-3, 6-1 victory.

* * * * *

Saturday and Sunday evenings were like a blur. Each day's preparation was basically the same. Breakfast with Enzo, Chelsea, Anja, Nicole, and Victor, followed by an early afternoon strategy session with Russo. Then, a light dinner and her evening match. She learned a long time ago never to change a winning combination.

Playing with newfound confidence and attitude, Syd dusted off Ramona Rawlings, an upcoming eighteen-year-old from Spain, by a 6-4, 6-2 score. Rawlings had recently vaulted all the way into the world's top-ten rankings, but she was no match on the big stage for Syd.

"You have become the player to beat in this tournament," said Russo. "Everyone's afraid to play you. They've heard about our strategy sessions. You're the one doing the playing, of course, but perhaps I've added something as well."

"You're going to be a wealthy coach after this tournament," said Syd. "You'll be handsomely rewarded. And if you don't accept the money, I'll have Nicole come after you with one of her spiders."

* * * * *

Sunday night's semifinal final match turned out to be nothing short of brutal. A nagging light rain fell intermittently throughout the match, causing several stoppages of play. The entire event lasted five hours, ending after 3:00 a.m.

Great Britain's Sandra White was also experiencing a modern-day Cinderella story. The thirty-two-year-old entered the event as the number-thirty-seven ranked player in the world and was fresh off a stunning upset of Japan's Nataliei Odessa. White had one of the most powerful games in tennis, whether she was hitting groundstrokes or transforming her big serve into a heat-seeking missile. She had never become one of the elite players in the world because she lacked the consistency to compete at the upper level. In her earlier rounds, however, she had not lost a single set.

White was the type of player who didn't need to strike the ball twenty times to win a point. When she was on her game, she could end a point with unbridled power.

Before the match, Russo admitted to Syd that he was nervous about facing White.

"She has the power of a Maserati GranTurismo," said Russo. "And the only way you can stop her is to knock her off course. So far, no one's been able to do that, but I have a plan that might work. But believe me, if it doesn't work, you'll be the first to know."

White cut through Syd like a knife in the first set, winning 6-2.

"I'm actually playing well," said Syd to Russo. "If she doesn't start missing, I'll be on my way back to Savannah before midnight."

Whether it was fate or dumb luck, the rain delays took their toll on White's focus and rhythm. After the second delay, which lasted about thirty-five minutes, the accuracy of her shots faded. Syd employed Russo's strategy of mixing in a variety of shots—a slice there, a drop shot here, and then a lob.

The helter-skelter strategy devised by Russo, combined with even more rain delays, unnerved White. She dropped the second set 6-4 and trailed 4-1 in the third. After another short rain delay, she begged the head umpire to suspend the match for the evening.

"No one can continue playing with all of this starting and stopping nonsense," she said. "Can't we suspend play until morning?"

Unfortunately for White, the tournament was already running days behind because of the investigation. The head official had no choice but to insist that the players complete their match.

Syd easily rolled to a 6-1 win in the third set, easily conquering an unfocused White. The finals were scheduled for 4:00 p.m. on Tuesday. Her opponent would be twenty-one-year-old Desiree Kitchens from Ft. Lauderdale, who was riding high after upsetting legend Sandy Willard in the other semifinal.

After the match, several tennis apparel companies asked Syd to endorse their product lines. The ESPN announcers lauded Russo as one of the best analytics-driven coaches in the world. Throughout the semifinal match, the cameras focused on Enzo, trying to capture his reactions to the big points. For the time being, Sydney Livingstone was the shining star of the women's tennis world.

And for a brief time during all the fanfare and hoopla, Sydney almost forgot that someone was trying to kill her.

CHAPTER 33

"I'm taking everyone to breakfast this morning!" said Enzo, jumping out of bed at 8:30 and heading for the shower. "It's time to celebrate!"

"That's quite a promise," said Syd, rolling over on the warm spot vacated by Enzo. "There are 329 million people in this country. I hope you brought your unlimited credit card."

Enzo stepped into the bathtub and pulled the translucent sliding doors to a close.

"I'm offering to pay for an entire group, and you make a joke," he said. "I'm talking about everyone in your players' box. You know who they are."

"Too bad we can't ask my dad to join us," said Syd, pouring a miniature pitcher of water down the back of the hotel-provided coffee maker. "My parents need to learn how to play nice."

Syd could see Enzo's outline as he rubbed shampoo onto his head and over his sleek body. She longed to join him but decided to save her energy for later in the evening.

"Actually," said Enzo, as the hot water ran down his backside, "you should be the person who's treating. Do you realize how much money you've earned in the past few days?"

Enzo was a business major at TCU, where he played three years of college tennis before turning pro. Syd thought he'd become an accountant one day because of his penchant for keeping track of every penny.

"Why don't you tell me, honey?" said Syd. "I'm surprised we haven't discussed this already."

Enzo slid the shower doors open, reached for a towel, and buffed himself dry.

"According to my calculations, you're guaranteed $185,000 by making it to the finals, with an extra $100K if—I mean when—you win it. And since you also qualified for the US Open, you're guaranteed $61K more just for showing up. You're the same person who worried about making your rent payment last month. Why don't you spring for a few extra stacks of pancakes?"

Syd grabbed a towel off the shelf next to the shower, rolled it up, and flicked it at Enzo, narrowly missing his buttocks.

"Obviously, you haven't checked out the prices at the restaurant downstairs," she said, wrapping her arms around his neck. "Won't you please go halfsies with me, darling?"

"Okay, you talked me into it," said Enzo, pulling Syd tightly against his naked body. "I guess I can belly up for a few extra hash browns and a croissant if I absolutely must."

Enzo lifted Syd off of her feet and brought her to the bed, where they both crash-landed.

Syd smiled, stretched, let out an overly dramatic yawn, and rolled on top of Enzo.

So much for conserving energy, she thought.

By the time Syd and Enzo arrived downstairs, Chelsea, Anja, Nicole, and Victor already occupied the large round table.

"You two are fifteen minutes late," said Chelsea. "Did you oversleep?"

Syd and Enzo stole a quick glance at each other.

"Something like that," said Syd. "What looks tasty on the menu today? By the way, Enzo is paying."

"Wait!" said Victor, rising from his chair. "Did you actually say that Enzo is treating? Whenever he opens his wallet, bats fly out. Today is truly legendary!"

After the laughter settled, Nicole made another announcement.

"Today is also something else," she said. "It's—drumroll please—Girls' Day Out!"

Syd looked at Enzo and shrugged.

"Yes," said Nicole. "Anja and I prepared a special treat for you, Syd. You don't have to play until four o'clock tomorrow, so we have the entire day!"

"How does this sound?" interjected Anja. "A picnic in a park. We can eat lunch, hike—nothing exhausting, of course—and swim in the lake. We'll chill out, eat some naughty food, and have a few laughs."

"Don't worry about Enzo," said Victor. "We have a practice court at 1:30. Peons like us, who lost in the early rounds, need to maintain our form for the US Open."

Speaking of early departures, Syd wondered if O'Malley was still in town. He'd lost a close three-setter to Jules Willems.

"I'll take care of Enzo while you three have fun," said Victor. "And who knows, Enzo and I may eventually stumble upon our own watering hole!"

Enzo nodded at Syd to let her know he was fine with the idea.

Syd looked over at her mother.

"Would you like to join us?" she asked. "It would be fun, all of us getting away together."

"I would love to," said Chelsea. "But Brian is flying into Columbus this afternoon to watch you play tomorrow. We plan to go shopping, find a nice restaurant, and check out the sites of Columbus. We may even take in a show if we can find one."

Chelsea put her hand on her daughter's shoulder.

"Have fun with your friends, but make sure you're never alone," she said. "There's safety in numbers."

Once a mother, always a mother.

Anja picked up Nicole and Syd at the front of the hotel. Her white Ford Escape rental had plenty of room for bags and a picnic lunch. Next to the basket was a large red cooler filled with ice and about twelve bottles of specialty beers.

On the way to the park, Syd received a congratulatory call from her father. She thanked him and mentioned she was taking some time away with friends.

"I'm so proud of you," he said. "You've taken the tennis world by storm."

But then, Michael's tone changed.

"There's something we need to discuss when you're alone. Will you call me tonight or tomorrow, before your match?"

"Sure," said Syd. "Is everything okay?"

"I think so," said Michael. "I have a meeting scheduled with Trent today. He considers me a suspect. But I'm going to tell him something he needs to know. That's what I need to discuss with you."

"Of course, Dad," she said. "I'll call you later tonight.

"And one more thing, Dad," said Syd. "I love you."

* * * * *

Fried chicken, potato salad, sugar cookies, and microbrews are not the staples of world-class athletes—or even world-renowned spider collectors. But a picnic, hike, and a dip into a swimming hole were exactly what Syd needed.

She forgot to notify security about her impromptu party plans. It didn't really matter, though. What could possibly happen in such a beautiful setting?

"Wouldn't it be great if it were nighttime already?" said Nicole. "We could build a campfire and tell ghost stories!"

Obviously, the microbrews were stronger than Nicole had expected.

"I hope you guys didn't plan for this to be an all-day event," said Syd. "I have a hitting session with Russo tonight. And not a word to Russo about the beer, Anja!"

"My lips are sealed," said Anja. "I need no more ene-mies, especially after having my cranium nearly caved in."

"Your head looks better than your forearm," said Ni-cole. "How did you get that awful scratch?"

"You can thank Russo for that," said Anja. "He's a wonder-ful coach, but his racquet stringing leaves a lot to be desired. When he cut off a knot, he left a sharp edge. While practic-ing, I scraped my forearm against it. If someone didn't know better, they'd think I tried to slash my wrist or something!"

The trio told more funny stories while washing down their cookies with beer. Anja eventually opened up about her split with Marisha.

"You know, I thought that she was my soul mate," said Anja. "But I really think she's gone forever now. But I'm happy you two seem to have found love.

"And Syd, you've found a new coach who's taken you to the precipice of greatness. So there's a lot to celebrate today."

By 5:00 p.m., Syd pounded bottles of ice water instead of microbrews. She needed a productive practice session with Russo tonight if she was going to perform at peak effectiveness tomorrow.

Anja emerged from the nearby woods after a quick na-ture break. She reached into her duffel bag and pulled out a sharp knife with a long blade.

"I really don't want to scare either of you," she said. "But when I was in the woods, I heard something rustling nearby. It's probably just a raccoon or coyote, but the noise spooked me. I had the feeling that someone or something was watching me.

"Will the two of you remain here while I check it out?" she asked. "Keep your cell phones nearby, just in case. I'm sure it's nothing."

"You're not going alone!" said Syd. "We're going with you."

"Not a good idea, Syd," said Anja. "Do you have that scratchy device? Tiger Paw or something?"

"It's called Tiger Claw, and it's in my bag," said Syd. "But you shouldn't go alone. Why don't I call Trent? He'll be pissed that I've wandered away, but what's he going to do, take away my birthday?"

Anja walked a little closer to Syd and Nicole.

"It's probably nothing," she said. "If I'm not back in ten minutes, you can call Trent. But that won't happen. I'll be right back."

Anja located a path leading into the woods and, in less than a minute, disappeared from sight. Nicole looked at Syd and shook her head.

"If I wasn't copping a major buzz, I'd be terrified right now," she said. "Anja is stubborn. I guess you have to be when you're a world-class athlete—independent to a fucking fault!"

Syd stared down the path where she entered the woods.

"She does that," she said. "If something is bothering her, she attacks it head-on, so she doesn't have to worry about it later."

Syd pulled out her phone and typed in a number.

"Are you calling Trent already?" asked Nicole. "I thought she asked us to wait."

301

"Not Trent," said Syd. "I need to speak to Russo. I'm down to two racquets with strings in them. Imagine if I break all my strings tomorrow. Jack McDuff would eat me for lunch!"

After three rings, Russo answered his phone. He sounded groggy like he just woke up.

"Yes, Syd," he answered. "We're on for eight tonight, right? I hope you're not partying with Anja and that spider lady."

The phone was still on speaker. Nicole looked at Syd and smiled sheepishly.

"I'm not partying anymore," said Syd. "I've morphed into Ice Mountain water now. We're heading back to the hotel soon. But I need two racquets strung. If I give them to you tonight, would you finish them before match time?"

"Yes," said Russo. "A guy in the players' lounge strings racquets for $25. I stopped stringing a few years ago because of a damaged tendon in my elbow."

Nicole sat up and looked at Syd.

"Wait a second!" said Syd. "Anja told me you string her racquets. Didn't she cut her arm on a racquet that you strung?"

"I haven't strung a racquet in years," said Russo. "I've never strung one for Anja."

Syd could feel her heart racing.

"But what about her arm?" asked Syd.

"I asked Anja, and she seemed evasive," said Russo. "I figured she had a confrontation with Marisha."

A rustling sound emerged from the woods. Anja walked on the trail toward them, a few hundred yards away.

"Quickly," said Syd to Russo. "Did you see Belov check out of the hotel?"

"No," said Russo. "Anja told me she'd left late at night. But that's not like Marisha. She's terrified of the dark. It was like a phobia."

"Okay, thanks, Russo," said Syd, loud enough for the approaching Anja to hear. "I'll see you tonight. I'll be ready to work hard."

Then, almost imperceptibly under her breath, she whispered to Russo.

"Call Trent."

CHAPTER 34

"Who were you talking to?" asked Anja as she returned from the woods. "It sounded like Russo."

Syd stood up and felt for her Tiger Claw, concealed in the pocket of her floral chino shorts she'd put on after swimming.

"Yes, that was Russo," said Syd. "I was just double-checking on our eight o'clock session. We need to leave soon."

Anja looked at Syd suspiciously.

"I've worked with Russo for almost two years," said Anja. "Once he schedules a practice time, he never breaks it. Did you think he'd alter his plans before a championship match?"

Before Syd could respond, Nicole interrupted. "Did you see anyone?" she asked, standing with her arms folded.

Anja nodded her head affirmatively but maintained eye contact.

"Some asshole has been watching us, ladies," she said. "When I returned to where I'd heard the noise, there was silence. Then I heard a twig snap. I swung around and saw someone—a male—scurry through the brush.

"I thought about pursuing him, but I thought I should come back and warn you guys."

"Maybe it was just a young kid," said Syd.

Anja stood erect with the knife in her right hand, with the blade pointing straight at the ground.

"It was probably some perv who watched us swim, looking for a cheap thrill. But given the circumstances, we need to leave this area."

Nicole checked her compass. "The car's parked about a mile in this direction," she said, pointing to the southeast. "If we speed-walk it, we can get there in ten minutes."

Anja squinted her eyes and shook her head.

"Whoever was watching is between us and the car," said Anja. "We need to take an alternate route. We passed a small cave to the north of here while we were hiking. Let's go back and find it. We'll hide there and call for help."

The carefree, fun-loving Anja, who had spent the entire afternoon with Syd and Nicole, seemed deeply bothered. "I'm concerned that someone was spying," said Anja. "We can be at the cave in five minutes. And it's in the opposite direction of the stalker."

"But you said it's probably a kid," said Nicole. "Why take a detour?"

"Syd said that," said Anja. "I said a perv."

Nicole pulled her cell phone from her pocket.

"Why don't I call 911?"

Anja snatched the phone from Nicole's hand and placed it in her own pocket.

"Let's not be sitting ducks," said Anja. "Follow me."

Reluctantly, Syd and Nicole trailed Anja until they arrived at a small cave. Leading into the cave was a dirt path flanked on each side by distinct sets of flora. A small waterfall flowed nearby, emptying into a narrow stream.

"I'm going to be honest," said Anja. "I'm not thrilled about closed-in places. You guys can enter before me. If there's enough room inside, I'll join you."

Syd and Nicole made eye contact, but not long enough for Anja to notice.

"After you, spider woman," said Syd, sticking her arm straight out with her palm facing up. "Once you clear the trail of creepy-crawlies, I'll follow you in."

The cave's small opening belied its actual size. Its ceiling climbed ten feet high, with the cave's depth extending to about half the size of a football field.

"It's fine in here," said Syd. "It's much bigger once you step inside."

Anja ducked below the cave's opening, relieved by its vast size. She removed Nicole's phone from her pocket and tossed it to her.

"Now would be the perfect time to call for help," said Anja. "If anyone comes into the cave, they'll have to face my knife and Syd's Tiger Paw."

"Anja," Syd interrupted. "it's called Tiger Claw. It got its name because it has claws that expand and retract, just like a cat. Tiger Claw is no match for your huge knife, but it's not something you'd want penetrating your eyes."

Syd hoped she had sold the benefits of the Tiger Claw, just in case Anja had ulterior motives.

Nicole entered numbers on the phone. Then she tried again.

"Damn it! I can't get reception. This place is like a vault."

Syd and Anja both tried their phones as well. Nothing.

"Let's wait in here for fifteen minutes," said Anja. "If that guy doesn't reappear, we'll make a run for my car."

Anja stood closest to the cave exit, ostensibly to be first to leave if the situation turned claustrophobic. Her eyes remained peeled on the entrance while she sharpened her knife against a rock.

Syd held her Tiger Claw in her right hand, with her thumb on the button, ready to expand the device's talons. Nicole sat on a rock near the back of the cave, wondering if she'd ever see Victor and her arachnid friends again.

After about ten minutes, Nicole summoned her courage, got up off the rock, and walked toward Anja.

"I'm leaving now," she said. "I know it hasn't been fifteen minutes, but if you're going to kill us, I wish you'd get started right now."

Anja stood up and faced Nicole, eye to eye.

"What in the flying fuck are you talking about?" she asked. "I know some of those foreign beers were around 9 percent, but they're not supposed to make you act bat-shit crazy."

"We know about your arm injury," interjected Syd. "You didn't get that scratch from some misaligned racquet string. It happened during a fight, didn't it? Possibly a life-and-death struggle?"

"Syd, what are you talking about?" said Anja. "I already told you how I got that injury!"

Anja looked sternly at both women. She didn't like being outnumbered.

"When I was a kid, I lost my two best friends," said Anja. "And do you know why? Because they teamed up on me, like you two she-clowns. How did we transform a perfect day into a shit-flinging show?"

"If Marisha Belov were present, the numbers would be even-steven," said Nicole. "But she's not. She vanished in the dead of night, despite being terrified of the dark! Or maybe, you're not telling the truth?" continued Nicole. "Maybe you conveniently got rid of her!"

"I'm losing my temper," said Anja, pressing the sharp edge of the knife into a large boulder. "Maybe I should allow you to leave so you can get slaughtered by this peeping-tom, psycho, son of a bitch. Isn't that what friends are for?"

"So you're going to let me leave?" asked Nicole.

"Go ahead, Nicole; leave," said Anja, pointing her hand toward the exit. "I have a knife, but I won't stab you. Be my guest."

As Syd started to speak, Anja's attention became diverted from Nicole, who used the opportunity to pick up a stone and hurl it toward Anja. The rock struck her in the temple, and she fell backward. As Anja's back and head hit the ground, the knife became dislodged from her hand.

Syd took three steps forward and dove onto the ground, grabbing hold of the knife. Anja also reached for the knife but ended up clutching Syd's left hand.

The two players who'd overcome so much adversity on the court as a doubles team now fought for their lives, trying to gain control of the knife. Syd's left hand slid near the blade as Anja pulled down on the handle. Warm blood running down her arm alerted Syd the knife had cut her, but she didn't feel pain.

Nicole picked up a rock and drew a bead on Anja's head. But every time she was about to strike, both women would adjust their positions.

Finally, Anja rolled back on top of Syd, whose hand was bleeding even more profusely. Nicole gripped the rock firmly in her hand and readied herself to bring the stone down with as much force as she could muster.

Click.

The sound of a gun being cocked.

"Drop the stone, or I swear I'll blow your head off," said a male voice.

Syd and Anja released their grips on the knife and stopped struggling. Nicole opened her palm and let the stone crash to the ground.

Standing at the entrance was a powerful man carrying a .357 revolver. Syd knew the man well.

He was Christopher Samuels, one of Trent's favorite detectives and a downright goon of a fellow.

"What the hell?" said Samuels.

The women were speechless.

"First, Syd sneaks away without alerting her security detail. Now, after I finally locate you with my tracking device, you three are about to kill each other. Forgive me for saying it, but this girls' day out thing seems a little overrated."

Samuels' phone rang. He answered it while keeping his weapon pointed toward the women.

"Trent!" said Samuels. "I located Syd. She's with Nicole and Anja in Big Bluff Cave, by the waterfall. If I arrived three seconds later, someone would be dead."

For the next few minutes, Samuels kept the women at bay with his gun. By the time Trent arrived, Syd and Anja had caught their breath.

"I received a call from Russo," said Trent. "He informed me about Anja Radonovic. He was absolutely heartbroken." Then he looked over at Samuels. "Good job, Chris. You prevented a dangerous situation from getting worse."

Trent placed Anja in handcuffs while reading her Miranda Rights. Anja protested vigorously, panicking at the thought of being shackled.

"I did nothing wrong!" she shouted. "Why are you arresting me? Take me out of these handcuffs, please. I can't breathe."

"Samuels, take Syd to the hospital," said Trent, looking at the blood cascading down her forearm. "I'll take Ms. Radonovic back to the station and book her. Murder one."

Anja struggled, but Trent's grip was too strong. She hung her head and walked toward his police car.

Nicole approached Samuels. "May I hitch a ride to the hospital? Anja drove, and I'd like to accompany Syd."

"Fine," said Samuels. "We'll walk to my car. It's parked on a gravel road three-quarters of a mile from here."

Syd asked Samuels if he'd spied on them.

"Yeah," he answered. "That was me. Trent freaked when he realized that you slipped away. Luckily, we had your cell number, and I could track you.

"I didn't want to interrupt your fun," continued Samuels. "That's why I hid when Anja came looking. I guess I wasn't stealthy enough."

On the trip to the hospital, Syd thought about Marisha Belov. She was a major presence at the beginning of the tournament. But suddenly, she was gone, like a nova burning itself from existence.

"Do you guys know anything about Marisha?" asked Syd. "It's odd how she's gone missing. You haven't stumbled upon any more bodies, have you?"

"Not Belov's body, if that's what you're asking," said Samuels. "But I heard on the radio today that someone found Hawthorne dead. He's that prick of a reporter who likes to throw his weight."

"Yes, we both know him," she gasped. "He's the guy that hassled me when I was warming up before my match. You had to knock him on his ass just to get his attention."

"That I did," replied Samuels. "I'm sure there's no shortage of suspects. Someone sliced him up in his own driveway this morning. His wife stumbled over him while she was walking outside to get the newspaper. If I didn't know better, I'd think Trent did it. Those two hated each other. But, of course, we know that's impossible."

CHAPTER 35

Syd and Enzo returned to their hotel at around eleven on Tuesday morning, five hours prior to her championship match. They had just completed a two-hour meeting downtown with Trent and her father, Michael.

Luckily for Syd, the cut to her left hand, suffered during her battle with Anja, was on the bottom edge of her palm, below the little finger. No tendons or ligaments were severed. The wound would only be a factor when she hit her two-handed backhand. A trainer would have to change the dressing and re-wrap the injury throughout the championship match. The cut would cause discomfort, but there was a reasonable possibility of finishing the match.

The meeting in Trent's office made Syd's head spin. The information was too much to comprehend, especially with a title match looming.

She replayed portions of her conversation with Trent.

"Given what's happened during the last day, we will not pursue charges against Michael," said Trent. "It's apparent someone planted the remote control device on his car.

"Mr. Livingstone, you are free to leave and enjoy your daughter's match. Hopefully, the Franklin County prosecutor's office will leave you alone from this point forward."

Syd leaned over in her chair and gave a warm embrace to her father.

"I think that's how we have to manage our father-daughter relationship," she said. "From this point forward."

Relieved that her father's name had been cleared, she remained apprehensive about how the case would unfold.

"I will notify the media this afternoon that we have a person-of-interest in this case," said Trent. "I won't mention anyone's name until your match is completed. I want you to focus out there."

Trent leaned over his desk and made direct eye contact with Syd.

"Ms. Livingstone, you will no longer go anywhere without security. Is that understood?"

Syd turned to Enzo and smiled.

"You have my word, lieutenant," she said. "I will welcome your crew's protection until I'm on my way back to Savannah."

"And hopefully, with a huge trophy in your back seat," said Trent. "You know, everyone in my office is rooting for you."

Toward the end of the meeting, Trent excused Enzo and Michael from the room so he and Syd could engage in a private conversation. At the end of the session, she thought about how much had changed since she'd embarked on the ten-hour trek to Columbus. In some ways, these past few days were difficult and heartbreaking. But in other ways, she'd experienced enormous growth, both personally and professionally.

Syd's heart ached over her fight with Anja. She could still envision a hyperventilating Anja being taken away in handcuffs.

Trent discussed the case with Syd, including the latest information provided by Michael. When the meeting ended, Syd didn't know what to believe. She needed to stay focused enough to cross the finish line. Hopefully, Trent and his crew could take care of the rest.

Syd was scheduled to meet Russo at three for a pre-match warmup. She dreaded it.

Russo told Syd he was devastated over providing information that led to Anja's detainment. "I feel like I've betrayed my own daughter," he said.

By the time Russo arrived at Court 9, hundreds of fans, writers, and photographers were waiting there. Russo's eyes were bloodshot, and large red circles underscored his eyes.

"I haven't slept since yesterday afternoon," he told Syd. "I've been studying notes, reviewing videos, and worrying myself sick over Anja. I have our master plan for this match," he said, pulling out a small binder. "Given the circumstances, we haven't had the chance to go over it, but we'll improvise during the match."

Russo brought out a ball machine to the court, spawning a few terrible memories for Syd.

"Don't worry about this machine," said Russo, attempting to inject mild humor in the situation. "I've examined the balls. Nothing metallic is in there."

Syd looked over at Samuels, who was standing nearby. He gave Syd a thumbs-up sign.

"We vetted the machine as well," said Samuels. "You'll be fine, although I wouldn't advise you to stick your head near the ball launcher."

By the time four o'clock rolled around, rumors were flying that Anja confessed to the crimes of the past week, including the murder of Monica Rivet. Some claimed the injury to Syd's hand was so serious that she would retire early in the final match and then withdraw from the US Open.

The television commentators tried to focus exclusively on tennis. Sydney Livingstone and Desiree Kitchens were modern-day success stories. One week ago, Sydney was an obscure, struggling player on the women's tour. Suddenly, she was one of the most popular players in the world. Kitchens graduated from historically black Tennessee State University, where she won an NCAA singles title. Her semifinal victory over number one ranked Sandy Willard legitimized her reputation as one of the world's top players.

Vegas bettors installed Kitchens as a 5-2 favorite in the match. Her supreme athleticism and all-encompassing net game gave her a substantial edge over Syd.

In a nutshell, Russo's plan was to use Kitchens' speed against her, a task that was easier to draw up on paper than implement. He wanted Syd to move Kitchens in one direction and then hit the next shot behind her.

"Fast players abhor changing direction," Russo told Syd.

"Make her run left and right, and vice-versa. Once you 'wrong foot' her a few times, she'll start second-guessing herself. If you can confuse her, you can win this match."

But nobody in the stadium was more confused than Syd. Her meeting with Trent left her numb, questioning what was real and what wasn't. She wished that she had a close friend at courtside. She loved Enzo, but their relationship was beyond friendship.

Anja would have sufficed, but recent events prevented that from happening. She needed her Italian friend, former doubles partner, and confidante. What if Milena had reached out before taking her life? Syd kicked herself for not extending an olive branch to Milena in order to save the relationship. Moments before the biggest match of her life, she sensed Milena's presence. She could almost smell her DNA.

Syd looked into her players' box. Nicole was all smiles, clinging to Victor and raising her fist to Syd as a sign of support. She longed for Nicole to join her at courtside, while Russo managed logistical matters. Chelsea and Brian sat directly behind Nicole and Victor. Syd wondered if her stepfather was as excited as he seemed or if he was playing a role to support Chelsea. She didn't know Brian well, but she valued him because he made her mother happy.

Sitting next to Enzo was an imposing figure who towered over everyone. It was Peter O'Malley, the guy who helped her improve her volley. Syd felt indebted to Peter since her accurate volleys played a major role in her success this week. But where had O'Malley been lately?

As much as Syd appreciated O'Malley's help, she didn't trust him completely. He played a pivotal role in ending her relationship with Milena. Her friend was now a sad memory. A visitor in a dream. A mere voice passing through her head during troubled times.

Compartmentalize and concentrate! Syd told herself. *You're facing someone who is flying high after upsetting the greatest player of all time. She's like a piranha, ready to rip the flesh from my bones. And for God's sake, quit thinking about Trent and the information he's uncovered. There's no time to process that. Focus on the pre-match warmup. Find your rhythm and acclimate yourself to her power.*

A solid warmup led to a fast start for Syd, as she raced out to a 4-1 lead in the first set. Russo's strategy of moving Kitchens back and forth and then hitting behind her was working. But Kitchens struck the ball as hard as anyone she'd ever faced. At 5-2, Syd's cut throbbed from beneath her bandage. She called for a medical timeout.

"Keep moving her," said Russo, as a trainer unwrapped the bandages. "She's recognizing what you're doing. If she stops overcommitting to our change of direction, we may have to alter our plan."

The trainer, an attractive woman in her late twenties, grimaced while examining Syd's cut. She gestured to the courtside doctor, a graying man in a blue suit. After examining the injury, the doctor spoke to Syd.

"I don't like what I see," he said. "Your injury is seeping green fluid, and there's swelling. It's definitely infected. What type of pain are you experiencing?"

"To be honest, it's throbbing like hell," said Syd. "But I can't walk away now."

Russo could tell the doctor was concerned.

"Sydney, you've performed magically at this tournament," he said. "You've had a great run and made an awful lot of money. Maybe it's time to put a wrap on everything. If you don't injure it worse, perhaps you can play in the US Open."

"I'm not in the finals of the US Open," she said. "I'm in the finals here. I may never get this opportunity again!"

The head umpire informed Syd and Russo that their three-minute injury timeout had ended.

"I'm going to keep playing," said Syd, getting up off her chair and walking toward the court. "I've overcome too much to stop now."

As each game went by, the two-handed backhand became more painful. Kitchens sensed the weakness and directed more shots to her backhand.

Extraneous thoughts flowed through Syd's mind early in the match, but the hand injury helped her focus on the task at hand—overcoming pain and moving to the ball.

Several crushing forehands from Syd, along with a few unforced errors from Kitchens, gave Syd a 6-3 first-set win. She continued to roll early in the second set, jumping out to a 3-2 advantage. Despite the trainer reapplying a new bandage at every court change, the pain became almost intolerable.

Kitchens broke Syd's serve to tie it at 3-all, held her own serve, and then broke Syd again to take a 5-3 lead in the second set. Although Syd recovered by breaking Kitchen's serve in the next game, three double-faults sealed her fate, giving Kitchens the second set, 6-4.

"You should retire now," said Russo, during the break between sets. "You're wincing every time you hit your backhand. Tell the umpire you're retiring, and let's get you some treatment."

The courtside doctor made an unsolicited appearance during the break between sets.

"Can you describe the pain to me?" he asked Syd.

"It feels like someone's doing hand surgery when I hit my backhand," said Syd.

The doctor looked at Syd and Russo. He reached into his pocket, pulled out a paper, and quickly signed his name on it.

"I'm writing you a prescription to take these," he said, holding three reddish pills in his palm. "It won't help the infection, but it may help the pain."

"What type of painkiller is it?" asked Syd, taking the pills into her hand.

"The type that works," said the doctor.

"Let's go with that," said Syd, tossing the pills into her mouth and chasing them with water.

Early in the third set, Syd's goal was to stay as close to Kitchens as possible in order to buy time until the medicine kicked in. Whatever the doctor prescribed didn't take long to work. With the players knotted at 2-all, the pain had diminished considerably. It now felt like a child's pinch, irritating but tolerable.

During a crucial game at 4-all, the two players battled through four points that lasted at least thirty-five shots, and Syd won three of the four. A two-handed swinging volley winner gave Syd a 5-4 lead, but she could feel the cut tear open as she followed through with the shot.

She plopped down on her chair as Russo and the trainer flanked her on both sides.

"That painkiller was some good shit," said Syd, as the trainer removed the tape. "But I felt something odd when I hit that last ball. Can you check it out?"

The trainer looked down and gasped.

"Don't look at it," she said. "You may become light-headed."

"If I can't see it, it never happened," said Syd. "Do you recommend that I continue?"

"If you were my best friend, daughter, or someone like that, I'd say no," she said. "But considering that you're one game away from becoming the MMO champion, I think it would be okay."

Russo looked over the trainer's shoulder while she attended to Syd.

"Sydney, I saw the cut," he said. "It's downright horrifying. If you don't close out this match within ten minutes, I will stop it. I have that authority as your coach."

"Please, don't!" said Syd. "Let me finish this. I won't get this chance again."

"You're winning on guts alone," said Russo. "She's adjusted to our change-of-direction strategy."

"I figured that out already," said Syd.

"I want you to do the exact opposite of what you've been doing," he said. "Instead of moving her side-to-side, I want you to hit every ball directly at her, deep and down the middle."

Syd looked at Russo as if he'd just arrived from outer space.

"Why would you want me to hit shots right at her?"

"By directing your shots deep and in the middle, she won't be able to hit those angles anymore," he said. "She'll need to win games the old-fashioned way, grinding out extended points from the backcourt!"

Syd nodded and headed to the court, too tired and worn out to argue. She would either win or lose with Russo's strategy—one ball at a time.

Kitchens seemed surprised by Syd's alternative plan. After chasing down hundreds of balls throughout the match, she was now fending off shots aimed at her. Once Kitchens realized that her angled shots weren't available, she approached the net on two shots but fell victim to a pair of Sydney's passing shots.

Just two points from victory, Syd then did the improbable. She not only double-faulted once but twice. Her wound was bleeding from below the bandages, and the throbbing had returned.

"She's choking!" yelled a rotund, intoxicated man from high up in the stadium.

30-all.

Syd knew that if blood seeped from beneath the bandages, they would halt the match. If the medical staff could not stop the blood flow in a timely manner, they would default her.

Few people in the crowd expected what happened next. Syd put her serve in play, and the point lasted for over seventy shots. She kept hitting the ball deep down the center of the court, almost under Kitchens' feet. Kitchens, now hesitant to approach the net, stayed back in a mind-numbing display of consistency.

The point eclipsed 120 strokes. Finally, Syd attempted a crosscourt angle shot, which clipped the top of the net and bounced on Kitchens' side.

Known for her explosiveness and speed, Kitchens sprinted forward and arrived at the ball before it bounced a second time. She directed a shot down the line, out of Syd's reach. But because the ball had bounced close to the net, Kitchens needed an upward trajectory to clear the net. The ball landed two inches beyond the baseline.

40-30.

The crowd stood on its feet and cheered, mesmerized over the most grueling and competitive individual points of the year.

Syd studied the scoreboard just to make sure she wasn't hallucinating. It showed her leading 5-4 and 40-30. Big yellow words at the bottom of the board displayed "Championship Point."

She was just one point from victory and a $346,000 payday, not to mention her first title on the WTA Tour.

Syd's first serve floated harmlessly into the net. The 120-shot rally sucked most of the life out of her body. Her legs felt like wooden pegs, and she could no longer thrust them upward to generate power on her serve. Another marathon point was completely out of the question. The pain in her hand was back in triplicate, burning and piercing.

The sands of the hourglass were running out, despite being one point from victory. Her only chance to get her serve into play was to guide a floating loop, completely bereft of power, into her opponent's service box. Kitchens, aware of Syd's pathetic effort on the first serve, moved well into the court, looking to pounce on any type of weak offering. Simply getting the ball in play wouldn't be sufficient. Kitchens would hit a winner, erasing Syd's match point. With her legs shot, Kitchens would eventually win this game and then the match. Her one chance to win a Masters 1000 title would vanish.

Syd bounced the ball several times, preparing to hit the second serve. Her thoughts turned again to Milena. She exhaled and closed her eyes. Milena's face implanted itself firmly in her mind.

What advice would Milena offer?

Like a shooting star in a clear sky, the answer appeared. Milena would tell her to gather up every ounce of energy in her body and attempt to crush a service ace, with no holds barred.

Go for it all or go home.

"Get your serve in play," Russo said, as the raucous crowd drowned out the sound of his voice. The umpire asked for silence. Soon, there was barely a sound in the entire stadium.

Syd bounced the ball two more times and lifted it into the air. She bent her knees as far as they would go, thrust upward with her legs, and struck the ball as hard as she could.

After the ball left Syd's racquet, her knees buckled under her, and she collapsed to the ground, her chest striking the concrete below her at full force. The impact knocked the wind out of her, and she lay sprawled out on the court, temporarily devoid of oxygen.

She still kept her head up to track the path of the serve. She saw the ball crossing over the net and heading down the middle of the court, toward the centerline. Kitchens, stunned by the powerful serve, stuck her racquet out, attempting to block the ball into play. The ball clipped the outer edge of the line and skimmed underneath Kitchens' racquet. It contacted the backstop with a resounding thud.

The line judge, manning the center service line, placed his hands in front of him with palms down, acknowledging the serve was good.

Enzo and Trent leaped over their seats and headed toward the court. O'Malley stood high above everyone else, arms thrust into the air. Chelsea, sitting next to Brian, laughed in amazement, her right hand placed over her heart. Nicole jumped to her feet and cheered while Trent and Samuels positioned themselves on the court to keep uninvited guests away from Syd.

In the upper echelon of the stadium, Michael Livingstone sprinted back and forth wildly, high-fiving everyone in sight.

Russo and several linespeople assisted Syd to her feet. When she arrived at the net, Kitchens placed both arms around her and gave her a congratulatory hug.

For five consecutive minutes, the crowd stood and cheered, chanting the name of their new favorite daughter: "Sydney!"

"Sydney!"

Once the commotion settled, TV announcer Pamela Stillwell stood next to Syd, smiling brightly with her microphone extended.

"How does it feel, Sydney?" she asked. "Can you put this week into words?"

Syd stopped and thought for a moment. She wasn't sure what words would flow from her mouth but eventually spoke.

"I've never been so happy, and I've never been so sad," she said, holding onto the net post for support.

"I've never been so fearless and yet, so fearful.

"I've never been so secure and yet, so vulnerable.

"I've never been so energized and yet, so exhausted,"

With that, Syd thanked the Columbus crowd, limped off the court, and headed into the tunnel, disappearing from view.

CHAPTER 36

S yd walked gingerly through the tunnel, her tennis
bag flung over her shoulder and her legs feeling as
if they each weighed 100 pounds. Trent and Samuels
flanked her as she took a right to enter the main part of
the tennis complex. Russo caught up to the threesome
and placed his right arm across Syd's shoulders.

"You proved today you are a true champion," said
Russo. "I only know of one or maybe two players over
my lifetime who have ever shown such courage."

Syd thought about asking Russo which players he was
referring to, but she was too exhausted to pursue that
line of questioning. Her goal at this point was to arrive at
the players' lounge, rip the bandages from her hand, and
melt into a hot shower.

It didn't take long for fans to spot Syd walking through
the facility. Hordes of swooning admirers surrounded
her, desiring a picture and an autograph.

"Please step back and give Ms. Livingstone room," announced Trent. "She's scheduled to arrive at the Cham-
pions Loft in about forty-five minutes for the trophy
presentation. She may address your requests at that time."

Several officers walked ahead of Syd, clearing her path to the players' lounge, which was several hundred yards in the distance.

A middle-aged female reporter, clad in a tight-fitting white bodysuit, jumped in front of Syd with her accomplice's camera rolling.

"Tell us about the murder investigation," she screamed. "Is your doubles partner responsible?"

"Please, I need to get to the showers," said Syd.

"Ma'am, you must maintain a clear distance from the athlete," said Trent. "She's not answering questions about the investigation."

As they moved closer to their destination, another male reporter shouted out a question. "Do you anticipate someone stalking you in New York during the US Open?"

Syd bowed her head and plowed her way to the door of the players' lounge, past a slew of fans and reporters hanging out on both sides of her pathway.

"Dang!" she said as the door slammed shut behind her. "You'd think someone would ask about tennis, especially since my last serve hasn't even bounced twice yet."

"Unfortunately, tragedy sells," said Russo, who followed Syd inside the building. "But despite those jackals, plenty of people are proud of you, including me."

Samuels, who had entered the players' lounge with Trent, bent down and reached inside a small refrigerator on the floor. He pulled out a fruit-flavored Gatorade and handed it to Syd.

"Why don't you freshen up?" he said. "We'd like to talk to you when you're finished. It will only take a few minutes."

As Syd started to walk away, Samuels spoke again.

"Ms. Livingstone," he said. "Since everyone is shouting questions at you, may I ask one before you shower?"

"I don't see why not," answered Syd. "I hope it's pertaining to tennis."

"Actually, it is," said Samuels. "My daughter is nine, and she's been watching you play on TV this week. Would you consider giving her a few private lessons? And how much would it cost?"

"More than a government worker can afford," joked Syd. "But Russo here is always available. Look what he did for me!"

Syd leaned her head back and downed the sports drink with four swallows. She grabbed her backpack and headed toward the door leading to the showers.

"Russo, promise me you won't go anywhere," she said. "I've brought my checkbook with me. I need to compensate you. I'll even throw in a bonus for working with Samuels' daughter."

She hesitated and then continued speaking. "It's the least I can do for you. You're truly a genius—a devious and evil genius."

While Syd showered, Trent looked through the tinted glass entrance door and spotted a small group of people waiting outside. He opened the door stealthily, allowing them to slip inside, and led them to a side room.

After a shower that lasted the better part of twenty minutes, the trainer inspected the cut on Syd's hand and applied fresh gauze and a new bandage.

"Get that checked before you leave Columbus," she said.

Syd found the shower soothing and healing, but her mind reverted to the picnic.

Syd thought about that long cut running up Anja's arm. Why did she lie about its origin? Also, where was Marisha? If she inflicted the cut during a struggle with Anja, she wasn't around to verify the fact. Was she dead? And was Anja to blame?

No, something wasn't adding up. Anja was a fiery competitor and a tough girl. But a killer? The idea seemed ludicrous.

"Are you ready to speak with us before the awards ceremony?" said Trent. "I asked them for a one-hour extension because of the length of the match."

"That's fine," said Syd, as Samuels motioned her to enter a side room.

As Syd broke the plane of the doorway, there was a loud yell.

"Surprise!" a group of people shouted in unison.

Nicole was the first to jump to her feet and plant a giant kiss on Syd's cheek. She carried a banner that read: "Syd Livingstone—A True Champion!"

Quickly scanning the room, Syd saw her mom, Brian, Enzo, Victor, Peter, Michael, and Russo all sitting around a big cake. Balloons floated everywhere, and streamers hung throughout the room.

She turned to Nicole.

"I hope you made several banners beforehand," said Syd. "There was no way you knew I'd win!"

Nicole put her arms around Syd's neck.

"To be honest, we had no idea if you'd win today," she said. "But to everyone here, you are a true champion."

Tears welled up in Syd's eyes, and for a moment, she was speechless. Then, she spoke.

"I love you all," she said, her words breaking up. "This victory is for all of us!"

The setting was ideal for an intimate gathering. A giant hoagie, courtesy of a local sandwich shop, was divided and placed on individual plates. Bags of chips and wrapped gourmet cookies accompanied the sandwich. Someone brought in beer and wine.

Syd's father, Michael, was sitting at the table, joking and laughing with Enzo, Trent, and Peter. She remembered the restraining order. She asked her mother to meet her on the opposite side of the room.

"Mom, were you aware Dad was invited?" she asked. "I can ask him to leave and meet privately with him later."

Chelsea smiled at Syd. "I've spoken to your father, and it's fine," she said. "We've all grown and matured from this experience. I think we all realize what's important now."

Syd couldn't stop thinking about Anja. She belonged here today. Was she really the monster everyone was making her out to be?

After about fifteen minutes of partying, Syd approached Trent.

"You fooled me when you said that you wanted to discuss the investigation," she said. "I thought you were serious."

Trent paused and then spoke.

"To be honest with you, Ms. Livingstone, I wasn't kidding. This is ideal for a meeting. You still have thirty minutes before the awards ceremony."

Trent announced an impromptu meeting to discuss the case. He advised anyone who needed a restroom break to take it. When they all returned, they would discuss pertinent facts.

"I'm sorry, Trent, but is this necessary?" asked Enzo once everyone had returned to their places. "Can't we just celebrate tonight and do this tomorrow?"

"That's possible," said Trent. "But are you okay with the murderer leaving this room and reappearing later? Let's take a show of hands. Will you help me count votes, Enzo?"

Enzo scanned the room. All eyes were focused on him.

"I get your point, lieutenant," he said.

Nicole raised her hand.

"I don't mean to be presumptuous, lieutenant, but isn't it obvious that Anja is the murderer?" she asked. "She lied about the scratch on her arm, and her lover is missing in action. And we have first-hand experience with her knife."

Samuels raised his hand, asking Trent to allow him to have the floor for a moment.

"Yes, Nicole; she had a knife in her hand," said Samuels. "But I also saw you holding a large rock, with your arm cocked, ready to bash her brains out. Think what would've happened if I hadn't arrived?"

Nicole appeared stunned. Then she turned her focus to Samuels. "I was acting in self-defense. She was blocking our way out of that cave. But since you brought that up, Detective Samuels, why were you spying on us? Are you a pervert, or were you looking to add to your body count?"

"That's enough," said Trent to Nicole. "I need you to sit down and listen. Everyone needs to remain calm."

One of Trent's deputies opened the door to the room. In walked Anja Radonovic.

Gasps emerged from all over the room. Russo rose from his seat to greet Anja.

"There will be plenty of time for that, Mr. Russo," said Trent. "Everyone, please remain seated."

Anja sat toward the front of the room, next to Trent, and away from everyone else. Her face was void of expression.

"I understand your surprise about Anja being here," said Trent. "For a moment, I also thought she was the culprit. Anja was in the middle of everything. She was in the vicinity when someone removed the locket from Syd's bag. She's also strong as a bull and could've overpowered Monica Rivet."

"But the flying object struck me," interrupted Anja. "How could I be involved?"

"The flying object struck you, but that was after Ms. Livingstone had ducked," said Trent. "She could have been your intended target all along."

Anja shook her head at Trent. "You're wrong, lieutenant," she said. "That's not what happened."

Trent looked over at Anja and smiled. "As a matter of fact, you're 100 percent right. But not just because you say so.

"When Samuels arrested you in the park, you were my number-one suspect. You were acting erratically and paranoid, standing at the cave entrance with an intimidating knife. But sometimes people act strangely after they've suffered a blow to the head. If that was the case with you, I truly didn't know."

"So what are you saying?" asked Peter. "If you're going cram me in the corner of this room, I'll need another beer."

"Help yourself, Mr. O'Malley," said Trent. "With your size, I don't think you'll be sneaking out of this room without anyone noticing."

Enzo spoke up. "So you're saying that it's feasible that Anja could be guilty even though the sphere struck her?"

"It is possible the ball could have struck the murderer," said Trent. "But in order for Anja to activate the ball machine, she would need to possess the remote control. She was unconscious and fighting for her life. How could she have planted that device on Michael Livingstone's car? Impossible. I realized that when she was incarcerated.

"But someone possessed the remote before it was attached to Michael's car. Unless it was Michael himself."

"That's ridiculous," said Michael, leaping out of his chair. "I wasn't anywhere near the ball machine!"

"No offense, Michael," interrupted Samuels. "But that machine was parked behind the wall for thirty minutes before they brought it to the court. Everyone had access."

Michael slouched back down in his chair, popped open another beer, and folded his arms.

"You were my top suspect for a period of time," said Trent. "I would've arrested you earlier, but your daughter continued to win matches. I didn't have the heart to prevent you from watching.

"But the more I thought about it, you didn't fit the profile. Someone would have noticed you invading your daughter's tennis bag or monkeying with the ball machine. Your presence at the tournament was suspicious, I'll admit. But you didn't strike me as a father who would stalk his own daughter. But again, I could've been wrong."

"You're still speculating?" asked Victor. "You don't know?"

"It all came down to Milena Lombardi," said Trent. "She committed suicide several years ago. She was Syd's closest friend and doubles partner."

Russo stood up and pointed toward Peter. "You were Milena's lover," he said. "Anja told me all about that. But you told Milena about your infatuation with Sydney, didn't you? A few days later, she was gone."

All eyes turned to Peter.

"What Russo is saying is true," said Syd, forgetting about her championship win an hour earlier. "You knew that I had no interest in you, but you forged ahead anyway. And that caused my relationship with Milena to end."

"What does that mean?" said Peter. "Everyone has relationship issues. Does that make me a murderer? Why the fuck are we discussing this? I loved Milena once. But her father forbade me from seeing her. They wanted her to marry someone in their little Italian village, kind of like an arranged union. Her father prohibited me from visiting her. The man terrified me."

"Can you elaborate, Mr. O'Malley?" said Trent.

"Everything was hush-hush all the time. A secret tryst here, a clandestine dinner meeting there, a prearranged jog in the park. I loved her, but I wanted a semi-normal relationship. I didn't want to peer over my shoulder forever."

"Anything else?" said Trent.

Peter shook his head yes. "Syd was beautiful and easy to talk to. I just didn't need a James Bond-type of relationship anymore!"

Syd looked over at Enzo. He didn't seem thrilled about what Peter was saying, but he obviously understood.

"So maybe it was you, Peter," said Nicole. "Unrequited love, perhaps?"

"I gave Mr. O'Malley a serious look," said Trent. "He tried to escape after the ball-machine incident and had access to everything else, including Sydney's tennis bag, the ball machine, and even Monica Rivet. He also tutored Syd at the beginning of the tournament."

"Maybe it's been Peter the whole time!" said Chelsea, quickly covering her mouth after her outburst.

"We didn't make the report accessible to the public, ma'am," said Trent, "but someone stalked your daughter while she was in her dressing room before the match. Syd saw the person's silhouette as it moved past her translucent shower door.

"Peter O'Malley, however, is six-feet, eight inches tall. Your daughter said she couldn't determine if the figure was male or female. Have you seen any six-foot-eight-inch women creeping around the tennis complex?"

Chelsea shook her head no.

"I didn't think so," said Trent.

Trent walked to a whiteboard. He wrote Marisha Belov's name at the top.

He pointed his blue marker at the name.

"Ms. Belov was present at the start of the tournament, but she's not here anymore," said Trent. "She was in an altercation with Anja the morning of the ball-machine incident. She was always close to the action, she's very fit, and she wasn't happy when Sydney and Anja spent time together off the court. She wasn't violent, according to Sydney, but pouted when she didn't get her way."

"Lieutenant," said Russo. "There is nothing illegal about pouting. I know Marisha. She is not a killer."

"Probably not, Mr. Russo," said Trent. "But we need to determine if someone made her disappear or if she left on her own volition."

"Anja was the only person who had a relationship with Marisha Belov," said Nicole. "If she disappeared against her will, it was probably Anja."

"Precisely!" said Trent. "I had to find out for myself. And then, lo and behold, guess who answered her phone this morning? None other than Marisha Belov!"

"But that doesn't let Anja off the hook," said Enzo. "Have her show you the scratch on her arm. It's pretty fucking nasty!"

"Stand up and show it to us," added Nicole.

"No need," said Trent. "I've already seen it."

"She lied about where she got it," said Nicole. "We know that for sure!"

"Do we really?" said Trent. "While everyone was at the tournament this afternoon, I had one of my detectives check out Mr. Russo's hotel room. Do you know what he found stashed under his bed? A portable racquet stringer. That's strange for someone who doesn't string racquets.

"Oh, I almost forgot to mention something. When I spoke with Ms. Belov today, I asked her if she was afraid of the dark. She laughed. She said she worked part-time as a nightwatch person in her own country."

Samuels looked over at Trent and smiled.

"Coach, we've noticed you've been hanging around the tennis center with long-sleeve shirts on. Would you mind exposing your forearms?"

"This is ridiculous," said Russo. "You have no right to force me to strip!"

"In this country, you have the right to *bare* arms," said Samuels, giving Trent a high-five.

Russo snarled but complied with Trent's request. On his left arm was a scratch running from his forearm to the biceps tendon.

"How'd you get that cut?" Trent said.

"I scraped it on a fence during the tournament. What,

you think this scratch proves something? Give me a fucking break."

Trent shook his head. "You know, I've seen you guzzle down a lot of Diet Coke in the past few days. You should be careful where you discard them. Someone—such as Detective Samuels or me— could gather up one of those cans and extract DNA from it."

"And like I said earlier, we found DNA under the fingernails of Monica Rivet. My tech called me a couple of hours ago. Guess whose DNA matches up with that skin?"

Russo stared at the ground. To his surprise, no one was moving forward to take him into custody. He reached into his pocket and pulled out a Smith and Wesson .38 special, which he had hidden in the restroom underneath the trash can. He pointed the gun at Syd and walked over to her. Trent wanted to fire his own weapon at Russo, but the crowded room made him reconsider.

Russo stepped behind Syd and wrapped his left arm around her throat. He moved the pistol up to her temple with his right hand.

"I guess it's going to end this way, isn't it, lieutenant Trent?" said Russo.

"Drop the gun," said Samuels. "Before more people get hurt."

"I'm not putting anything down," said Russo, wedging his back against the room's doorway opening.

"But since you know the answers, lieutenant, tell everybody more, starting with my real identity."

Trent's expression turned serious, almost somber. He

never expected Russo to stash a gun in the restroom. Russo was more clever than he had given him credit.

"Okay," said Trent. "I'm advising everyone to stay calm. Nobody panic."

"All right, that's out of the way. Let's hear more information," said Russo.

"Michael Livingstone got the ball rolling," said Trent. "He said you resembled someone from his past. He wasn't 100 percent sure, but I promised I'd investigate."

"First, you are not from Yugoslavia like you claimed," said Trent. "Your homeland is Italy, the same as Milena's. During my research, I found that your name is what you say it is, except for one insignificant detail. Your name isn't really Paul Russo; it's Paulo Russo."

"You're on the right track," said Russo, tightening his grip around Syd's neck.

"You mentioned to me once that your significant other never married you because you were obsessively compulsive. Therefore, the woman you were living with probably carried a different last name. And what if there was a child? Which name would he or she carry?

"We eventually got a hit with your name on a birth certificate," said Trent. "But the certificate wasn't your own, Mr. Russo. It was your daughter's. A person named Milena Lombardi."

"Holy shit!" exclaimed Syd.

Peter jumped out of his seat. "You're Milena's father?" he asked. "But that can't be. Milena told me that her father was a big, tough man, as strong as a bull. She said he had arms the size of boulders! This guy's an imposter," said Peter.

"You're wrong, Peter," said Russo. "Lieutenant Trent knows what he's talking about. But it's a good thing I never found you with Milena. I wouldn't have killed you, but you would have spent considerable time in a hospital."

"But look at you," said Peter. "You're a frail, weak man. How can that be?"

"That's a good question," said Russo, looking at Trent, who subtly moved his hand toward his pistol.

"Don't do anything cute, lieutenant. You don't want next year's event to be the Sydney Livingstone Memorial, do you?"

"No problem," said Trent, moving his hand away from his jacket. "We'll do it your way, Russo."

"Wait a dang minute!" said Syd, moving her neck sideways to prevent Russo from crushing her windpipe. "How did I become the centerpiece in all of this? Milena was my friend. I loved her."

"I find that hard to fathom," said Russo. "You knew that she would fail that drug test. She asked you for one small favor. Just to pee in that cup. One time and done. And you refused! That's when her downward spiral started."

"They would have thrown me off the tour!"

"They never would have fucking found out. There was no risk for you! They suspended her for three years. That's nearly an entire career for a young tennis player.

"And then, after they suspended her, you moved on with your career, with another doubles partner. Then you and Milena stopped talking. She became deeply depressed, and

I couldn't change that, no matter what I tried. She took her life, and you didn't have the decency to attend her funeral!"

"You have to believe me," said Syd. "I didn't know about the suicide until a week later."

"I'll tell you one thing I know," said Russo. "My Milena would still be here if you were a loyal friend."

"But you look nothing like her father," said Peter. "Why? How can you be Paulo Russo?"

"I met Syd one time, several years ago. I couldn't take a chance on her remembering me. And yes, it's true that I was a big burly tough guy. In my prime, I was a sight to see.

"But I wanted to make Sydney pay. I overhauled my appearance, but I knew it would take time. I stopped lifting weights, a lifelong passion of mine. I began an extreme diet combined with heavy cardiovascular exercise."

"I know how tough that is," interjected Trent. "Why don't you place the gun down and continue your story?"

"For eighteen months, I walked a minimum of 27,000 steps per day and consumed only 1,500 calories," said Russo. "Do you understand how unsatisfying 1,500 calories is, lieutenant? Take a fucking deep breath, and you're halfway there. But in the end, I'd lost 110 pounds.

"Then, I had a nose job and did something extremely painful. I had my face reconstructed by a doctor whose specialty was altering underlying bone. It took me two months to smile again.

"I grew a thick beard, wore sunglasses, and befriended an acquaintance of Syd. That's where Anja came in."

"But you're one of the best coaches in the world," said

Syd, her legs trembling from stress. "Why didn't you forge ahead and make that your career?"

"You're right, Sydney. Perhaps I am one of the best. But my only goal, my only passion, was to develop my own daughter into becoming the best. I don't give a rat's ass about you or Anja, or anyone else.

"After Milena died, my sole purpose in life was to get even. And I will fulfill my dream today. Even with your best friends and several cops all around you, you are going to experience a terrible death. And I am so glad you now know the reason."

"Wait!" said Trent. "We can arrange for you to go free if you don't hurt anybody else. But I have one more question if you don't mind, so I can close my book on this investigation. Did you kill Hawthorne in his own driveway?"

"You are very good at your job, Trent," said Russo. "Yes, I did. I pretended like I was a weak little pipsqueak while he bullied me in the hospital and outside that stadium. But despite my diminutive appearance, I am still a powerful man. When you lift weights for most of your life, you never lose all of your strength. Your muscles go into a state of hibernation.

"So I tracked that mother-fucker down in his driveway. He knew who I was. He laughed when he realized that I was there to confront him. I never used a knife on him, lieutenant, until he was unconscious. I conquered him with my bare hands. His last memory was getting his ass kicked, not bullying a little man outside of the stadium."

"What about Rivet?" asked Samuels.

Russo looked down at the ground.

"Yes, I sliced her throat, drove her car to that bridge, and catapulted her over that railing and into the water. She didn't deserve that. But she probably would have beaten Sydney. I needed Sydney to stay in town longer.

"Monica Rivet's blood is on your hands, Sydney. And so is Milena's."

Russo looked at Trent.

"There's another murder you haven't accounted for, lieutenant," he said. "During our restroom break, one of your detectives walked in on me when I was removing my gun from the trash can. He's still there, but not as healthy as when he entered."

Trent nodded at Gonzalez to check the restroom. When he returned, the color was missing from his face.

"It's Norton," said Gonzalez. "He's gone."

"I hope that's enough proof I'm not playing around," said Russo.

Sweat streamed down Russo's face, and he bit into his lower lip. The gun dug deeper into Syd's head. The trigger finger on his hand moved. Something was about to happen.

Samuels lunged toward Russo and threw a shoulder into his midsection. Russo withdrew the gun from Syd's head and slammed the barrel against Samuel's temple, sending him to the floor with a thud.

With the gun away from her head, Syd reached for the Tiger Claw she stuffed into the pocket of her jeans after the shower. By the time Russo turned around to face her, Syd held the device in her patented forehand grip and raked it across Russo's face, claws exposed.

Russo screamed as the claw ripped open the side of his right eye socket. As blood cascaded down his face, he pointed the gun at her, trying to locate her head amidst a sea of red.

Trent pointed his weapon at Russo's midsection and fired three shots, each penetrating his ribcage. Russo collapsed to the floor, his gun dropping harmlessly to the ground.

Russo's breathing became labored, and he let out one last word as he passed away.

"Milena!"

Syd found Enzo amongst the scramble of moving bodies and wrapped her arms around his neck.

"Are you okay?" he asked. "Did that bastard hurt you?"

"No, I'm fine, just a little shaken up," she said. "It's about time I put that Tiger Claw to good use," she said. "That damn thing cost thirty-four bucks."

Police waiting outside the players' lounge rushed into the room, now that the threat posed by Russo had been vanquished. Chelsea and Michael comforted Syd, and Nicole embraced Anja.

A puzzled Samuels approached Trent.

"Chief," he said, "I didn't know the DNA results from those fingernails were available yet. When did they let you know?"

"They didn't let me know," said Trent. "Quite frankly, I lied."

EPILOGUE

Syd waved goodbye to Chelsea and Brian as she dropped them at the airport. She wished her father farewell earlier in the day as he packed up his car and headed back home to Michigan. Chelsea, Brian, and Michael promised to attend next week's US Open, where Syd had earned the twenty-first seed because of her MMO title.

Breakfast was more difficult, as she met with Anja and Nicole. Syd apologized for her behavior at the picnic.

"You're my dear friends, but there were times when I doubted your innocence," she said. "Please forgive me, so we can move forward together."

"Well, Anja and I weren't exactly reading scripture during the picnic," said Nicole. "We're just fortunate we didn't kill each other. Suspicion and paranoia ruled the day. But you have to admit that those cookies were pretty damn good!"

"I propose a new rule," said Anja. "We agree to trust each other 100 percent from this day forward."

"Friends to the end, no matter what comes our way!" said Nicole.

"Group hug!" shouted Syd, as the trio formed their own intimate circle. "Friends to the end. That's our forever motto!"

Syd even made time to speak with Peter privately.

"I'm sorry about everything that transpired with Milena," she said. "I know she cared for you."

"I know," said Peter. "I was arrogant and selfish. Now she's gone forever. But unfortunately, I can't change the past."

"None of us can," said Syd. "We only control the present. But the advice you provided on the volley brightened my future. Your instruction was amazing."

"Maybe you can repay me some time," said Peter. "Why don't you watch a few of my matches on YouTube? Advise me on how I can become a better player."

"I'm on it," said Syd. "Now, rest up for the US Open. I hope we shock the world in New York."

"Don't be such a hog," Peter mused. "You've already shocked the world. Now, it's my turn."

* * * * *

Syd dropped off her rental car in Columbus. The company issued a new one and didn't charge for the vandalism.

"We don't accept money from heroes," said the rental agent. "We hope you return next year and win the tournament again."

Instead of flying home, Enzo opted to ride with Syd to Savannah, where he would stay before flying to New York the following week.

"Why don't you buy the entire apartment complex and fire the manager?" suggested Enzo. "Isn't she the one who's been riding your ass about late payments?"

"Yes, she's the one," said Syd. "But she's only doing her job. Hopefully, she'll be more understanding when I encounter my next financial crisis."

With her car packed and Enzo riding shotgun, Syd pulled out of the hotel's parking lot and headed toward the freeway.

She'd missed two calls from Trent earlier in the day but decided to answer his third attempt.

"I wanted to say congratulations and good luck at next week's Open," said Trent. "Let's pray your next trip to Columbus is less adventurous."

As stressful as her life had become during the past week, Syd realized she'd miss Trent.

"Thank everyone at headquarters for me," said Syd. "I'm so sorry about what happened to Norton. I hope you can find peace."

Trent became silent. Syd thought she could hear him take a hard swallow.

"I love your spirit and your spunk," he said. "I understand you studied criminology. If you need a job after tennis, I'd love to interview you."

The call was on speaker. Enzo gave her a thumbs-up.

"Sounds great," said Syd. "You may receive a call sooner than you think."

As their car pulled onto the freeway, Syd interrupted Enzo as he sang along with the radio.

"I almost forgot. I have to visit the hospital."

Enzo appeared surprised but then nodded.

"Oh yeah, you're supposed to get that arm checked," he said. "Are you going straight to the emergency?"

"No, we're going to a different part of the hospital," she said. "We'll take an elevator to the third floor."

"Why?" asked Enzo.

"I met an elderly old man named Emile after my visit here," said Syd. "He's recovering from open-heart surgery. We have unfinished business. I called him today. He's expecting us."

"You mean the guy who wanted to play chess?" asked Enzo. "I didn't know you actually played such an intellectual game."

"For your information, I was a third-grade legend," said Syd. "Don't challenge me when we get home. I'll rock your world."

"Sydney!" exclaimed Emile as she entered the room with Enzo. "I watched you on television. You won the championship! I was cheering so loud that the nurses threatened to turn off my TV. But I couldn't help it. I was so excited.

"I told my family you'd return to play chess. They said I was foolish."

"Well, they must feel foolish now," said Syd. "Here I am in the flesh, ready to play a three-out-of-five game match. Oh, and by the way, this is my boyfriend, Enzo."

"Hello, Enzo," said Emile. "Do you play tennis?"

"Only a little," said Enzo. "Syd's the athlete in our relationship."

Emile pulled the board out, and Syd pulled up a chair next to his bed.

"I will take the white pieces," said Emile. "If you don't mind."

"Not at all," said Syd. "It's not how well you start; it's how well you finish."

Emile made his first move: the king's pawn two spaces forward.

Syd studied the board for a minute. And then for another. She leaned over and whispered into Enzo's ear.

"One quick question, sweetie," she said. "Which pieces are allowed to ride on the backs of those cute little horseys?"

ABOUT THE AUTHOR

Greg Milano writes under the pen name of Orion Gregory. He is an award-winning writer in the newspaper and advertising industries, and is a nationally published magazine contributor. He is a graduate of Wright State University with a degree in Communication Arts, and resides in Southwest Ohio. You can visit him at www.oriongregory.com.